T0147882

THE TAKEN LAND (RIRO TE WHENUA)

ROBIN O'REILLY

iUniverse, Inc.
Bloomington

The Taken Land (Riro Te Whenua)

This is a work of fiction. All of the characters, names, incidents, organizations, and dialogue in this novel are either the products of the author's imagination or are used fictitiously.

iUniverse books may be ordered through booksellers or by contacting:

iUniverse
1663 Liberty Drive
Bloomington, IN 47403
www.iuniverse.com
1-800-Authors (1-800-288-4677)

ISBN: 978-1-4697-3875-8 (sc)
ISBN: 978-1-4697-3876-5 (e)
ISBN: 978-1-4697-3877-2 (dj)

Printed in the United States of America

iUniverse rev. date: 3/22/2012

Dedication Page

I dedicate this book to my family, especially my grand children who haven't yet started out in life. Only through hard work will you achieve anything. Follow your dreams and anything is possible. You just need to want it badly enough.

English / Maori Translation

Wharenui   Meeting House

Korowai   Ancestral cloak of a chieftainship covered in Kiwi, Takahi and various other native bird feathers

Marae   An Iwi's enclosed grounds or meeting place

Iwi   A section of a tribe that live in a separate location. Several Iwi make up a tribe

Pa   A village or fortified stockade

Hui   A meeting of the tribe for social or political discussions

Mana   Influence of great importance

Pakeha   Foreigner, referring mainly to white people

Aotearoa   Maori word for New Zealand

Patu   Maori hand weapon

Haka   Maori war dance

Pirau Corn   A Maori delicacy. Made by fermenting corn in a container over a long period of time.

CHAPTER 1

"I have called you all here today to discuss the matter of the three mountains and the adjoining land surrounding them. We have discussed this many times before in the past." Pausing, Amohia studied the faces of the warriors seated before him for a second or two. "If we do not gift this land it will be confiscated without any doubt. We are all aware of that, because we supported our neighbouring tribes during the war. That is in our past and should remain there."

After the Maori land wars, there was enormous pressure on the new colonial regime to acquire land and many tribes were deceitfully manipulated into selling at ridiculously low prices. A directive from the Governor General targeted those tribes who forcibly resisted the colonial forces during the land wars and, if they resisted again or refused to sell, would be the first to forfeit land through confiscation.

Ships from the United Kingdom arrived at ports and safe anchorages all around New Zealand crammed with people filled with hope of a new life and the desire to escape the aristocracy created by the lords and noblemen who, for

1

centuries and countless generations, denied the middle and working classes the right to own their own home and land and the right to earn a decent living.

A high percentage of these settlers were from farming backgrounds, hoping to obtain land at an affordable price to settle on and forge a living.

Several tribes had resisted this unruly land requisition and were themselves subjected to land confiscation. One tribe in particular was to forfeit what is known today as the Tongariro National Park which was made up of Mount Ruapehu, Mount Ngarahoe, Mount Tongariro and all the immediate surrounding land.

The paramount chief of that tribe, Amohia, was of the opinion that if he could reach a consensus from all his iwi, (sections of the tribe) rather than have their sacred mountains seized, it was far more beneficial as a tribe to gift them. The conditions of this gift however, was not for the government, but for all of Aotearoa, (New Zealand) allowing the tribe to retain its mana (pride) and save face within Maoridom itself.

Amohia wasn't a tall man but he was mentally and physically fit with a solid build and well-toned muscle. On his face, he wore a chieftains tribal tattoo. His hair was graying slightly around the edges but he still trained daily with his warriors for the purpose of defending his village and lands. He was a proud leader, and his status within the tribe was indisputable. His manner was one of fairness, and his consideration of the opinions of his chiefs was one of professional expedience.

To all his chiefs, Amohia had sent out invitations to a final hui (meeting) at his marae (village). It was his view and the view of his chiefs that it made good sense to gift the land rather than to forfeit it through confiscation. This in itself would demonstrate the tribe's wholehearted commitment to the Treaty of Waitangi, signed in February, 1840, and their united show of goodwill.

To make a stand against the land requisition would be futile. A terrible loss of life would be imminent, and the final result would be that the colonial regime would undoubtedly confiscate the land anyway.

This hui would allow any grievances against the gifting of the mountains and land to be aired openly. It was imperative that Amohia consolidate all his iwi and unite them as one. He had to be 100 percent certain that he had the confidence of the whole tribe behind his initiative in order to achieve a consensus and he spent months formulating the conditions of his proposal.

Ten weeks earlier, he had spent many days with the governor general and senior government officials in long tedious discussions and was insistent that his conditions regarding this momentous gift were non-negotiable. Finally, he convinced them to unanimously accept his proposal without amendment or extra provisions added to the agreement.

At an earlier hui six months prior, there had been some minor resistance concerning the gift, but his brother, Iwikau, had assured him that once all the conditions had been laid out and explained thoroughly and openly to the members of the tribe, it was possible to gain a unanimous consensus. Amohia made it quite clear that the result of a vote would be their irrefutable and final decision and could not be overturned at a later date.

A hush came across the gathering of chiefs and warriors seated in front of the meeting house as Amohia appeared and for many long seconds, he regarded them with an appraising eye.

It was all part of his personal ceremony and rhetoric, allowing him to observe the attitude among them all. Feeling moderately comfortable and relaxed, he pondered the words of his prepared speech.

Amohia took a deep breath. "It is time to show our goodwill to our pakeha chiefs." He paused, taking two steps to his left. "As much as it goes against the grain, we cannot turn back time. It is my view, and many among you, that the time has come to address this issue and gift the three mountains and its surrounding lands to all the people of Aotearoa. I repeat, we gift the three mountains and the surrounding land to all the people of Aotearoa. At no time will it be gifted to the government."

Taking his time, he took a step to his right before continuing. "It will demonstrate our wholehearted commitment to the treaty we signed so many years ago, and it will show our sincerity to that document." For a moment, he looked reflectively over the gathering. "There are some among you here that do not agree with this gift."

Again, he paused, looking down at his feet before continuing. "But it is my view and the majority of us here today at this hui that this show of goodwill does demonstrate to our pakeha chiefs that this gift will seal our commitment to the treaty."

Lifting his chin musingly, Amohia stood there for many long seconds, allowing those who disagreed with his proposal to stand and voice their objection.

One man stood, a warrior of no actual stature or status within the tribe and one who had no speaking rights at the hui.

Shouting angrily at Amohia, Huri Te Ngongo said, "I disagree with such a gift of our mountains and lands. Let them try and confiscate it. We will fight them for it. It is our right."

Amohia looked at him perceptively, and then, acknowledging him with a nod, he turned to the gathering, waiting for anyone else to voice his objection against the proposal.

Before anyone else could object, Amohia's brother, Iwikau,

jumped to his feet and shouted, "Sit down, Huri Te Ngongo. You have no speaking rights at this hui. Only your chief can speak on your behalf. You were only invited here to listen."

Full of resentment, Huri Te Ngongo glared at Iwikau for being told to sit down like some lowly warrior. Lifting his chin defiantly, he continued, "I will not sit down. This land being gifted is sacred land. It should not be taken by the pakeha or given away as if it is worth nothing." He put his fist in the air rebelliously. "I say, let the pakeha come. This is our tribal land, part of our treaty settlement. They can not just come in here and take it."

A startled murmur rose among the gathering. Amohia, putting his hand in the air to silence them, turned to Huri.

Again, and before Amohia could respond, Iwikau was infuriated at Huri's defiance and disrespect for Amohia. He took several steps toward him.

"If you do not sit down, you will be removed, forcibly if necessary. It's your choice," Iwikau shouted. "You lack respect for your chief, Eramiha."

Huri's eyes narrowed, his loathing for Iwikau etched into his face. Turning on his heel, he stormed out of the hui. Hesitating at the gates, he cast a scornful eye over his shoulder at Iwikau.

Iwikau, angry at Huri's bad manners and defiance, waved him away contemptuously.

Ignoring the disturbance, Amohia turned back to the hui. "Who else disagrees with this decision to gift the mountains and the surrounding lands?"

Two more warriors stood to have their protest noted. One sat back down, but the other walked hurriedly away.

Amohia nodded, acknowledging their protest, and then continued, "This land is sacred, I recognize that, but have no fear; it will be taken if we sit here and do nothing. However, I have spoken to our pakeha chiefs, and they have agreed to my conditions, which, I have expressed most ardently, are non-negotiable." He took three steps to his right, pausing momentarily, looking at the seated warrior who had protested. "One of the conditions is that we have full access to the land and the mountains at any time." He drew a deep breath, taking two steps to his left. "And that the mountains and their surrounding lands be preserved as a national park in their present state and for all people of this land to have full access with due respect to its spiritual value and significance to all Maori."

Again, he paused, allowing the significance of what he was saying to be absorbed. "The pakeha chiefs have agreed to this and have given their solemn word that they will maintain the mountains and the surrounding lands as a national park. They will sign an agreement that will affect our demands."

Then, putting one hand in the air, he called out in a loud clear voice, "Do we have an agreement?"

Acknowledging their commitment to the agreement and the treaty, all the Chiefs put their hands in the air.

That evening, after their meal, Amohia, Iwikau, and two other chiefs, Eramiha and Tairinga, were walking together along the lake edge, just down from Amohia's village, discussing the "deeds of gift".

Wading along in the shallows, still sulking from his humiliation at being ridiculed in front of the whole tribe, Huri Te Ngongo saw the four chiefs walking slowly toward him in serious discussion, unaware of his presence. Flexing his jaw muscles nervously, he slipped his 'patu' (close-quarter hand weapon) from his flax belt.

It was then that Eramiha noticed him watching them and observed the angry young warrior for several seconds. Sensing his antagonism, Eramiha glanced at Iwikau, pointing with his head at Huri. "Hot head. Never could hold his temper."

With his nostrils flaring with anger, Huri slowly approached the four chiefs. He glared at Eramiha and said,

"I am a loyal warrior. We have fought many battles together. Is my opinion worth nothing?"

"We have fought many battles together, granted," Eramiha replied, soberly. "So have all the other warriors. They do not doubt my judgement."

Huri glanced at the other three chiefs, his mouth twisted with resentment. "Your judgement is clouded by these others."

Taken aback by the young warrior's continuing insolence, embarrassed, Eramiha glanced at the other three chiefs and then said to Huri, "How dare you question our judgement? We have a common interest for the good and welfare of the tribe as a whole."

Not wanting to be pushed aside like a common expendable warrior, Huri lowered his eyebrows and squinting ominously, said, "The mountains are sacred and should not be given away to the pakeha. Never." He hesitated for a second, looking at the other three chiefs contemptuously. "You are deceivers and should not be chiefs. You all lick the arses of the pakeha."

Resenting the insult, Eramiha pointed to the lake. "Go for a swim and cool off. You never could control your temper."

Huri stood his ground, glaring into the faces of the four chiefs.

Annoyed at the young warrior's continual defiance, again Eramiha pointed to the lake. "Go and cool off. What do you care what's good for the tribe?" He tapped the side of his head. "You need to use this more instead of that patu and you just might learn something." Angry now and grossly embarrassed, he waved Huri away. "Leave us."

Without warning, Huri's right hand blurred in the air, his patu striking Eramiha on the forehead, burying it deeply into his skull.

Eramiha staggered backward, and for a second, he just stood there, rigid as a board. Huri wrenched his patu from Eramiha's skull. Blood oozed from the deep gash and ran down his face like a rivulet. His legs gave way under him, and he collapsed to the ground.

Huri flew at Amohia; but Amohia, defending himself, grabbed Huri's hand holding the patu with one hand, and punched him in the face with the other, twice.

Huri staggered back from the blow but managed to remain on his feet. He broke Amohia's grip and lunged at him again, swinging the patu.

Iwikau leaped to Amohia's defense, attacking Huri from the side. He thrust his elbow into Huri's throat, forcing the young warrior back, and then, taking hold of his arm, flipped him onto his back.

Before Huri could react, Iwikau dropped his left knee onto Huri's sternum with all his weight, snatched the patu from his hand, and drove it into Huri's forehead, killing him instantly.

Shaken, Amohia and Tairinga stood there for many seconds staring at each other, dumbfounded at the sudden unprovoked attack. They looked appreciatively at Iwikau, impressed at the swiftness in which he had defended them.

Disdainfully, Iwikau looked down at Huri's body. "Good warrior in battle. Always fought like a demon but only thought of himself. It was a shame he was such a hot-head with nothing between his ears." He went down on one knee beside Eramiha and, with deep respect, said, "This is a very sad day indeed for the tribe." He paused, brushing his hands lightly over Eramiha's eyes, closing them. "Today, we have lost a good warrior, a brother, and a loyal, wise chief. He will be sadly missed."

CHAPTER 2

Mannie Te Ngongo had just arrived home from work. Having completed a carpentry apprenticeship four years prior, he was now a qualified carpenter and employed by a commercial builder in South Auckland working on modest apartment blocks and small shopping centres.

Being six foot two inches tall, broad across his muscular shoulders, narrow at the hip with thickly cropped hair cut moderately short, and handsome in a rugged sort of way. He did, however, have aspirations as a Maori radical and activist with many grievances with the Treaty of Waitangi.

Jo was five foot ten, had a slim shapely figure with a finely sculptured jawline and wavy dark hair that ran down just past her shoulders. She could be single-minded at times but mostly, she was a very caring and maternal person.

Mannie was in an extra good mood, and as he opened the back door, he called out jokingly, "Hi, my little cupcake. I'm home."

Mannie and Jo had been sweethearts since their fifth form school years and enjoyed a close, caring, and physical relationship; like two peas in a pod, they were meant to be together.

Having just arrived home from work herself, Jo was standing by the fridge and, putting her arms around his neck, she kissed him tenderly, laughing at his term of endearment. "Cup cake! Is that what you think I am?" After a quick giggle at his demented joke, she added, "You have a good day?"

Having put his lunch box on the sink bench and taking her in his arms, Mannie replied, "Yeah, not too bad." He gave her a cheery smile. "How was your day?"

"Yeah," she replied. "Not too bad."

Jo appeared a little skeptical for a moment and he asked, curiously, "You look as if something's bothering you. I mean, is everything okay?"

"Yeah, everything's fine here, with us I mean. It's Jackie, my friend from work."

"What's wrong with her?"

"Something's not quite right," Jo tried to explain. "She used to be a real laugh once but now..." Jo broke off and looked out the window summing up the situation. "She's been distant lately, not her usual self, if you know what I mean?"

"Sort of. Is she upset with you about something?"

"No. It's nothing like that." Jo paused for a second, searching for the right words, not wanting to sound like a gossip. "She came to work this morning wearing sunglasses. I thought that was a bit odd, then I saw her black eye. When I asked how she got it, she said she walked into a door." She looked at Mannie quizzically. "That's the oldest excuse in the book."

"You think something's happened at home?"

"Yes, I do. I think Matt's given her the bash again. She looked so embarrassed, and when I queried her about it, she wouldn't say anything. So I asked her straight up, 'Did Matt hit you?' She put on a forced laugh, and of course, she denied it. I know I hit a nerve. She wouldn't look me in the eye."

"What about their daughter, Li?"

"She's almost fifteen. I have a gut feeling she's got something to do with what's happened."

A frown crossed Mannie's face. "What do you mean?"

Jo sat down at the dining room table, wondering if she should tell him her suspicions. "I'm not sure exactly but I've just got this terrible feeling. I asked if Liana was okay, and that's when she almost burst into tears."

"So you think there's trouble between Jackie and Li?"

"No. That's not what I mean," she said soberly. "I think Matt might be interfering with Li."

Mannie was aghast. "Bloody hell, Jo. That's real serious stuff. Are you sure? I mean, you just can't accuse Matt of something like that without some serious evidence."

"I know, I know. It's just a gut feeling. Call it a woman's intuition. It's Jackie's body language that's got me thinking. She's not herself these days and so stand-offish and has been for a few weeks now. It's not like her at all." Again, she broke off, looking around the room at nothing in particular. "And each time I mention Matt's name, she shuts up tight as a drum. We've always been so close. She was always so happy and jovial. I could talk to her about anything once." Jo paused for just a moment. "I'm telling you, there's something not nice going on in that house."

Mannie had been studying Jo as she conveyed her suspicions. This wasn't just some woman's gossip. Jo wasn't into gossip, and her face was deathly serious when she asked, "What do you think we should do?"

"I don't know, Jo," Mannie told her. "Is there someway you could ask her quietly, as a friend? I mean, that's what you tell me to do when I have a problem."

Jo thought about Mannie's advice. "I don't want to appear like I'm butting in or anything like that, you know, intruding. It's not an easy subject to broach, especially with someone who's your close friend. I don't want to upset her."

"I see what you mean, but if you really want to help her, you're going to have to broach the subject somehow."

"I'll sleep on it. I don't want to upset her and lose her as a friend. You know, despite the nineteen years between her and I, we're the best of friends. She's something special to me."

Mannie tried to sound positive about the whole debacle. "You know. This could be something that's been totally misinterpreted."

Jo was very serious. "I'm telling you, Mannie. This is not something I've imagined." She eyed him seriously. "You do know Matt drinks a lot, and I mean, a lot. Not just a couple of beers after work. His trouble is he doesn't know when to say when, and from what I can gather, he's got one hell of a mean temper."

The following day, when Mannie arrived home from work, he found Jo preparing their evening meal. With a big smile, he greeted her with his usual, "Hi, honey, I'm home."

After giving him an affectionate kiss, she asked, "How'd your day go?"

"Not too bad," he replied. "More to the point, how did your day go with Jackie?"

"Okay, I suppose. I've managed to get Jackie to acknowledge that there is a problem at home and that I'm here for her when she's ready to talk." She closed the fridge door and turned to him with a sigh. "I'm not pushing her at this stage. I've never seen anyone so embarrassed. The bruise on her right eye has spread down her cheek and it's gone a dark bluey yellow. Geez, Mannie, it sticks out like dogs balls, poor woman."

Jo put the roast of beef in the oven, and then switched on the jug for a cup of coffee. "I did what you said and asked her straight up if Matt had hit her. She nodded, not wanting to actually say the words out loud."

"Well, that's a start. Some progress, I suppose."

"I also asked her what caused him to hit her, but she

wouldn't say. So, I asked her if Li was the trouble? Again, she only nodded."

"Well, at least she's got some of it off her chest. Opened the door, you could say. And another big plus for her is that she knows she's not on her own any more. That's gotta be a huge bonus." Mannie scowled, and then went on, "I'd like to give that bloody Matt a bit of his own back, the bloody arsehole, geez...!"

"That's not all either," Jo said as she poured the coffee and sat down. "I asked her straight up if Matt had interfered with Li. That's when she broke down and cried her eyes out. Shit, I felt bloody terrible after that."

"She didn't say any more though?"

"No, and I didn't want to push her either. She's had a real shit of a day, I can tell you."

"You did good, girl. You did good."

"I hope so. At least now, she knows I'm on her side and that I'm there for her if she wants someone to talk to."

"Even though she didn't say it, she insinuated he's been interfering with his own daughter...?"

"Not in so many words, but that's what I took she meant. She also told me that they haven't had sex now for over twelve months. Basically it was after they lost their house that she first had her suspicions."

"Geez...! What an arsehole. His own daughter...! I don't believe it. Somebody needs to sort that bastard out good and proper."

"Yeah. That must have been devastating for her. It's a wonder she didn't leave him then! But, she's one of those people who stay with their partners no matter what. You know, she made her bed and now she has to lay in it."

"Have to admit, it hasn't done her any good." Mannie shook his head, disgusted. "I'd like to give him a smack around the head, the bastard."

"Promise me you won't go sticking your nose in where

it's not needed," Jo asked him sternly. "Nobody's supposed to know about this. No one. You hear me? No one," she repeated. "I'm the only person she's told, and I don't want that trust destroyed, okay?"

Mannie nodded dispassionately.

Jo went to work earlier than usual the next morning in the hope of having a heart-to-heart talk with Jackie over a coffee before they started work and get to the bottom of Jackie's problem. Unfortunately, Jackie wasn't there. She was never late for work. Never.

This concerned Jo, and she decided to ring Jackie's home. She let the phone ring and ring until it cut itself off. She rang Liana's school and asked the receptionist if she could speak to Liana's teacher and that it was urgent. The receptionist told her that she would get Jeanette to phone her back and asked for her work number. Jeanette rang her fifteen minutes later.

"Is Liana at school today?" Jo asked, anxiously.

"No she isn't," Jeanette replied. Jeanette picked up a tone of urgency in Jo's voice. "Why, what's the matter?"

"I'm not sure," Jo told her. "Jackie, her mother hasn't arrived at work either. She's never late." She broke off for a second. "I've rung her home but there's no answer. I'm concerned, that's all."

"If Liana does turn up here, I'll phone you, okay?" Jeanette said, sensing Jo's anxiety.

"Yeah, thanks," Jo replied and hung up.

At the morning tea break, Jackie still hadn't turned up at work, and Jo told her supervisor she had a doctors appointment. She rushed out to her car and went immediately to Jackie's home.

She knocked at the door several times, and waited for a good four minutes. There was no sign of life and no sound of movement from inside. She went around the house peering in the windows, but the curtains were still drawn. Strange, she thought. She had mixed feelings— on the one hand, she was relieved because no one appeared to be home, but on the other hand, she was apprehensive because the curtains were still drawn. This is definitely not like Jackie. She was always "'Miss Tidy Britches'."

Liana didn't appear to be inside either, so where are they? She didn't have a car, as Matt had written it off on his way home from one of his benders while under the influence eight months prior. There had been no insurance cover because of his drink-driving, leaving Jackie without a car. She had been using the bus of late.

At the time, Matt had been given a hefty fine and lost his license for six months. That was then, but he had a van now, which he used for work. That was still in the driveway, unlocked, and with the drivers window down.

Alarm bells started going off in Jo's head. She knew for certain now that something was amiss. She knocked on the back door again, calling out, "Jackie, Jackie. Are you there? It's Jo. Open up." She listened for a few seconds and then knocked again, this time harder. "Jackie, open up. It's Jo."

After waiting for thirty seconds or so, Jo decided go back to work. Jackie may have turned up by now. She turned, about to walk back to her car, when she thought she heard a faint sound inside. She knocked again, calling out, "Jackie, Jackie. Open up. It's Jo." She hadn't thought to try the door handle, and when she turned it, the door was unlocked. She pushed the door open cautiously, peering around the kitchen. The sink-bench was clean, but what appeared like the groceries from the day before were still on the bench beside the fridge.

Cautiously, she made her way to the lounge. Shock struck her a crushing blow when she saw Liana sitting on her heels on the floor, cradling Jackie's head in her lap, stroking her mother's hair; her school blouse was torn down one side and from where Jo was standing, she could see that Liana had no underwear on.

Liana was almost fifteen years old, average height for her age with a strong athletic body. She had wavy shoulder length hair and had the most angelic face with finely sculptured cheek bones, a younger version of her mother, and to those who knew her, she was a happy child.

Jo rushed over, and, putting her arms around her, she cuddled her tightly. Upon glancing quickly down at Jackie's bruised face, to her horror, she noticed even more bruising than she had the previous day. There was no doubt in her mind that Jackie was dead. Something terrible had happened.

Liana hadn't acknowledged Jo's presence in the slightest. She was in a trance-like state, sobbing and mumbling incoherently. Jo couldn't understand a word she was saying; her eyes were glazed and unfocused. It's weird, Jo thought to herself. What the hell's happened here?

She took Liana's face in her hands and looked her in the eye, trying to get her to focus. "Liana. Liana," she said in a slow clear voice. "What's happened to your mother?"

Liana kept mumbling to herself, not acknowledging Jo at all. Poor girl's traumatized, Jo told herself. She quickly glanced around the room. The room was quite dark. A chair had been upended, and the coffee table was upside down, lying in the centre of the room.

She opened the curtains and then rushed to the phone in the kitchen. After dialling 111, she asked for the police and an ambulance and gave the operator the address. Her next thought was of Mannie, and she dialled his cellphone number.

"Hello," Mannie answered, jovially. "What ever you're selling, I'm not interested, okay? So bugger off."

"Mannie," Jo snapped at him. "This is not a joke, please. I'm at Jackie's home, and something terrible has happened. I mean something real serious. The place is a mess." It was then she lost control and burst into tears.

"What's happened?" Mannie asked anxiously. Jo had never lost her composure like this before. "What's wrong sweetheart?"

"Jackie's dead. Liana's here and she's in one hell of a state."

"Where's Matt?"

"I don't know. His van's here, but I haven't seen him yet."

Stunned at Jo's explanation, he replied, "Don't move. I'm on my way. Okay?"

Jo was too distressed to answer and just hung up.

Mannie dropped his apron where he stood on the work site and, rushing to the site office, he said to his employer. "I'm sorry, mate. Major trouble at home and I've gotta go. Can't talk now. I'll tell you about it later, okay?"

His boss nodded, taken aback at Mannie's disturbing request. He watched Mannie rush to his vehicle.

As Jo went back through the lounge, she noticed another body on the floor through the hall doorway. She knew instinctively it was Matt. The realization of the horror that had taken place was almost inconceivable. She glanced at Liana, who was still mumbling incoherently to herself, her face wet with tears.

Jo felt herself beginning to shake, her nerves stretched to breaking point. She edged her way slowly along the hall to where Matt lay on his stomach. Her distress increased when she noticed he had nothing else on but a dirty T-shirt. She gagged at the pool of blood on the floor around his head and recognized immediately the heavy black caste-iron poker lying on the floor beside him. It was usually on the iron stand beside the fireplace in the lounge.

She had to physically restrain herself from screaming. Her

knees felt like jelly as she staggered her way back to Liana. Gripping the young girl by the shoulders with both hands, she shook her severely to try and bring her to her senses. "Liana, Liana!" she shouted. "Come on sweetie. Snap out of it."

Liana's eyes slowly began to focus. Jo kept shaking her and then grabbed a cushion from the lounge settee to put under Jackie's head. She then helped Liana to her feet and sat her down on the lounge settee.

At that moment, Mannie came rushing in. He quickly assessed the situation and put his arms around Jo who, upon seeing him, burst into tears. He put his arm out and was about to cuddle Liana. Liana, on realizing what he was about to do, slid frantically along the settee, punching at his hands with closed fists, terrified that he was going to touch her. Her mouth was wide open, her face displaying extreme panic as if she was about to scream, but no words came out. Her eyes were dilated and glazed in absolute terror.

That was when Mannie noticed dried, crusted blood between her bare legs. "Oh shit, Jo. Bloody hell. Look at the insides of her legs."

Slapping her hands to her mouth, Jo eyed Liana in absolute horror, knowing only too well what the terrified young girl had gone through. "God almighty, you poor little child," she said through her streaming tears.

Mannie then saw the cast-iron poker beside Matt's head.

Two police officers knocked at the back door. They came in and introduced themselves. The first officer asked, "Has anything been moved or touched since you arrived?"

"Only the girl," Jo replied, nervously.

"Who are you?" the second officer asked Mannie.

"My wife here," he replied, pointing to Jo, "is the dead lady's close friend."

A forensic photographer came in and introduced himself. He nodded to the two police officers and began to assess the scene.

Jo looked up at the two police officers from the settee. "When I arrived, Liana here," she said, pointing to Liana with her head, "was sitting on her heels with her mothers head on her lap. Poor kid's in shock, as you can see."

Mannie pointed to Matt in the hallway. "The father's in there."

A sound at the back door made everyone turn and see a paramedic and the ambulance driver came in.

The second officer put a hand up. "I'm sorry, guys. This is a double homicide. You can't touch a thing until forensics has done their job." He pointed to Liana. "You might want to take a look at this young girl here. She's in shock."

The paramedic quickly assessed Liana and noticed the blood crusted between her legs. He looked gravely at Jo. "Do you know what's actually happened here?"

Jo glanced at Mannie and then the police officer and said, hesitantly, "I have my suspicions and I hope I'm wrong. I just don't want to think about it at the moment."

"We're going to have to take her to hospital to be properly examined. Can she walk?"

Jo took Liana's face in her hands and said softly, "Sweetie, you're going to have to come with us to the hospital. Do you understand? We need to examine you." At first, Liana just stared at Jo, her eyes unfocused and blank. "I'll come with you and make sure everything's okay. Is that alright?"

Tears were still running down Liana's face as she gazed across at her mother lying on the floor. Upon glancing at her father's body in the hallway, her face turned to one of horror, and, with her eyes tightly shut, she clung to Jo.

Jo pointed to the paramedic and the ambulance driver. "These very nice men are going to take us to the hospital. Will you come with us, please?"

Liana glanced up at the two men, and after a second or two, she looked back at Jo and nodded, just slightly, but enough for them to see she understood.

"Good. Come on then. We'll get you sorted, eh?" Jo wrapped an arm around the young girls shoulders and led her to her bedroom. That was when she saw the blood on the bed. Jo froze for a split second and then looked away, forcing herself to ignore the state of the room. It was obvious Liana had put up a struggle, as her room looked like a hurricane had gone through it.

She grabbed a small carry bag from the wardrobe and put a change of fresh clothes in it, and then, upon heading back to the lounge, she grabbed a blanket out of the hot-water cupboard in the hall to wrap around Liana. "There. That's better," she said in a calm, maternal voice. "That'll keep you nice and warm. Come on. Let's get going, eh?"

She led Liana out to the ambulance. Mannie was beside them and said, "Don't worry about your car. I'll get it home. I'll meet you at the hospital."

One of the policemen interrupted. "How far away is your home from here?"

Mannie turned to him, mystified. "Why?"

"I'll drive your wife's car home if you like. My colleague can follow and pick me up at your place."

Mannie smiled. "Oh, thanks, mate. That'd be great. Home's only about five minutes away." He turned to Jo. "See you at the hospital."

The paramedic went over to the first police officer. "Get someone to give us a call when forensics is done and we'll come back for the bodies, okay?"

It was late in the afternoon when Jo and Mannie arrived home with Liana after being at the hospital. Jo smiled as she sat Liana down and turned on the TV. "I'm glad they let you come home with us." Liana didn't say a word. She was still not willing to talk, and it had been a trying time for all the medical staff at the hospital. Liana would not let a male doctor near her let alone touch her or examine her and it was some time before it was made clear why and a female doctor was called.

Jo said jokingly to Liana, "I'll get us something to eat. I'm starving and I bet you're so hungry you could eat a horse and chase the rider."

Liana appeared not to have acknowledged a word. Jo went into the kitchen and spoke to Mannie, quietly. "I'm so glad CYF's (Child Youth and Family) decided to let her come home with us for the next couple of days. I don't know what would have happened if they had tried to put her somewhere else. No one seems to know how long she's going to be like this. I mean, the poor child's been through so much." She shook her head, dispassionately. "Raped by her own father...! Geez...! What a bastard of a guy!"

Mannie agreed. "And he was the one person she should have been able to trust the most. For all we know, he might have ruined her permanently." Mannie clenched his fist angrily. "I'm glad the bastard's dead." He glanced into the lounge to make sure Liana couldn't hear what they were talking about. "Do you think it was Li who hit Matt over the head with that poker?"

"Who else could it have been?" Jo replied soberly. "It couldn't have been Jackie or she wouldn't be dead, would she? It looks like it was Li to me."

"We'll know in a few days' times anyway, from what the cop said. Finger prints don't lie."

"Do you think we should apply to Child Youth and Family to become Li's foster parents?"

"I was wondering about that myself earlier when we were at the hospital. If you're happy with that, then so am I."

Jo gave Mannie a kiss and a big hug. "You're a good man, Mannie Te Ngongo." She glanced at Liana in the lounge. "I'd better get us some grub before we all starve eh?"

Liana broke down totally at her mother's funeral, and to

calm her, a doctor had to inject her with a strong sedative. She refused to go to her father's funeral in the afternoon and so Jo and Mannie remained at home with her. Thanks to the sedative, she slept most of the afternoon and all that night.

The coroner had ruled that an inquest be held into the deaths of Liana's parents. At its conclusion a month later, it was found that Liana had been raped by her father, who had excessive alcohol levels in his blood, late in the afternoon and that the mother had come home and witnessed the gruesome act. The father had then attacked the mother when the mother tried to get Liana out of the house.

It was ruled that in her mother's defense, Liana had grabbed the cast-iron poker from the lounge, the first item she saw in the house to defend her mother and herself with, and hit her father over the head with it three times to get him to stop hitting her mother. The death of Liana's father was considered a crime of passion, committed in a moment of insanity on her part to save her mother from the brutal beating.

For Jo and Mannie, it was a slow pains-taking and agonizing task applying for custody as foster parents of Liana, and it took several months to have everything signed over completely. The couple had temporary custody and had been scrutinized severely before CYF's finally agreed to let Liana live with them on a permanent basis once they had completed a trial period of three months.

They had a separate bedroom for Liana and Jo had bought her a complete new set of clothes along with several pairs of shoes. Both she and Mannie had gone out of their way to convince CYF's that they would be good and fitting parents.

Liana still had not spoken a word, and a report from a panel of physiologists sent to CYF stated that Liana suffered from a conditiom called delayed speech recall: a condition that has been experienced by certain child-abuse victims. It was not known if the condition was temporary or permanent. Only time would tell in her case.

Financially, and thanks to Jackie, both Liana's parents had wills; so in essence, everything was left to her. As it was, there was not a lot to inherit. Matt and Jackie had owned their own home twelve months or so prior, but due to Matt's gambling problem, which was unbeknown to Jackie, his debts were so great that they lost their house. Jackie was not aware there was a problem until it was too late. It wasn't until the debt collectors turned up on the doorstep one afternoon that she was faced with the fact that they had two options. They could sell their home and pay his debts or Matt could file for bankruptcy.

All gamblers are trapped into doubling their bets in the hope of eventually winning their money back, but this was not to be the case with Matt. Their house was sold and they were forced to rent.

This left their combined estates to be worth approximately $15,000 if all the assets were sold at current value, but at auction value, the total sum Liana received, after funeral costs, auctioneer fees, and other incidental fees were taken out, was $2,755.

Jo put this money in a savings account on a long-term fixed deposit for Liana, with the condition that she not withdraw it until she was twenty-one years old. Liana was happy to agree and the investment was signed with Liana as the sole beneficiary and Jo as her guardian.

CHAPTER 3

FOUR MONTHS LATER

Mannie arrived home from work and literally charged in the back door, and with his usual, he called out. "Hi, honey, I'm home. How's my two favourite girls been today?" Then smiling proudly, he continued before Jo could say a word. "I got a pay rise today." He paused for a moment to kiss Jo. "Am I a smart so-and-so or what?" He burst out laughing. "And that's not all. I'm being promoted to foreman. What does that make me? Don't answer. I'll tell you both. One big bloody smart-arse, eh."

Jo and Liana laughed at his crazy sense of humour. Jo replied, "Geez, Mannie. I thought you were a crazy bull or something, charging through that door like that." She looked at Liana, laughing, and then back at Mannie. "Hey, that's great news. How much did you get?"

"A dollar eighty an hour extra." He looked away for a second, frowning. "The funny thing is, the boss said times are getting tough. He's laying off four labourers at the end of the month. There'll only be qualified men left on the job."

"So how many guys will still be working with you?"

24

"Nine including me."

"Wow. I'd say this calls for a celebration. I should ring Marlene and invite her and her hubby around eh?" Jo glanced at her watch. "You know, that new girl at work who replaced Jackie? Remember me telling you about her? The one who got married last year."

"Yeah, I remember. Celebrate, eh? Sounds good to me."

"Marlene's husband works for some engineering company. They build truck trailers, stuff like that."

"Oh, okay."

"I'll call her, shall I?"

"Yeah. Go for it."

Liana had been doing her school home work when Mannie arrived home with his good news. Over the last three months, she had settled down considerably and was fitting in well with their lifestyle. She got on well with Mannie, even though she wouldn't allow him to touch her in any way, not even a paternal kiss when he came home from work.

One of Liana's problems now was that she couldn't cope with a crowded classroom since her parents' deaths. It was all part of her condition, and she still hadn't spoken a word.

It was agreed that she attend a special-needs class at the school which had only three other students in it. The principal of the school and her teacher, along with Mannie and Jo, agreed that she needed time and space to get herself on track to recovery. It was necessary to isolate her, to a small degree, during class. Socially, she mixed happily with three other girls during breaks, who had been her close friends before her parents' deaths. They also protected her from the less compassionate and ignorant students. These three girls understood that the last thing Liana needed was teasing about her lack of speech.

Jo turned to Li, and holding her gently by the shoulders, she looked her in the eye. "Would you like to come out with us tonight to a restaurant for dinner, Li? We have to celebrate Mannie's pay rise."

Liana thought about it for a moment and then smiled, nodding shyly.

"Fantastic. It'll be great and I'm sure you'll enjoy it. Get you away from my cooking and out of the house for a change. It'll do us all good." She laughed happily, wanting everything to be just right for Liana. "Right then. I'll phone Marlene and Nga Rangi."

Jo picked up the phone and was about to dial the restaurant, when Liana put her arms around her waist and cuddled her. She looked into Jo's eyes, smiling, and then stepping back half a metre, she pointed at Mannie first then at Jo and with her hand, she did a 180-degree sweep around their home. She looked back at Mannie with a huge smile and then at Jo again and wrapped her arms around Jo and held her tightly.

Jo was taken aback for a few seconds while she summed up what Liana was trying to say then; when she thought she understood, she took Liana's face in her hands and kissed her tenderly on the forehead. "You're welcome."

Confused, Mannie asked, "What's she trying to say?"

For a moment, Jo felt her throat restrict as her emotions took over and a tear ran down her cheek. She replied, "She's saying thank you to us for taking her into our home."

Mannie knew better than to hug her, but he too was overcome with emotion with Liana's gesture. "You're more than welcome. You're my little princess, did you know that?"

Liana looked at him affectionately and then gave him a shy nod accompanied by a young girlish giggle.

Jo had to gather her emotions. She wiped her tears and phoned Marlene. After a serious debate, they decided to leave it up to Jo to pick the restaurant.

She glanced at Mannie and asked, "Where do you reckon we should go?"

Mannie rubbed his cheek, thoughtfully. "Can't afford anything too flash." Then, puckering an eyebrow, he replied. "What about Chinese? You always get a good feed and it's not too expensive."

Smiling, Jo looked at Li for her approval. Liana nodded. Jo picked up the telephone directory. "Getting a pay rise is real good news," she said to Liana as she flicked through the yellow pages. "It means we'll have our own home in next to no time. All three of us." She shot a glance at Mannie. "How long do you reckon before we can afford a deposit?"

Putting his arm over her shoulder, Mannie planted a kiss on her cheek. "Two, maybe, three years at the most. I'll be getting an extra sixty-three dollars in the hand more a week to put toward what we're already saving."

Jo made a booking for five at a Chinese restaurant not far from where they lived. "Shit mate. Just think. In three years we'll be inviting friends around to our own home. Our very own home. Yours, Li's, and mine." She put her arms around his waist and gave him a bear hug.

Mannie replied conservatively. "Don't get too carried away now. It won't be a mansion, you realize. It'll be just a normal house like everyone else's."

Jo couldn't help herself and kissed him passionately on the lips and then said, "Whatever it is, it'll be a mansion to me. Some place we can bring up some kids, that's what I want. All three of us and a few kids."

Mannie gently took her face in his hands and kissed the tip of her nose. "Lets not rush things, eh. We got plenty of time for kids."

Mannie and Jo had had many discussions with the female psychologist about Liana and asked if showing open affection for each other would be good for Liana's recovery. The psychologist agreed that it was a step in the right direction and at the very least, it should help Liana slowly gain back confidence in the male gender.

Smiling and wiping her hands on a tea towel, Jo added, "I don't mean have kids right now, you big ox." She laughed at Mannie's assumption. "When the times right, we'll know. I'll tell you." Giggling, she nibbled his ear and whispered, "You know what though. We could practice making kids, like now, if you like."

Caught totally off guard by her seductive suggestion, Mannie replied, "Geez girl. Get outta here." He glanced at his watch. "What time did you say these buggers are coming around?"

"In about an hour or so. We got time, you know. And we could shower together after." She smiled at him challengingly, flashing her puppyish eyes.

Observing her mood affectionately, he said, "You know how to pull a mans strings don't you, you sexy wench?"

Taking him by the hand, she led him towards the bedroom. "Yeah, well. That's what women do."

Grinning approvingly, Mannie replied. "You enjoy having your way with me. You got an evil streak in you, did you know that?"

She chuckled. "Yeah, not all the time though, just sometimes." Then turning to Liana, she said, "We're going to have a shower, sweetheart. You get out your best outfit and we'll see if it needs ironing, eh? We won't be too long."

Nga Rangi and Marlene knocked on the front door an hour and a quarter later. Smiling contentedly, Jo opened the door. "Come in. Come in."

As they entered, Marlene turned to her husband. "Jo, this is the other half, Nga Rangi. Nga Rangi, Jo."

Nga Rangi flashed his eyebrows, returning Jo's homely smile. "Nice to meet you. I've heard a lot about you."

Mannie came to the door and immediately put his hand

out. "Gidday, mate." He turned to Jo, smiling. "I know this bugger. We went to school together years ago down country. How's everything, mate? You're lookin' good."

Nga Rangi was surprised to meet an old friend from their childhood days and shook hands. "Gidday, mate."

"What a shocker, eh?" Mannie said cheerfully. "Fancy meeting you again after all this time."

Jo took Mannie's hand. "Mannie, this is Marlene."

"Hi, nice to meet you," he said, laughing jovially. "You don't want to hear what I've heard about you."

"Yeah...!" Marlene said, laughing. "What have you heard?"

Jo cut in, slapping Mannie's arm, "He's only joking, silly bugger. Take no notice." Then turning to Liana, she said, "And this is Li."

Nga Rangi said hello. Liana smiled shyly.

Then Jo asked, "You fellahs want a drink? You can have anything you like so long as it's wine or beer." Laughing, she asked Nga Rangi, "Beer?"

"Yeah, thanks."

Nga Rangi was as tall as Mannie but not as solid. He was wiry with more defined facial features and wore moderately long hair.

Marlene was five foot eight, attractive, had a slim figure with shoulder-length hair and sparkling brown eyes. She had a good sense of humour and enjoyed nice things. She and Nga Rangi shared a strong physical but private relationship and were very close.

Settling in the lounge, the two men began talking old times. Jo poured their drinks and joined them. Looking at Marlene, she gestured toward a chair. "Sit down. I've booked us at the Hoo Wa Chinese restaurant just down the road. I hope you guys like Chinese?"

"Yeah, great," Marlene responded cheerfully.

"This your home?" Nga Rangi asked casually.

"No mate," Mannie replied. "Just renting. It's a Housing New Zealand home."

Jo cut in excitedly, "We hope to have our own home in about three years."

"Good one," Nga Rangi said. "We're just renting at the moment too. State house. It's not bad. Got three bedrooms."

Chuckling, Jo added, "We want at least three bedrooms and I'm gonna fill them up with kids."

It was obvious a good friendship was developing. Both couples had a lot in common, and before they knew it, it was time to leave for the restaurant.

Getting ready to leave, Mannie announced, "We can all go in my van if you like." He had a Ford Econo van he used for work.

Raising an eyebrow, Jo said, a little concerned, "It's clean in the back I hope?"

Mannie replied, "Yeah. Seats are fine. It's nothing flash. Just a work vehicle."

"I've got an old Mazda to go to work in," Nga Rangi said with a shrug. "Having a flash car isn't a priority at the moment."

"You work for an engineer, I hear?"

"Yeah. We build truck trailers. You know, transporters, logging trailers. Heavy duty stuff like that."

"Got plenty of work?" Mannie asked.

"We were real busy a while ago but things have slowed up a bit lately."

Marlene cut in, "We've got two friends boarding with us at the moment. They say they can't afford to rent just yet."

Pondering the scenario, Mannie said soberly, "My boss says things are getting a bit tight lately too. But things can't be too bad or he wouldn't have given me a rise."

Jo pondered their options. "We could do like Marlene and

Nga Rangi are doing if things do get tough. We could take in a boarder. It's not a bad idea."

"Well yeah, that's an option."

As the night progressed, so did the friendship and as time went by, they spent a lot of their leisure time together.

CHAPTER 4

New Zealand troops were in East Timor, assisting the United Nations peace-keeping forces. Indonesian militia was being forced back across the Indonesian border southwest of Suai and as they retreated, they tortured and killed East Timorese civilians and burned everything in their path.

A New Zealand Iroquois helicopter was returning from Dili to their military base near Suai with eight New Zealand Special Air Service troops on board under the command of Lieutenant John Amohia. To communicate between each other as a unit, the troops wore 'wireless radio receivers'.

The commander of the New Zealand Forces in East Timor, Colonel Cooper, was in his command post at the military base. He had just received a message from the British command source in Fohorem that the village near the hospital on the outskirts of Suai was under attack from Indonesian militia.

Colonel Cooper put on his wireless radio receiver headset. "Eagle one. Eagle one. Copy?"

Lieutenant Tony Scott, the pilot, took the call. "Eagle one. Go ahead."

"Got a problem at the hospital near Suai, Scotty. Retreating Militia are attacking the village and burning everything in sight. They haven't made it to the hospital yet but it's only a matter of time. I need to divert section 4 to the hospital to evacuate medical staff ASAP before the militia reaches them. Is that a problem?"

"No problem, Colonel. Can do. Should take around ten minutes to get there."

"You there, John?"

John Amohia, a tall, muscular intelligent Maori, answered, "Colonel. Heard that loud and clear Sir."

"The village around the hospital near Suai is under attack from retreating militia. They're creating havoc. We need to evacuate the medical staff immediately."

"Roger that, Colonel."

"Remember the rules of engagement, John," the colonel reiterated. "Do not engage the militia unless fired upon."

"Copy that loud and clear Colonel. Do not engage the militia unless fired upon."

"Be careful, John. Bring your team home safely."

"No worries, sir. I'll get them home safely."

"Carry on, soldier. Do your job."

John turned to the pilot. "You heard what the colonel said, Scotty. Turn this bird around."

"Be there in ten minutes," Scotty replied. "I'll pull back once I've dropped you off and wait for your call."

John nodded and then, turning to his men, ordered, "You all heard that. Our job is to evacuate all medical staff." John looked at his men. "Remember the rules of engagement. Do not engage the militia unless fired upon. Copy?"

Each man acknowledged with a nod.

Scotty cut in, "Two minutes out."

"Red team, take starboard, blue team, on me," John said as they prepared to disembark through the open side doors.

Red team was led by Sergeant Tui Paloa, John's close and

trusted friend. Tui was part Cook Islander, part Maori, six foot tall, wiry but muscular, a dedicated soldier.

John and Tui had struck a strong friendship and had stuck together right through their Military careers.

Scotty turned to John, pointing with his head. "There's the hospital. Twenty seconds to drop off." John gave his men the hand signal to get ready to disembark.

The helicopter swooped low over the jungle into the clear space beside the jungle 150 metres from the hospital.

Through the smoky haze they could see huts in the village on fire. It was a chaotic scene. Villagers were running in all directions, screaming at the horror surrounding them. Some were trying to flee to the temporary safety of the jungle. Many villagers were already dead, shot by militia, their bodies strewn on the ground around the village. The ominous sound of AK47 automatic rifle fire echoed through the small valley.

John signalled to Tui. Tui nodded. As the helicopter briefly touched down, they leaped out and, keeping low, sprinted towards the hospital. Scotty quickly lifted off and pulled back out of range to wait.

The militia opened fire on them as they ran towards the hospital. John shouted into his wireless radio receiver, "Return fire. I repeat. Return fire."

As they raced toward the hospital they heard the whine of a missile and went to ground. A mortar exploded in a huge fireball fifty metres behind them sending shrapnel whining menacingly around them. Leaping to their feet, they continued to the temporary safety of the hospital.

Tui's team was against the right hospital wall. One militia soldier ran out from the closest hut only thirty metres away and threw a lighted torch onto the thatched roof. The militia soldier spotted Tui as Tui glanced around the corner of the hospital and fired his AK47. Tui drew back as the corner beside him erupted in a cloud of shattered wood and splinters.

Going down low, Tui rolled out onto open ground and fired a short burst of automatic fire. The militiaman went down with two bullets in his chest.

John, sneaking a peak inside through a side window, saw a militiaman with his arm around a nurse's neck. He was pointing his AK-47 rifle at four medical staff huddled together beside a hospital bed.

John spoke into his wireless receiver. "One hostile inside with hostages. You see him Tui?"

Tui was on the opposite wall and stole a peak through a side window. "Copy that. What do you want to do?"

"I'll go in this side and distract him. You take him from behind."

"Affirmative. Give me the word."

"Going in .... now."

John and the blue team burst in through the side door pointing their rifles at the militiaman. The militiaman swung the screaming nurse around, using her as a shield and retreated backwards towards the opposite side door.

"Let the girl go!" John shouted to him. "Let the girl go."

Not understanding English, the militiaman kept retreating. Tui had his rifle slung over his shoulder and slipped quietly in through the side door. The militia soldier caught sight of him out of the corner of his eye. He swung his AK-47 around, but before he could bring it to bear, Tui grabbed the barrel with one hand, the butt with the other, and wrenched it out of the militiaman's hands then drove the pistol-grip into the man's temple. He slumped to the floor unconscious. Tui grabbed the terrified screaming nurse's arm to calm her and took her over to her colleagues.

Tui's team rushed in as a mortar shell burst in a massive explosion, blowing an enormous hole in the front corner of the wall, sending fragments of timber and debris flying in every direction.

The northern end of the thatched roof caved in without

support from the shattered corner wall and began to burn, quickly filling the room with smoke.

The medical staff consisted of two doctors and three nurses. John pointed to the rear of the building. "We're here to evacuate you to the military base. Everybody to the rear. Come on, move it, move it." With a calculating eye, he quickly assessed the situation. "Is there anyone else in here?"

A doctor shook his head.

John spoke into his wireless receiver. "You there Scotty? Evac now. I repeat. Evac now."

Scotty answered immediately. "Rodger that John. Standby to evac."

Putting up covering fire, John's team led the medical staff out through the rear door. Another mortar exploded on the open ground in the front of the hospital. Fragments of shrapnel ricocheted off the walls.

Appearing through the screen of smoke, the helicopter swooped in low over the jungle onto open ground, landing 150 metres from the hospital.

Keeping low, John led the medical staff while the other six members of the team formed a line and retreated, running backward, putting up covering fire.

"Keep moving but hold the line," John ordered. "Hold the line."

A mortar shell burst between them and the helicopter. A nurse screamed in terror as they went to ground, and then she was hurriedly dragged to her feet and urged to keep going.

"Keep moving!" John yelled at them. "Keep moving!"

A mortar exploded in a huge fireball on the southern end of hospital roof blowing part of it away. Sparks and flames from the explosion blew over the building setting the whole building alight.

They reached the helicopter. John quickly helped the medical staff onboard. As the rest of the team reached the helicopter, another mortar shell exploded between them and the burning hospital. They leaped up into the helicopter as it lifted off. John manned the M60 machine-gun and opened fired on the attacking militia soldiers as they charged across the open ground.

John called to the pilot. "Get us outta here Scotty. Take us home, mate."

Scotty swung the big war bird low over the dense jungle and disappeared from sight of the burning hospital.

CHAPTER 5

SOUTH AUCKLAND , 2005

Wall Street crashed over night, sending a world wide monetary collapse across the globe with catastrophic results. The New Zealand economy plunged on the international stage forcing the nation into recession. The Reserve Bank was forced to step in in an attempt to slow a fragile economy without result. Finance companies crumbled into liquidation, receivership, or bankruptcy. Thousands of mum and dad investors either lost their hard-earned savings or had them frozen.

The building industry plunged into disarray, with developers and building companies closing their doors; some were forced into liquidation and bankruptcy with trades people being laid off by the hundreds nationwide. Trade related companies also fell into financial chaos, forcing yet further job lay off's.

The project Mannie had been working on came to an end. Reluctantly, his boss had to lay him off, forcing him to apply for the unemployment benefit. Having a healthy bank balance complicated matters and he was given an eight week stand-down period, meaning he wouldn't get any assistance from Work and Income for at least eight weeks.

Jo was devastated when she arrived home from work and Mannie broke his sad news. Frustrated, she threw her hands in the air. "Eight bloody weeks' stand-down period...! Geez! I don't believe it. How ridiculous is that?" Slapping her hand down hard on the sink bench, she shouted. "The bloody moment we get anything saved, they want to take it off us!" Again, she thumped the sink top. "Apart from the rent, we still got hire-purchase payments to make on the fridge, the washing machine... Shit...! This really pisses me off. How the hell are we going to get by without having to dip into our savings?"

Biting his bottom lip, Mannie replied, "I've applied for another job, but I'm not holding my breath. The guy has been inundated with applications. He said his phone hasn't stopped ringing."

"That's just it. I'm not angry at you. It's the bloody system. I mean, what's the damn point in trying to get ahead when this sort of shit happens."

"At the moment we don't have any options." Mannie said, regretfully.

"Just when things start to come together for us, we get lumbered with this crap. I can't believe our luck."

Liana was now almost eighteen. She had left school and Jo managed to wangle her a job with the same company she worked for as office assistant. Their employer had been sympathetic to Liana's plight and so, when she left school, he offered her the job. Jo was so appreciative of his gesture and it was good to be able to keep an eye on Liana during the day. She was still very sensitive to males and had not yet spoken a word.

Just two weeks prior, Nga Rangi lost his job, as the transport industry floundered in the doomed economy. Applying for the unemployment benefit was the only option.

His stand-down period was six weeks. To keep up the rent payments to Housing New Zealand, he was forced to sell his car. Marlene's wage wasn't enough to cover their expenses and they decided to take in yet another boarder, making it a total of three boarders to help with the rent.

* * * * *

For eight months now, Mannie and Nga Rangi had been on the dole and to supplement their meagre existence, most Saturdays they went fishing at South Head, just inside the mouth of the Manukau Harbour.

To buy vegetables at reasonable prices, Marlene and Jo went to the Otara market most Saturdays and were still unpacking their purchases when the two men walked in earlier than usual with only one fish between them.

"Weren't expecting you guys back for at least another two and a half hours," Jo said, a little bemused. "What happened?"

"DoC officers were all over the bloody place this morning," Mannie informed her. "We didn't want to get caught up with that lot. They were searching everyone's bags and measuring the catches. They gave some people a real hard time."

Marlene cut in, "I suppose with so many people unemployed, a lot of them are taking whatever catch they can to put food on the table."

"We can kiss our house good-bye," Jo said, angrily. "All our dreams and hopes gone, just like that," she said, clicking her fingers. "Geez, man, this pisses me off." She put her hands on her hips and pondered their demise. "You know what the problem is, don't you? There's too many bloody pakehas running this country."

Marlene added. "She's right. Maori don't have enough say in parliament."

Shooting a quick glance at Mannie, Nga Rangi said sombrely, "They're both right, but what can we do about it?"

Mannie shook his head and said, "Nothing mate. Not a bloody thing." Frustrated, he looked quizzically at his watch and then at Nga Rangi. "You feel like a beer?"

"You mean go to the pub?"

"Yeah. Just a quick one, eh? Just one."

Feeling a little guilty, Nga Rangi turned to Marlene for her approval.

Frowning, she looked at her wristwatch. "Just so long as it's only one beer. We don't have money to waste at the pub."

"We'll be about an hour."

Mannie and Nga Rangi were standing at a leaner table in the local tavern, quietly drinking their beer. Being on the side of the table that faced the door, Mannie observed three men as they walked in, one seemingly to be somewhat familiar.

Noticing, Nga Rangi followed Mannie's gaze to the men who had just come in. They ordered a drink each at the bar and went to a leaner table just two along from where he and Mannie were standing.

Curious, Nga Rangi asked, "Who're you lookin' at?"

Mannie kept studying one particular person. "That tall bugger. I know him from somewhere but I can't remember where." He turned to Nga Rangi. "You know him?"

Nga Rangi shook his head. "Nope."

Mannie kept studying the tall guy, and then suddenly, his eyes narrowed. "I know that bastard. Yes, now I remember him."

Now stationed at the Papakura Military Camp, John Amohia had recently returned from his second tour of duty of East Timor. He had come in to relax and enjoy a quiet drink with two friends, who were local to this bar.

Mannie walked over and stood behind him. "Your name Amohia?"

John Amohia half turned to Mannie. "Yeah. What can I do for you?"

With a hint of cynicism in his tone, Mannie replied, "Your old man's a paramount chief?"

"Yeah."

Mannie's mouth twisted into an angry snarl. "It was your bloody ancestors that gave away the Tongariro National Park, our sacred mountains, and all it's surrounding lands to the bloody pakeha." He hesitated, shaking his head. "Seventy-nine thousand, five-hundred bloody hectares in total. Now that's one hell of a lot of land to just give away. My great-grandfather disagreed with that decision and your gutless lot murdered him for it."

Taken aback by the accusation and looking at Mannie quizzically, John replied, "Who the hell are you then?"

Mannie sneered. "You obviously don't know your history very well, do you?"

John did know his tribal history. He frowned, thinking seriously about what Mannie had said. "You must be the great-grandson of Huri Te Ngongo. Am I right?"

"Yeah. How'd you guess?"

John looked him over for a second or two before replying. He could understand his anger if Mannie's account was correct, but it wasn't, and he tried to reason with him. "It wasn't like that at all. Huri, your great-grandfather, attacked his chief, Eramiha, and killed him with his patu. He then turned on the paramount chief, my great-grandfather, and tried to kill him as well." Pausing for a moment, John studied Mannie's face to see if he was listening to what he was saying. "In defending his brother and chief, Iwikau, my great uncle, fought the patu from Huri and killed him in self-defense with his own weapon."

Furious at John's version of the story, Mannie shouted into

his face, "Bullshit. They murdered him because he disagreed with them. That's why he was murdered."

John was getting annoyed and very agitated by Mannie's accusation and turned fully around to face him. "That's not what happened at all." He could see how angry Mannie was, and again, he tried to reason with him. "The government was going to take the land anyway, one way or another. Don't you understand that? It was all going to be confiscated." Sensing Mannie's disbelief at his version, he went on, "You need to listen to your true history, the way it was, not that crap story your family has been telling you." Angry, he threw his hands in the air. "If you don't believe me, look it up for yourself. It's in our history books."

Mannie lifted his chin condescendingly. "That's what your lot say just to save their own arses. Gutless arseholes, the bloody lot of them."

Keeping his anger in check at the insults, John replied. "Ask any chief in our tribe then. They'll tell you the truth. Ask someone independent from your family. They'll tell you what really happened."

"They've all been brainwashed by your bloody lot. You're so full of shit."

Disgusted at Mannie's outburst, John turned back to his two friends. "Come on, fellahs. We don't have to listen to this idiot." He waved his hand in dismissal. "Go away. Bugger off Te Ngongo and take your crap with you. Leave us alone."

Embarrassed, Nga Rangi grabbed Mannie's arm. "Come on, mate. Don't make a fuss, eh. It's not worth it."

Shrugging Nga Rangi's hand away, Mannie stabbed a finger at John. "Stuff this prick. It was his family that murdered my great-grandfather."

John looked at his two friends and, with his head, pointed to the door. "Come on fellahs. We don't have to listen to this dumb bastard."

John and his two friends started walking towards the

door. Unable to control his temper, Mannie lunged at John, punching him on the back of the head. John staggered and then turned to face Mannie, but before he had time to do anything else, one of John's friends stepped between them, pushing Mannie away.

"Come on, man. Bugger off, eh. We don't want any trouble." Glancing around the bar, he noticed other patrons were staring at them. "This isn't the place to sort out your problems. Go on, bugger off."

Determined, Mannie stood his ground. "You bugger off, you bloody wanker."

Feeling very uncomfortable, Nga Rangi put his hand on Mannie's shoulder. "Come on Mannie. Don't do this. Let's go before there's some serious trouble."

Mannie shrugged Nga Rangi's hand away as a bouncer walked over to them.

"What's going on here?" the bouncer asked. "We don't want any trouble, understand? If you can't hold your liquor, leave."

Without another word, Mannie stormed off toward the door. Nga Rangi followed, apologizing to the bouncer as he went.

Outside, Nga Rangi grabbed Mannie's shoulder, stopping him, and asked, "What the hell was all that nonsense about? His grandfather murdering your grandfather...?"

Feeling miserable and upset at his lack of self control, Mannie started walking home. "I'll tell you one day when I'm not so pissed off."

"Geez, man. You were so angry. What the hell got into you?"

CHAPTER 6

Back at home, Jo sensed Mannie's despondent mood. Frowning, she asked, "What's happened? Did you get into a fight or something? You look so damn grumpy."

Not wanting to tell her, Mannie turned away and gazed out the window.

Nga Rangi decided to tell the girls about John Amohia and the way Mannie had attacked him.

Worried and concerned, Jo went over and put her hand on Mannie's shoulder. "That's not like you...! I mean, what did he do that upset you so much?"

"I'll tell you later," Mannie replied, still annoyed at himself for not keeping better control of his temper.

Nga Rangi, wanting to leave Jo and Mannie to sort out their problem, took Marlene's hand and gestured toward the door. "Come on. We better get going anyway. The boarders'll be home soon." Nga Rangi and Marlene then left.

Jo took Mannie's hand, feeling a little disconcerted. "What's happening to you? You've been so quiet and distant lately. What are you thinking about? Come on mate. I'm one person you can talk to. Tell me."

With a forlorn face, Mannie slowly turned to her. "I'm just so pissed off with things. You know, being on the dole and all that. We had our plans about buying a home, having kids. It's just not possible any more."

Jo, putting her arm around him, rested her head on his shoulder "What do you want to do then? I mean, what can we do? At least we have each other and Liana. That's not so bad."

Two weeks later, Nga Rangi was walking home from the local Four Square supermarket, when a black 1963 Ford Galaxy pulled up just ahead of him. There were four passengers; one rather grubby-looking man got out. He was wearing a black leather jerkin and black sunglasses. He took a couple of steps toward Nga Rangi and then stopped, blocking his path.

"How's it?" he asked.

Ignoring the question, Nga Rangi tried to walk around him but again, he blocked his path. To Nga Rangi, the guy appeared either intoxicated or high on drugs or both. Another thing he couldn't help but notice was the man's putrid body odour. His clothes were filthy and grimy; the shirt collar had a permanent stain from the lack of washing, and his bad breath would stop a charging bull elephant.

Frowning, the man asked, "What's your problem? I just wanna have a little chat."

Getting agitated at the way the man was acting, Nga Rangi replied, "Whatever it is you got, I'm not interested."

"You don't know what I've got."

"Like I said. Not interested."

The man turned to his friends in the big Ford. The passenger in the left front seat whispered something to the him.

Nga Rangi noticed the patch on the back of his black leather jerkin. Black supremacy. He also noticed the back of his right hand had a large skull tattooed on it.

The gangster turned back to him and said, "We're

recruiting new gang members at the moment. Thought you might be interested."

Nga Rangi shook his head. "Like I said, not interested."

"You like being on the dole doing nothing?"

"Not particularly."

"Join us. You'd have a patch in no time."

"You mean rape a couple of girls and my reward is, you'll give me a patch?"

"Don't be a smart-arse."

"Piss off."

"We know where you live, fellah."

"Go play your stupid games somewhere else."

"You just might regret saying that, arsehole."

"Whatever."

The gangster got back in the big black Ford and gave Nga Rangi the one-fingered salute as they drove off. Feeling somewhat uncomfortable and ignoring the derogatory gesture, Nga Rangi carried on home.

Jo and Mannie had been forced into taking in two boarders to try and cope with the everyday living. Pucky and Chappy had been with them for two months.

Mannie was standoffish, not his usual self and had been for some time, his mind seeming to be far away. Jo was in the kitchen. He was standing in the dining room looking out the window, his face serious. He turned to her. "You were saying a while ago 'there's too many pakeha running this country'."

Jo studied him for a moment, wondering what he had in mind. "Yeah. What's that got to do with anything? We can't change things."

He pondered, thinking about the incident. "That bastard I met at the pub the other day. You know, the one I had the argument with. He's given me an idea."

Jo corrected him. "You mean the fellah you took a swing at?"

Mannie sat down on the lounge suite. "You know what I mean. His great-grandfather was the paramount chief of our tribe at that time and he gave a lot of land away to the bloody government. You know, the Tongariro National Park. It was once Maori land. Our tribal land." He hesitated, mulling over the idea. "We could go there and claim some of it back."

Unsure and confused about what he was getting at, Jo said. "What the hell are you talking about? Claim back some land...? From whom? The bloody government...? I don't understand what the heck you're talking about."

Mannie patted the lounge suite for her to sit down and then began to explain his story about how his great-grandfather was murdered because he was against the gifting of the three mountains and all its surrounding land. That was the reason he was so angry and upset the other day in the bar. It was John Amohia's great-grandfather who was the murderer.

Jo looked deep into his eyes, not fully understanding what he was on about. "You want to go and claim back some of that land. To live there? How the hell do you expect to get away with that? You just can't do that these days." She waved her hands in front of his face. "Hello...! Wake up Mannie." She hesitated momentarily. "We're in the twenty-first century for God's sake. Not the eighteenth century."

"This land, there's nothing on it but scrub, bush, and wild game," Mannie went on. "No one lives there. No one even goes there apart from the odd hunter."

"So what are you proposing then? I still don't understand what you're really getting at."

"We could build some huts there and live off the land." He looked at the floor for a second, considering the idea. "We could do it, you know. No one would even know we're there."

Jo shook her head, not at all convinced his idea would work. "Geez Mannie. Get real. We couldn't do it on our own. And we've also got Li to consider. We'd need to have more people than just you, me, and Li. And it wouldn't be easy either. If you just think about it for a minute you'll realize just how much work would be involved."

"I know that, and I do know how much work would be involved," he replied impatiently. "We'd need about nine, maybe even as many as eleven people with the same sentiments and purpose as us. We could do it. We could really do it."

Again, and shaking her head, Jo said, "Who's going to wanna come with us? It's on the side of a damn mountain for Christ's sake. It'd be as cold as buggery in winter. Who would want to live up there? You tell me? And another thing. If we were ever found out, we'd be kicked off quick smart, no ifs or buts about it. What then?" She paused, adding up the disadvantages. "And where is this place anyway?"

"It's a place called Pokaka." He paused for a moment, deep in thought. "Look, I know there's a few things that need to be ironed out, but I'm sure it could be done."

Looking at it from another perspective, Jo interrupted, "Hang on a minute. We couldn't just build huts on the side of the mountain without someone noticing. And another thing. Where would we get the materials from for a start, and how would we get it there?"

"We build the huts in the bush."

"Mount Ruapehu is a tourist destination. There'd be planes and helicopters full of tourists flying around the place all year round. Have you thought about that? Someone's bound to notice, surely to God. We'd never get away with it."

Mannie smiled as his idea expanded. Jo had brought up something he hadn't thought about, but one that would be easy to remedy. "It's too far from the ski fields to get a lot of planes flying around. There might be the odd one, but not many. But you're right. You've brought up a very valid point." He turned away, thinking about the scenario. "We could build huts that are partially underground. It'd be easy to insulate them too. They'd be reasonably warm inside during the winter, and the big thing is, the way I'd build the roof, they wouldn't be noticed from the air."

He smiled, eyeing her up speculatively. "It'd be easy to disguise the entrance. We could use camouflage nets with twigs and foliage wound into them. The walls would be built the normal way, you know, with studs and nogs, and I'd fit polystyrene between the walls for insulation. I could make them up in plywood sections so they'd be light and easy to carry." He pondered his options with a positive mind. "For the roof, we'd use small trees cut from the bush with a waterproof membrane like Butynol pulled over them to keep it dry inside. Then we'd put dirt on top of that and cover it with grassy turf so it looks natural from the air."

Jo cut in, still not convinced. "Underground...? You expect me to live underground like some damn cave woman...? Be your mole...? Is that it?" She scratched her head dubiously. "For a start, they'd stink like hell! Geez, Mannie...! Get real. Pull your bloody head in."

"It wouldn't be really underground. We'd build them so they appear to be underground. As long as we keep them clean and tidy inside, they'd be fine." He paused as a picture formed in his mind; his idea was beginning to sound feasible. He smiled positively. "Look, I've been to this place hunting in my teens several times. I've got the perfect spot in mind. It's on a big plateau with a moderate slope that would drain the water away from the huts when it's wet."

Jo shook her head. The idea of what he was suggesting still wasn't clear. "It sounds crazy. You're going to have to try a hell of a lot harder than that to convince me. Trust me."

Three days passed without Mannie mentioning the move to Pokaka. Jo didn't broach the subject either, and he naturally thought she had put the idea out of her head.

She had been out at the washing line, and as she came in, she dropped the basket on the table. Mannie noticed her sombre mood. She was deep in thought, just standing there, looking at the basket of washing. Turning to Mannie, she said, "Been thinking about your idea about moving to Pokaka. It's been playing on my mind these last couple of days." She broke off and sat down beside him. "You know, the more I think about it, the more I like it. I know it sounds crazy and totally out of character for me, but it's not a bad option. Let's just say I'm warming to the idea. I've also been thinking about how Li would like it. I'll run it past her, eh?"

Mannie nodded with a smile. Well, that's something. At least she's thinking about it, he thought.

"Hey, Li. Come in here for a moment, will you. We have something very important to ask you."

Liana had been tidying her bedroom and came into the lounge. Jo gestured for her to take a seat. Liana sat down beside her.

"Mannie and I have been thinking," she started. She could see she had Liana's attention. "We've been thinking of moving out of the city and going to a place called Pokaka. It's down by Mount Ruapehu." She looked at Liana quizzically to see if she understood. Liana nodded her head questioningly.

Jo had grown used to Liana's body language, and she could see that she understood. "So you understand what I'm saying then?" Again, Liana nodded. "Good. We've been thinking that if we could get enough nice people we could trust, say like ten or eleven, we could build some huts down there and live off the land. Do you think you might like that type of life? They'd be a lot of work, but it would be rewarding work. I think I would like it myself and so does Mannie."

Liana was deep in thought, studying Jo's face. She had her lips pursed, a sign Jo had come to recognize that she was seriously mulling over the idea. Liana suddenly got up and took Jo by the hand and led her to her bedroom and looked Jo in the eye with her hand out from her side with her palm side up. Jo was studying her face for a moment, trying to fathom what she was meaning.

Mannie had followed them and was watching Liana staring at Jo quizzically. He guessed immediately what she was asking. "She's wondering if she'll still have her own bedroom." Liana turned to him and he looked Liana in the eye. "Yes, Li. You'll have your own bedroom, just like you have here. It might not be as nice as this one, but you will have your very own bedroom."

Jo looked at him, surprised. "How'd you guess that?"

"Don't forget, I live here too, you know," he replied.

"Well," she said. "You never cease to amaze me. For a big oaf, sometimes you display some intelligence, even if it is in a primitive sort of way." She laughed at her own joke and then looked back at Liana. "Is that what you were asking?"

Liana grinned at Mannie and then glanced at Jo, nodding.

"Well, that settles it then." They went back to the lounge.

Mannie looked at her musingly. "It'd be a lot better I reckon than living like this, on the dole, like damn beggars."

For many long seconds Jo sat there, summing up his idea. She could see Liana wasn't going to be a problem with the change in lifestyle and she said, "I'm still not 100 percent convinced. You reckon you could build something with normal studs, a normal wooden floor, insulate it all with polystyrene walls and ceilings with dirt over that, and you reckon it wouldn't stink?"

"Yeah. No problem at all. The dirt would be on the outside. The inside would be totally isolated from the outside." He explained to her his basic thoughts of the construction. "It'd be quite simple really and I'm sure it'd work. In fact, I know it would if it was done right."

Several days later, Jo had been going through the accounts

payable. She sat back on her chair, mulling over his idea. Mannie was very quiet, sitting in the lounge. He looked very serious, obviously thinking about his idea.

Frowning, she cocked an eyebrow and asked, "You really think this idea of yours would work?" She paused for a moment, rubbing her chin. "I know the whole idea sounds crazy, but just maybe, you might be onto something." She looked down at all the unpaid bills, summing up their financial situation. She was slowly beginning to come around to Mannie's idea and that, if they did things right, it just might work. "Let me think about this for a bit eh. I'll sleep on it. Gotta get my head around a few things, if you know what I mean."

"Yeah, that's fine," Mannie replied, smiling at her and switched the television on.

Mannie was sitting at the dining table opposite Jo during breakfast the following morning. Liana was sitting at the end of the table, eating her breakfast. Mannie looked at Jo as he cut into his fried eggs. "You given any more thought to the idea?"

"Yeah, I have," she replied and put down her knife and fork. "Tell me more."

Grinning and sensing she was beginning to seriously consider his idea, he sat bolt upright. "Let me do a couple of sketches and I'll show you."

"Okay. That's a good idea. I'll get a pad and pencil, and you can draw it out for me." She found an A4 pad and pencil and laid them on the table in front of him. "Okay. Convince me."

Liana finished her breakfast, and putting her plate to one side, she watched Mannie sketch out a basic floor plan of the type of hut he had in mind on one page. Then on another, he drew a cross section of how the hut would fit together, from the top of the floor up, including the beams cut from the bush and the way the smaller branches would support the Butynol.

He even drew in the dirt roof with turf on top to form a grassy appearance.

He looked up at Jo with a serious face. "See. Quite simple, really. It wouldn't really be underground. Just looks like it is. We'd pre-cut everything out here first, strap each hut together individually so nothing gets left out or left behind."

Jo studied the roughly sketched plan for several minutes and then asked. "What about the floor? I couldn't put up with a dirt floor."

Turning a page, Mannie drew another cross section. "We make up floor sections 3.6 metres long, 600 millimetres wide out of 150 millimetre dry tantalized pine with plywood screwed on top for the actual floor."

He looked up to see if she understood. She nodded; he went on. "We sit each floor section on top of ground treated tantalized blocks one and a half metres apart. We'd need six sections for each floor per hut. The sections could be screwed together on top of each other in packs of three so they could be carried without too much trouble. There'd be two packs per hut. We'd unscrew them once we are ready to lay them down. They'd be light, easy to carry, strong, and effective. I'm telling you, this'll work."

"Explain the walls to me again."

Mannie explained how the walls would be built, how the polystyrene would be fitted between the studs and glued to the back of the exterior plywood sheet with the interior sheet fitted over that, forming one panel, and so on.

He sat back, feeling satisfied and happy with his basic design. "See. It'd be quite simple. It'd take three or four days to carry everything in. Then after the digging is completed, it'd be just a matter of time to put it all together."

She eyed him with a serious face, partially convinced and then, cocking her head to one side, she said, "I've been going over our bills and boy, we have a lot to pay this month. You know, we wouldn't have to pay rent, power, phone. That's one good thing in its favour."

Mannie sensed her optimism. "There's a lot of wild game there too. Deer, pigs, pigeon, probably pheasants. We wouldn't run short of meat. It's the vegetables that could present a bit of a problem initially. A vegetable garden would take a while to get established, but we could take in canned and freeze dried veggies to tide us over in the mean time. Once we have the vegetable garden established, we'd be in business."

Unconsciously, she wiped her mouth with her hand, studying his sketch. "We should have a talk with Marlene and Nga Rangi. They just might entertain the idea."

"So you're actually thinking seriously about it then?" Mannie asked, rather excited with his proposal.

"The idea does have some merit, I'll give you that. It's the garden that worries me. I mean, what types of vegetables grow in that climate?"

"I know carrots grow there for a start. Then there's potatoes, brussel sprouts, stuff like that. I'm not sure about kumara though, but in the summer, there'd be cabbage, lettuce, peas, beans and corn for sure."

"But what about opossums? Wouldn't they eat all the new plants?"

"We could take in wire netting to put around the garden to keep the blighter's out. We could also lay poison just to make sure. We'd soon stop them. I don't think they'd present a problem at all."

"Where's this place again? Show me on a map."

"It's called Pokaka, and there's a large north island map in my van. I'll get it."

Mannie rushed out to his van, and returning thirty seconds later, he lay the map out on the table. He showed her where Pokaka was situated on the map and where the plateau was and why he thought it would be the perfect place. "See, it's quite a distance in. About five hours walk from the road in actual fact. It's very isolated. That's the reason bugger all people go up there. It's so far in."

"Long way to carry all our gear too," Jo added cynically.

"Yeah, but once it's all there though," he said with a wide grin. "I know it sounds like a lot of hard work initially, and it would be, but once everything was done, we'd have a pretty good, healthy life style. No more worrying about having enough money for rent and all that other stuff or living on the dole."

"Come on. Let's go see Marlene and Nga Rangi," Jo replied.

"Yeah, and if they're keen, Nga Rangi and I could go down there and check the place out just to be 100 percent sure."

Feeling moderately positive, even though she still thought the idea was outrageously crazy, Jo said, "Okay. Let's go around to their place now and see what they make of it. Maybe I'm going crazy, but I'm starting to moderately like the idea. Growing our own vegetables and all that appeals to me. I really think I'd enjoy that. Be like being my own boss in a way."

Mannie took Jo's hand and, wanting to strike while the iron was hot, picked up his sketches and van keys and called Liana. "Come on. Let's do it. Let's go see them."

At Nga Rangi and Marlene's home, Mannie explained his idea of moving to Pokaka and living a life of self-sufficiency in the bush.

Marlene's initial response was negative. Shaking her head, she cast a doubtful eye at Nga Rangi. "Sounds crazy to me." She pondered for a second. "What about cooking? Where would we cook?"

"We'll build a communal cooking area in the bush," Mannie told her with a confident tone. "We'd all cook together. Be like one big happy family. The way our ancestors did in the good old days. They all cooked together."

Jo interrupted, "The secret to it is that we'd need to have a good vegetable garden. If you're worrying about that, I did quite a bit of gardening when I was living at home with my parents. I helped my dad all the time. He had a monster vegetable garden with everything you could think of in it. I could teach you."

Nga Rangi's opinion wasn't what Mannie had expected either. "I've never hunted before. I don't even own a rifle." He was sitting at the dining table in a quandary. "Do you have a rifle?"

With an air of optimism, Mannie nodded and said, "Yeah. There's nothing to it. I can show you how to use a rifle."

Still doubtful, Nga Rangi asked, "Who else have you got in mind? I mean, it'd need to be people we can get along with and trust. Living in such close quarters wouldn't be easy."

Marlene interrupted, "How many people do you think you'd need to make it viable?"

"Maybe ten, eleven at the most," Mannie replied.

Nga Rangi scratched his head. "Living in huts sounds bloody primitive to me, and everyone cooking together. It'd be like being a caveman."

Mannie replied, "That's basically what Jo said at first." He laughed. "We'd be living like our ancestors did. We'd be warriors again."

Marlene chuckled. "That's a bit of a laugh. I mean, that's like trying to live two centuries ago today, if you get my drift."

"The idea does have a few drawbacks, I admit, but there are more advantages than disadvantages. Think about it for a second. We wouldn't have rent money to find each week, insurance, power bills, phone. And Jo's keen to take charge of the garden. Once we have that established, we'd be up and running in no time."

Marlene was looking at Liana and cut in. "And what about

Li? How does she feel about it? It wouldn't be much of a life for a young girl."

To everyone's surprise, Li stood, and pointing to herself, she put her hands out with her palms up and gave them all a big smile.

Mannie smiled at Li and said, "That's Li's way of saying she's happy with the idea. We've spoken to her about it in depth, and she does like the idea."

Marlene wasn't going to take their word for it. She looked at Liana with a very stern face. "Are you sure about this, Li? It's one hell of a different way of life to what you're used to."

Liana looked at Marlene and nodded, showing a big open smile.

Nga Rangi was still dubious, unsure about the location. "What if someone found out about us?"

"Who's gonna find out? Nobody goes there any more."

"Somebody's bound to find out sooner or later. It might not be this year, but eventually, someone will discover us."

"But what could they do?" Mannie said, casting the suggestion aside. "What could they really do about it? We wouldn't be bothering anybody."

"What troubles me is, it's not our land. We'd be trespassing. I'm sure if the authorities found out, they'd kick us off, and they wouldn't mess around doing it, I might add."

"It used to be Maori land years ago until the paramount chief gifted it to the bloody government."

"You sure about that?"

"Yeah, I am, and no bugger wants it now. That's what pisses me off with the bloody pakeha. It didn't cost them a brass razue. They take it and don't do a bloody thing with it. If we have to, we'll claim squatter's rights."

Nga Rangi laughed. "Well, that's one way of looking at it."

"Why don't you and I go down there this weekend and take a look? We could go down on Friday if you've got nothing else on." Mannie suggested, sensing Nga Rangi's marginal interest, "We'd have to sleep down there for the night, but that's okay. It'll take us five hours to walk in and five hours to walk back out again, not counting for any time to have a good look around the place."

Marlene was weighing up their options and advised, "Why not? We're not doing anything. You could go if you wanted to. See what you think. We've nothing to lose."

With Marlene's obvious semi-approval, Nga Rangi replied, "Okay. You're on. Like she said. We've nothing to lose."

Happy with the outcome, Mannie added, "But we've everything to gain, mate. I reckon you'll like the place once you've seen it."

Nga Rangi suddenly hesitated, his face serious.

Mannie noticed his sudden change in mood and asked. "What's wrong? You having second thoughts?"

Nga Rangi looked up. "No, nothing like that. It's got nothing to do with the weekend or your idea."

Marlene could see something was bothering him too. "What is it then?"

He drew in a deep breath and, sighing, said, "A guy from the black supremacy gang stopped me in the street the other day, wanting me to join their gang."

Surprised at his statement, Mannie asked, "They wanted you to join their gang...?"

"Yeah."

"So what'd you say?"

"I told him to bugger off and go play his stupid games somewhere else."

"Shit, mate. That wasn't very wise. What'd he say to that?"

"He made a few threats."

"What sort of threats?"

"He said he knew where I lived."

"And...?"

"I walked off. I wasn't listening to his bullshit."

Mannie mulled over the scenario for a moment. "Not a good move."

Marlene turned to Mannie, concerned and unsure what he meant. "Why? What do you mean?"

Not wanting to sound pessimistic, Mannie replied, "Everybody knows they're a bunch of bad buggers. They don't make idle threats. I wouldn't trust those buggers as far as I could spit."

"All he said was, we know where you live. I'm a bit concerned about Saturday night, you know, with me being away."

Jo interrupted, "Marlene can stay here Friday night. I don't trust those gangsters either."

Mannie rose at five o'clock on Friday morning. After a hasty breakfast and having said goodbye to Jo and Liana, he drove to Nga Rangi's home to pick him up, and off to Pokaka they went.

Excited about the prospects of moving out of the city, the two men discussed all sorts of options and ideas. Time seemed to fly, and it was just before the second bridge past the Makatoki viaduct that Mannie parked his van off the road out of sight, behind the stock pile of crushed river metal that Transit New Zealand had put there for road building and road repairs.

Nga Rangi took out their backpacks while Mannie locked the van, and eager to get going, he asked, "How long did you say it'll take us to walk to where we're going?"

"About five hours, normally."

"Quite a way to go then."

"Yeah. That's the beauty about this place," Mannie replied. "It's too far in for anyone to bother us." Getting his backpack comfortable on his back, he pointed with his head toward the bush. "Come on. We're wasting time standing around here yapping."

Nga Rangi followed Mannie over the railway line to the start of the track into the bush. Twenty-five minutes later, they came out by a river and stopped for a rest.

Nga Rangi went down to the river and bent down, about to dip his hands in and have a drink.

Smiling, Mannie stopped him and said, "Never drink the river water, mate. It comes off the mountain. There's a hint of sulphur in it. Apart from the taste, it's like drinking salt water. You know, you no sooner have a drink when you want another one. It dries the mouth out." Mannie pointed along the track. "There's heaps of fresh water springs around the place though. One's just up there. You'll soon discover where they are." He pointed upstream with his head. "Come on. We'll have a quick drink up there and then we'll get going. You'll find that the riverbank has a clean grassy area about five metres wide each side of the river once we get up further. Makes walking real easy."

As they walked up to the spring, Mannie added, "We have to cross the river back and forth a couple of times further on upstream to avoid some of the rubbishy patches of bush. The river's thirty to forty centimetres deep most of the way." Grinning, he pointed to the river. "You'll notice that with the sulphur in the water there's no algae on the rocks. They're clean as a whistle. That means the river bottom isn't slippery like other rivers." Nga Rangi looked questioningly at Mannie as if to say, what the hell are you talking about? Mannie just grinned and said, "You'll soon see."

It was just after one of their river crossings an hour later, and as they stepped out of the river onto the riverbank, Mannie spotted fresh hoof prints in the damp soil. Smiling confidently, he turned to Nga Rangi and pointed. "Take a look here, mate. Deer prints. That's the sign of fresh meat."

Studying the prints, Nga Rangi grinned and said, "Just like you told me. We wouldn't have to worry about meat."

With Mannie leading, they continued at a steady pace. Periodically, they stopped briefly at a spring for a rest and a quick drink and then carried on.

It was early afternoon when they approached a long sweeping bend in the river. Mannie pointed out the large plateau ahead up a steep face, 120 metres high.

"That's where we're going, mate. That's what I call paradise."

Nga Rangi slowed his step as they gazed along the river. To his left was the plateau Mannie had spoken so much about. Ahead of that was a huge waterfall 100 metres high to the right of but a little further up the valley from the plateau.

Each side of the waterfall was covered in lichen, with dozens of varieties of small native shrubs and ferns of all sizes and clematis clinging to the damp rocky escarpment. Some shrubs were out in bloom, giving the perpendicular face the appearance of an operatic backdrop on a wondrous stage of nature.

Nga Rangi smiled at the splendour of the valley. "What an amazing place. I could quite easily live with this."

"It's not too bad, eh?" Mannie agreed.

They stopped at the base of the steep rise to the plateau and sat down, resting the bottom of their backpacks on the ground to take the weight off their shoulders. Nga Rangi noticed that with the angle of the sun, a double rainbow had formed in the misty spray generated by the waterfall.

Satisfied with what he'd seen, he checked his watch. "Four hours fifty minutes from your van to here."

"It usually takes about five hours, but we've been pushing the pace a bit today." Laughing, he peered up the steep scrub-covered face. "Last stretch to the top is always the hardest."

"Come on then," Nga Rangi said. "I'm keen to see what's up there."

Getting his backpack comfortable on his back again, Mannie gazed around, taking in the grandiosity and the splendour of the valley. "What do you think so far?"

Nodding with a smile, Nga Rangi replied, "Yeah. The more I see of the place the more I like it." He pondered, momentarily, staring at Mannie inquisitively. "You really think we could get away with living up here?"

"I've no doubt at all, mate. I wouldn't be here if I thought otherwise."

"The more I think about it, the more I like it. It's really a great idea. I've got a good feeling about this."

"It'll mean a lot of hard work initially, but once we get set up, there'd be no holding us back," Mannie said, slapping Nga Rangi on the back. "The garden's the first priority though. That'll be Jo's domain. Once it's been dug she's pretty confident she and Marlene can handle it."

At the summit, they stopped to get their breath. To Nga Rangi's surprise, the flat area was larger than he had visualized. He could see where Mannie had explained they would build the huts. It was the perfect spot. The ground had a gradual slope up toward the bush, creating the ideal run off for water in bad weather.

Smiling, Nga Rangi said, "Man, this place has everything and more. It's absolutely bloody awesome."

Laughing, Mannie added, "I told you it was a great place, didn't I?"

They spent the rest of the day exploring the plateau and the surrounding area. Mannie pointed out the spring at the back of the sloping area by the bush and where the huts would be built in front of the spring. He then pointed to another spot just down from the spring. "That'd be perfect for a communal fireplace." Then thinking about the spring, he added, "You know, if we got smart, we could put a pipe in the spring and let the water gravity feed to a tap by the fireplace. Be good for when we're cooking and doing the dishes."

Nga Rangi liked at the idea. "Brilliant idea."

"We couldn't do that for a toilet though. That'll just have to be an old-fashioned long-drop up there somewhere in the bushes."

Nga Rangi laughed. "Can't have all the mod cons, mate. Not if we're to live like our ancestors."

Nga Rangi went suddenly quiet, and Mannie sensed the change in mood. "What's up? You having second thoughts?"

"No," Nga Rangi assured him. "Remember I told you about those two gangsters the other day?"

"Yeah. I remember."

"I'm a bit concerned about that threat they made."

"Those buggers don't make idle threats, I told you that."

"Yeah. That's what worries me. I know Marlene's okay, but what about our boarders?"

"They should be okay."

"You sure?" Nga Rangi replied, not as confident.

"Gotta think positive, mate. You gotta stay positive."

CHAPTER 7

With a fire blazing away that night, they sat around it making plans for their move to Pokaka. Nga Rangi felt very positive and enthusiastic about the whole concept, and he knew Marlene would too, once he explained everything about what the area had to offer.

Puckering an eyebrow, he asked, "When do you want to move down here?"

Mannie sat there, summing up their options. "I suppose, when you think about it, the sooner the better. There's nothing really stopping us. We'll get together Monday when we get back and write a list of essentials that we'll need to bring." He hesitated, deep in thought. "First though, we need to work out how many people we want to come with us." He counted silently on his fingers. "I've got six others I know who would definitely be interested, including Liana."

Nga Rangi replied, "Apart from Marlene and myself, two of our boarders are keen to give it a go. They get along with everyone, you know, real easy going types."

"So that's twelve of us then," Mannie said. "That'd be a good number so long as everyone pulls their weight. The next thing we need to work out is how much it's going to cost. The huts will cost the most. I'll take some measurements in the morning. That'll be enough to draw up a schedule of materials when we get back to cost out. If we all pool our money, it shouldn't be too expensive." He shook his head, frowning. "Our savings have dwindled over the last couple of months. It's amazing where all the money's gone." He broke off for a moment, contemplating the scenario they were in. He went on, "We'll get everyone together tomorrow and have a serious talk about it. A lot depends on how much each person can put in."

"I know our boarders haven't got a lot saved," Nga Rangi had to admit. "Some might have to put in more than others.

The following morning, they had a good look around the immediate area, absorbing as much as they could. Then after Mannie took several notes, a lot of approximate levels and measurements, they set off on the long walk back to the vehicle.

It was late Sunday afternoon when they arrived back at Mannie's home. The three girls heard the van pull up and rushed out to greet them.

"Well, how'd it go?" Jo asked enthusiastically with an arm around Liana's shoulder. Marlene was standing beside them, smiling, waiting in anticipation for a positive answer.

Mannie stepped out of the van and stretched his limbs. "Yeah, not too bad. It's been a bloody long day."

Nga Rangi put an arm around Marlene. He sensed she was keen to hear his thoughts. "I like the place," he started, smiling. "It's got everything there we need and more, right down to having a freshwater spring smack bang right where we need it."

"We'll have a talk tomorrow after we've had a good sleep and see who's coming and who isn't," Mannie said.

Marlene was eager to get the ball rolling. "Two of our three boarders, Himi and Tuku, are keen to come. They've really had a gut's full of city life. You know, being on the dole and all that. The other one, Danny, isn't so keen. He's still got his job and seems pretty settled. But there's Bud, our other friend. The way he was talking over the weekend, he might be interested."

"That's good. We need to know exactly how many are coming."

Jo took Mannie aside and explained that she and Marlene had gone around to Marlene's home and met Tuku and Himi and got on fine with them. They both seem like real nice guys.

Mannie smiled at the news and said, "That's good. I actually like them too. Just the sort we need to have with us."

Tired from the trip and keen to get home and have a meal, Nga Rangi pointed with his head at his old Mazda. "Come on, girl. Let's get home. I'm tired and hungry."

It was Sunday and Nga Rangi and Marlene were sitting in the lounge when Himi and Tuku came in. Danny, the only one who had a job, was sitting in a lounge chair in the light beneath the window reading a Buy, Sell, and Exchange magazine. Bud, a close friend, had just come in the front door.

Bud's face lit up when he saw Nga Rangi. "Hey, mate. How'd the trip go?"

"Good," Nga Rangi replied. "It was well worth going down there for the night. Gave me a real good look around the place."

"You sound like you were impressed."

"Yeah, I am, and I really think it'll work."

Bud was quite excited and said, "Tell me about it. I want to know everything."

Danny cut in, "Sit down and listen. We all want to know what it's like, mate."

Marlene stood and asked if anyone wanted a cup of coffee. They all put their hand up.

Suddenly and without warning, the whole lounge window smashed inwards in a massive shower of glass; a Molotov cocktail exploded in an enormous fireball on the fireplace hearth on the opposite side of the small room. Marlene leaped back and lost her balance and fell against the wall with the force from the concussion. Partially winded and terrified, she tried to scream but couldn't. She covered her face with her hands as the room burst into flames and chaos.

Sitting in a chair below the window, Danny was showered with broken glass and received several cuts to his hands and upper legs. Shocked, he leaped to his feet to look out the shattered window. He wanted to see who had thrown the petrol bomb.

Two men with beanies pulled down over their faces with slits cut in them for their eyes, were standing facing the house brandishing sawn-off shotguns. They had set fire to Danny's car as well.

One of the masked men called out, "Hey dick-head. How's this for a stupid game?"

Danny shouted at them, angry at seeing his car on fire, "You bastards! You've set fire to my bloody car!"

Nga Rangi stole a glimpse outside. Even though the two gang members wore masks, he recognized one of them instantly from the previous week when they wanted him to join their gang. One had a large skull tattooed on the back of each hand, and the big guy outside on the left had the same tattoos. He also noticed the green Mazda van parked beside them with the motor running.

Nga Rangi yelled at Danny, "Get down! Get down!"

The masked men with the sawn-off shotguns open fired. Danny, a split second too late, took the first blast in his left shoulder, shredding his collarbone, tearing away muscle, tendons, and tissue. The second blast took off the top section of his skull, and with the impact, his body was hurled backward into the burning inferno behind him.

Marlene was screaming hysterically, overcome with terror at the unexpected violent attack. She was huddled in the corner of the room on the floor with her knees drawn up under her chin, her hands over her head.

Bud, upon seeing Danny's car ablaze, had rushed for the front door.

Nga Rangi screamed a warning. "Don't open the door! Don't open the bloody door! It's the black supremacy!"

His warning was too late. Bud already had the door half open. The other masked man fired. The shotgun blast hit Bud in the chest. The force from the impact threw him backward two metres onto his back.

Mortified at the chaos and devastation surrounding him in the small room at the sudden unprovoked attack, Nga Rangi grabbed Danny's left foot and tried to drag his body out of the blazing inferno but was hindered by the lounge chair against the front wall.

With the heat from the flames and no space to move in, Nga Rangi, now in a panic, slipped his sleeve down over his hand. He took hold of Danny's left arm and tried to drag him sideways. The part-wool, part-nylon shirt had melted onto his skin, and as he pulled, the skin peeled back off the arm like taking off a sock.

Shocked and shaken to his core, Nga Rangi let go of Danny's arm and stared down at the mutilated body. Danny's lips were almost burned off, exposing his teeth; where his nose had been there was now a lump of sizzling, crispy flesh. His scalp and the top of the skull were completely gone.

Lying just inside the front door in a pool of his own blood, Bud, now in total shock, forced his hands into the huge cavity in his chest in a feeble attempt at trying to stifle the flow of blood.

Nga Rangi looked helplessly across at him, knowing there

was nothing he could do to help without putting himself in mortal danger from the lethal shotguns. He was in a complete quandary at the roar and heat of the deadly flames that were quickly filling the room and the dreadful smell of sizzling, burning flesh. Engulfed in panic and at hearing Marlene's screams, he tried desperately to think clearly. He dared another glance outside. One masked man was laughing at his friend Bud, lying on the floor inside the front door in a pool of blood. The other was laughing at the raging inferno, which was quickly filling the small room.

The flames in the lounge had taken a firm hold, having crept up the inside wall to the ceiling, and were burning uncontrollably in both directions.

Horrified, Nga Rangi cast an appraising eye around the small room. Bud was holding out a hand, begging for help. Another shotgun blast tore a huge hole in the wall beside the chimney, purposely made helping Bud impossible.

Nga Rangi turned to his traumatized friends, milling nervously against the southern wall in the dining room. Tuku was yelling something at him, but he couldn't understand a word. He screamed back at Tuku, "See if the anyone's out the back!"

Cautiously, Tuku put his head out the window to check if the rear of the small section was clear. He shouted back to Nga Rangi, "Can't see anyone!"

Nga Rangi shouted at everyone. "Out the back door! Get out the back door!"

As much as he wanted to, he couldn't get across to Bud and drag him clear. The flames had now spread across the whole room. Huddled in the corner, Marlene was petrified and shaking uncontrollably, semi-paralyzed with terror and with her hands over her head, she screamed hysterically at the burning bloody scene.

Nga Rangi dashed across to her, and taking hold of her hand, he dragged her to her feet, and together they raced through the dining room to the back door, following Himi and Tuku out.

Nga Rangi pointed to the back fence. They both leaped the fence together, encouraging Himi and Tuku to follow. "To the next street!" he yelled. "Get across to the next street."

A blood-curdling scream from the burning interior of the house stopped Nga Rangi in his tracks as flames slowly engulfed Bud. Marlene, covering her ears, was sobbing uncontrollably as they started racing after the others. Nga Rangi froze again as Bud let out another blood-curdling agonizing scream. He had such an overwhelming sense of guilt and loss, followed by a crippling sense of utter helplessness.

Himi took Marlene's trembling hand and led her across the section and around the back neighbour's house. Tuku hesitated beside Nga Rangi, urging him to keep going. He could see he was in a state of shock at the horrendous nightmare they were escaping.

"Can't stay here," he shouted, grabbing Nga Rangi by the arm. "Come on. You gotta keep going. There's nothing we can do." He could physically feel Nga Rangi's body shaking with terror as he turned him away from the scene and pushed him to a run.

Together, they raced across the back yard of the neighbouring property, around the house, across the front lawn, and out onto the next street. Nga Rangi caught up with Marlene and grabbed her hand. Himi was standing nervously in the centre of the road, unsure of what to do or where to go.

Nervously, Nga Rangi glanced around, making sure there was no black supremacy in the street and said, "Where the hell do we go from here?"

They could hear the sirens of police cars and fire appliances as they arrived at the burning conflagration that had been their home.

"Mannie's!" Marlene yelled through her terror. "Let's go to Mannie's!"

Encouraging Tuku and Himi to follow and taking Marlene's hand, Nga Rangi began running. "Come on. No good staying here. We'll go to Mannie's."

Afraid and not wanting to be seen by the gang members if they cruised the neighbourhood, they sprinted the three blocks to Mannie's house and burst in through the back door, horrified and out of breath.

Jo and Liana heard them as they rushed in and came out of Liana's bedroom. Marlene was clinging to Nga Rangi's arm, crying her heart out.

Not understanding what had happened and why they were there and in such a state, Jo took Marlene into her bedroom to console her.

Upon hearing the commotion in his kitchen, Mannie came out of the bathroom, putting on a shirt. "What the hell's happened? What's going on?"

Nga Rangi, eyes dark with terror, turned to him. "Black supremacy." He hesitated, gasping for air. "You said they were nasty buggers. The bastards hit us with a Molotov cocktail." Again, he paused, catching his breath. "They shot Bud and Danny. Shot both of them in cold blood." He looked around to make sure everyone was there.

"What...?" Mannie asked, flabbergasted.

"They even burned Danny's car."

"Geez...! And they shot Danny and Bud?"

Nga Rangi sat down at the dining table, still shaking in absolute confusion. "We've lost all our stuff, our gear. Everything's gone." He gasped for breath. "And it happened so damn quick."

"What are you going to do?"

"Dunno. Haven't had time to think."

Mannie cast a sympathetic eye around at the small

traumatized group. "You'll have to doss down here for a while until you get yourselves sorted out." Then, pointing at Marlene, he said, "You can sleep in Liana's bedroom but it'll have to be on the floor." He pointed at Nga Rangi, Tuku, and Himi. "You guys can have turns on the couch. Two will have to sleep on the floor. That's the best I can do for the moment."

Nga Rangi nodded, but he wasn't at all comfortable with the arrangements, but under the circumstances, they didn't have any other choice.

Angry and confused, he began to pace. "Geez, this really pisses me off," he said, shaking his head. "This is absolute shit." He glanced around at everyone. "I'm sick to the bloody teeth with what's happened to us lately." He slammed his hand against the wall. "There's no work for us anywhere. Is this what life's going to be like...? Is this what we have to look forward to?"

Three days later, everyone was sitting in the lounge after dinner. They were still in shock at their predicament.

Marlene glanced at the front page of the Auckland Star news paper lying on the coffee table. She held it up for everyone to see. "You all seen this?"

Nga Rangi nodded. "Yeah. The cops are asking for anyone with information to come forward." He looked around the faces in the room. "Any of you want to go forward?" He picked up the paper and read another paragraph. "And it looks like that green van those bastards were in was stolen. All the neighbours would have seen the patches on their jackets. Do you think anyone will remember anything when the cops ask them? I don't think so. They'll all be shit scared it'll happen to them next."

Nga Rangi stood, looking around at everyone. "I'm not talking to any bloody police. No way. It won't do any good, and they won't catch those arseholes who did it, so what's the point. So what the hell we gonna do now eh? Where do we go?"

Marlene looked up at him, sombrely. "I still can't believe it. I know it was a rented house, but everything we owned was in it. We've absolutely nothing left, not even a damn bed."

"It all happened so damn quick," Tuku cut in.

Himi cast a confused eye around the room. "So, what now?"

Nga Rangi suggested they all buy air beds and use them while they were at Mannie's. At least they would be reasonably comfortable.

Marlene was thinking about Bud and Danny and burst into tears. "I keep seeing the image of Danny lying on the floor in the flames and Bud looking at me with his hand out. I can't get it out of my mind." She broke off momentarily. "What a way to go, poor buggers."

"If the cops find out where we are," Tuku said nervously, "we'll have some pretty heavy explaining to do."

"Just hope no one saw where we went," Himi added.

No one answered. "So what do we do then? We can't stay sitting around here forever."

"We all go to Pokaka," Jo interrupted.

Mannie cut in. "It's like you said. You can't sit around here forever. Why don't we discuss it now while everyone's together? I'll ring Ritchie and Manu and see if they're home. If they are, I'll go around and get them and the others at the same time."

Within thirty minutes, Mannie was back with four others who had expressed interest in their move to Pokaka. Ritchie was the youngest at seventeen, with Zac twenty, and Pucky and Chappy both twenty-one, three years younger than Mannie and Nga Rangi.

Mannie introduced them all, and once everyone had settled down, he began discussing their move to Pokaka.

Mannie wanted everything to be planned properly and logistically.

"Sounds good to us," Tuku said, looking at the other two.

Nga Rangi glanced at Mannie. "Now you've got everyone's attention, explain how we're going to build the huts, set up the garden, how we'll live, all that sort of stuff so everyone has a clear picture of what to expect."

Mannie showed them his sketches, and then explained in detail the construction of the huts, about the communal cooking, and so on. He then turned to Jo to explain how she planned on doing the garden with Marlene's help.

Ritchie put his hand up. "I can help with the garden too if you like. I don't mind getting my hands dirty."

Jo was happy to have someone volunteer to help her and Marlene. She gave him a cheerful smile. "That'd be great, Ritchie. I'll hold you to that." She now had Liana, Marlene and Ritchie, more than enough helpers to keep the garden in tip-top shape.

"No worries," Ritchie replied, returning her smile. He had never volunteered for anything in his life, but he was keen to learn, especially with helping Jo in the garden. He had never had a female to look up to before, not even his mother. Being a drug addict, she had abandoned him before he was one year old. He grew up with numerous relatives, being fobbed off around his extended family, not feeling welcome anywhere for all his adolescent years.

He was so happy to have found a group where he could form some sort of attachment. "At least we'd be together and outta this shit hole of a city. Working as a family should be good."

Even though their traumatic experience and fears with the fire was still vivid in their minds, there was a mild expectancy among the small group as they discussed their move to Pokaka.

Mannie put his hands up for everyone to keep quiet. "If we pool our money, we should be able to afford to do this quite easily but we have to be 100 percent committed. It's no good going there and then thinking after a month or so, well, bugger this, I'm off. If anyone has any doubts, even the slightest doubts, now's definitely the time to voice them. We only want committed people coming with us. Otherwise it's going to be a total waste of time."

"When do you wanna go?" Manu asked curiously.

"As soon as we're organized. The sooner, the better, I reckon. May even be as close as three or four weeks."

"What do we sleep on in the bush?" Marlene interrupted. "I, for one, don't wanna sleep on the ground. No way."

"We each buy a good quality air bed," Mannie told her. "One that's not going to deflate every night. You'll also need a puncture repair kit as well. Most come with a foot pump as well."

Nga Rangi was still a little dubious about the ownership of the land. He wasn't having second thoughts; he was just concerned. "What if someone discovers us? I'm just worried we'll get kicked off."

"We've talked about this before, you and me, and I'll tell you the same thing I told you then. Who's gonna discover us? No one goes there any more. You saw how isolated it was down there."

"Call it last-minute jitters but are you 100 percent positive? I'd hate to go through all this trouble and effort and 'DoC' discovers us six months down the track. I know for a fact they wouldn't let us stay there."

"I can assure you, no one goes there any more apart from the odd hunter, and they won't bother us either." He rubbed his chin, recollecting when he and Nga Rangi were there. "Can you recall seeing any foot prints anywhere other than the ones you and I made? That's the same track that hunters or anyone else for that matter, would use."

Nga Rangi thought back to their short time at Pokaka and had to admit it. "You're right. There weren't any other prints anywhere but ours."

Himi was thinking about the financial aspect. "We can't just up sticks and bugger off like it's a Christmas holiday. For starters, we all need a rifle and ammunition and God knows what other gear we'll need. You've mentioned building huts, buying good quality air beds, vegetable plants, a rifle and ammunition etc. How much is this all going to cost?"

Mannie grinned. "Got that covered, mate. We're going to make up a list and cost it all out." He looked around and asked, "Do any of you have a firearms license?"

No one put their hand up.

"I've got one, so it'll have to be me to get the rifles then."

"Isn't that a bit risky?" Nga Rangi asked, a little concerned about the police getting involved.

Mannie smiled. "The gun laws in this country are crazy, mate. I'll buy one at each sports shop until we have enough. They don't record how many guns you buy. All they're interested in is if you have a firearms license."

"So no alarm bells are going to go off if you buy nine or ten rifles?"

"Nope. Quite sure," Mannie replied and then glanced around the room. "Any more questions?"

"How much do we all have to put in? I haven't got very much saved at all," Tuku had to admit.

"Don't know yet. The girls and I'll make a list of all the gear and equipment we'll need. We'll let you know tomorrow."

Marlene interrupted, still a little shaken. "One thing's for sure. We won't have to give notice for our house. It isn't there any more."

Mannie glanced at Jo and spoke in a serious tone. "I'm deliberately behind with our rent too."

Jo's face went a pale ashen colour. "We could get kicked outta here...?"

Mannie grinned. "No, we won't. Let me explain. For the last two months I deliberately stopped paying the rent. I knew we couldn't stay here forever, and I wasn't going to be duped out of any more money if it could be helped. Anyway, I rang the rental agency the other day. I told them I'm starting a new job shortly and I'm arranging a loan at the bank to pay the balance in arrears, but it's going to take about a week so."

Jo cut in. "You're what...? You never said anything to me about any of this. Shit, how much behind are we?"

"Just over twelve hundred dollars."

"Who's gonna loan you that sort money and how the hell do you intend paying it back?"

"I'm not getting a loan, sweetie. It's a ploy to buy us time so we can get organized. I'm not paying the buggers a cent. No way. It's the bloody government's fault we're in this predicament. It's not our fault. I'd rather put the money toward our venture at Pokaka."

"So we're just going to leave without paying any more rent?"

"That's right," Mannie replied. "Do you think they're worried about us? I don't think so, so stuff them. It's like I said. I knew we couldn't stay here while we were living on the dole. I didn't know at the time what we were going to do, but it was obvious we would have to do something and now we are. We're moving to Pokaka."

"That's stealing though," Jo said, feeling a little guilty.

"Yeah, well. Things are desperate now," Mannie replied with a half-hearted grin. "We can't afford to pay rent and buy the stuff we need to take with us to Pokaka."

"What about our savings?" Jo demanded.

"Half that's gone already paying the power, phone, that new fridge, and washing machine you bought on HP and every other bloody thing we had to have. Your earnings and my dole money's not near enough to live on, you know that, especially when I had an eight-week stand-down period before I qualified for the dole."

Pucky interrupted, changing the subject. "Who owns this land we're going to anyway? You say no one goes there, but someone must own it."

Mannie frowned, recalling its lost ownership. "It used to be Maori land. It once belonged to my tribe. Way back in the late 1800's, the government forced the paramount chief to either let them take it by confiscation or to gift it to them. They decided to gift it. I say we just move there, and if anyone tries to kick us off, we claim squatter's rights." Mannie laughed, and slapped Pucky on the shoulder. "All the same, no one'll know we're even there."

Chappy wasn't convinced about the way the huts were going to be built. "Why can't we build ordinary huts? I mean, why do they have to be underground?"

Mannie grinned. "So they're less conspicuous to any planes flying over. If we built new huts out in the open, that would be inviting trouble. Do you understand that?"

"Yeah, sort of."

Pucky nodded congenially. He could see Mannie had it all worked out. "And as Ritchie says, we'll all be together, and we won't have to worry about losing a job again."

Mannie cast a perceptive eye around the room. "So you all agree it's not a bad idea then?"

Glancing at each other, they all nodded.

"Good. Looks like we have a consensus." He hesitated for a second. "It'd be like living in the old days, you know, like our ancestors did. But I can guarantee you this, it won't be easy. Everyone'll have to pitch in. Some days'll be hard, some days'll be easy."

Smiling happily, Himi cut in. "Not much different from being here. I like the idea. In fact, it'll be a whole new experience. I've never even been out of the city."

"Okay," Mannie went on. "There'll be about eleven of us

altogether. First priority is to get the garden dug. Once that's done, the girls can get the planting right away, and while they're doing that, we'll get started on a temporary shelter for us to sleep in. After that's up, we'll get on with the huts. If all goes to plan, it should take us maybe three weeks to have everything done properly if we get stuck into it."

Zac put his hand up, interrupting them, counting everyone. "Did you say eleven of us? I've counted twelve."

Smiling, Mannie corrected himself, "Okay. twelve then."

Mannie described the area in detail and explained that they would have to hunt for their meat on a regular basis, which would add to their adventure. Everyone felt positive with the idea of leaving the city behind and moving to a quieter life of self-sufficiency in the bush. If it could be done successfully, then they were all for it.

The following morning, Mannie gathered the group together in the lounge. "We've decided that everyone put in as much money as they can. We need to know exactly how much we have altogether so we can work out a budget. You'll have to go to your bank and draw everything out. You then give the money to Jo."

Tuku interrupted. "Like I said before. If everyone puts in as much as I do, we won't be going anywhere. I got sweet stuff all to put in."

Mannie put his hand up to quell any questions about the monetary discrepancies. "I know, some of us will be putting in more than others, but that can't be helped. So long as you put in as much as you can. Okay?"

Everyone agreed and went off to their respective banks. As they arrived back they gave their money to Jo, who, in turn, wrote down the figures beside each name.

Later on that morning and standing beside Jo, Mannie looked over the figures. "Not a bad sum. We can top up the balance if we need to from what's left of our savings."

Jo sat there, somewhat disgruntled. And for many seconds her mind seemed far away.

Mannie noticed her sombre mood and asked, "You're not having second thoughts about this, are you?"

Jo looked up, shaking her head. "No. It's just that when I think about how hard we've both worked to save that money. It took so long, and we sweated our guts out for it."

"At least it's going to a good cause." He turned, about to leave, and then remembered an appointment he'd arranged. "Oh, by the way, I'm going to be out for a while. I should be back some time mid afternoon. I've left a list of stuff that needs sorting." He turned to Nga Rangi. "Can you and Tuku organize that for me?" He hesitated for a second and said, "I've sold my van. There's a guy coming around later on this afternoon to pick it up."

Mannie arrived home at 2.30 PM that afternoon with his face tattooed like that of an ancestral warrior.

In dismay, Nga Rangi jerked his head back and gasped. "What the hell've you gone and done?"

"This is how I feel on the inside. It's my family heritage, my whakapapa," he stated. "I'm a warrior. A warrior of the people."

"You've taken it a bit far, haven't you?" Nga Rangi responded.

Jo came into the room, and the moment she saw him, she put her hands to her face, shocked. "Shit, Mannie. That's a bit drastic, isn't it?"

"Don't you like it?" he asked, a little taken aback.

"No, no," she said, not wanting to hurt his feelings. "I just think it's a bit over the top, that's all." She indicated a small measurement with her thumb and index finger. "Just a little bit." She studied his face for a few seconds. "You're making one hell of a statement, that's all I can say."

Mannie replied proudly, "I know there's a few scabs at

the moment, but once they've healed, it'll look better. It's a depiction of my whakapapa. If we're to live like our ancestors, we should look like them."

"Not me, mate," Nga Rangi said quite adamantly. "I feel okay the way I am."

"Me too," Tuku said. "I don't need tattoos to make me feel good on the inside."

Mannie was a first-class organizer, and within a week they had most of their gear and vital equipment together. He only had the timber and materials to purchase, pre-cut it to length, nail and screw everything together, and put it in their separate lots, ready to go. A truck had been booked to take them and their gear to Pokaka, allowing them nine days to finalize their planning.

Five days later, they were all in the lounge going over the final preparations. There was a loud knock on the door. Mannie jumped up. "I'll get it."

As he approached the door, there was another very loud knock. "Hang on a minute. Keep your pants on."

He opened the door to a tall white man in his early thirties who was dressed in a dark suit, a white pin-stripped shirt with a very colourful tie and wearing very expensive sunglasses.

"Yeah?" Mannie asked, surprised at such a well dressed person standing in his doorway, holding a document in his hand.

The man asked in a stern tone. "I'm from South Harbour Real Estate. Are you Mannie Te Ngongo?"

"Yeah. What's your problem?" Mannie replied, glancing at the document in the man's hand.

The man handed it to him. "I'm here to serve you an eviction notice. Our company handles all the government housing corporations rental homes for this region."

Taken completely by surprise at the young man's

announcement, Mannie took the document and quickly studied it. "You can't evict us."

"Yes we can," the young man replied, very matter-of-factly. "By the end of this week, you'll be over two months behind with your rent. We've sent out overdue statements, but you've not responded."

"I've been out trying to get work. I spoke to your boss last week."

"Yes, and you said you were arranging a loan through your bank," the well dressed man broke in. "We've made inquiries on that subject, and your bank has instructed us that they are not processing any loan in your name. We think you're lying." He watched Mannie examining the document. "This is the only avenue left open to us. We've no choice."

Mannie appraised the man's nice flashy suit. He felt the hair on the back of his neck rise with anger and thought back on what Jo had said about the government. "I'm trying to get work, but there's nothing around at the moment." He paused and again, cast a scrutinizing eye over the man. "You know something. It's always a bloody honky telling us what we can and can't do." He held the document up to the man's face and tore it up. "Bloody pakehas. Always bloody taking." He was now in a rage and threw the torn document into the man's face.

The real estate man pointed nervously at the torn document fluttering to the ground. "What'd you do that for...? You can't do that."

Mannie replied bitterly, "You can shove that where the sun don't shine, honky, and tell that to your colonial bloody boss. Go lick his white arse why don't ya." He scowled bitterly. "We got rights, you know. You just can't boot us out like that."

Flabbergasted, the young man said, "You haven't paid any rent for two months. You can't expect us to sit around doing nothing. You've had every opportunity to talk to us if there's been a problem. We've bent over backward to try and help."

The man wavered nervously, collecting his thoughts. "You can't live here free forever. There are people out there desperate for a home. People who will pay the rent." Again he hesitated, astonished at Mannie's negative and arrogant attitude. "And we've got rights too, you realize."

Sensing the man's nervousness, Mannie exploited his advantage. He put his face up close to the man's face. "Piss off. Go lick your boss's white arse. Tell him we'll leave when we're ready, not before."

"Unless you come up with the money in seven days, you've got twenty-one days to vacate the property."

Nga Rangi walked slowly over and stood beside Mannie, eyeing the real estate man up narrowly. "So you're bootin' him out?"

"Got no option," the man replied. "Pay up or get out. Simple as that."

Sneering, Mannie looked the young man over. "Bloody white arse. Piss off. You pricks're always pushin' us around. Bloody pakehas, always taking. Take, bloody take. Nothin' ever changes." Again, he stepped up close and shouted into his face. "Piss off, pakeha. You're not welcome here." He then slammed the door in the man's face and shouted, "Piss off."

Nga Rangi shook his head, astounded at Mannie's attitude. "What did you expect...! If you don't pay the rent, you get kicked out. I know that, you know that."

Mannie waved his hand dismissively at the door. "Bloody pakehas running the damn country. It's just as the girls said. Too many of the bastards if you ask me. They really piss me off. Maori own nothing." He glared at Nga Rangi, his anger slowly receding. "The white bastards took most of it."

"You had no intention of paying the rent, did you?" Nga Rangi asked.

"Nah. Stuff the bastards. Not once I made up my mind. I'd rather put the money into our little venture."

Nga Rangi was a little reticent at the reason he was behind

with his rent. "You've been thinking about this for a while now, haven't you?"

"I've been trying to think of something for ages, but until I came up with the idea of going to Pokaka, I had no idea. But one thing was certain, we had to do something."

The next week was a very busy one for the small group, Mannie especially. He pre-cut the walls and floor sections out for the huts, including the plywood and polystyrene. Under Mannie's supervision, Nga Rangi and Tuku nailed and screwed them all together. After that was completed, they bound them up into individual lots.

Jo, Liana, and Marlene had all the vegetable plants and food packed into boxes ready for the truck. Jo had also packed her wallet with eight hundred dollars in cash just in case they required something urgently. The rest of their money, she and Mannie put in a long-term fixed deposit account.

The other members of the group helped purchase everything else that was required, and as the items were packed away, they were crossed off the list. Then finally, with one day left to go, they were ready for their move to Pokaka.

Having strapped the last pack tightly together, Mannie looked encouragingly at Nga Rangi. "That's it, mate, the lot. Everything's ready for the truck."

They went inside to check on the girls. "How're you getting on? We're pretty much done out there."

Marlene said proudly, "That's the last one for us too. Geez mate, we've got one hell of a lot of gear."

"We have to be prepared for everything and anything if we're to pull this off."

Jo, with a serious face, went over and stood beside the two men. "I won't be happy until it's all been carried in to where we're going and the garden's dug."

"You're not the only one thinking about that," Nga Rangi

replied with a wry smile. "It's gonna take quite a few trips to get all this stuff up there."

Chuckling, Mannie added. "Yeah, but once it's all there, mate, we'll be in business. But there's a lot of work to do before we can sit down and take things easy."

Frowning, Jo cut in. "No one'll be taking it easy until after the garden's been dug."

"That's our first priority," Mannie assured her. "And with a wire netting fence around it as well. Don't you worry your pretty little head about that."

Jo's face went suddenly serious. "I been thinking a lot lately about you and me."

"Yeah," Mannie replied curiously. "What about?"

"Remember we had plans about starting a family?"

"Yeah!"

"Do you think we'll ever have a family? I mean, we can't even think about it while we're in Pokaka."

"Why not?"

"Not on the side of a bloody mountain, I'm not. And another thing, Marlene and Li are the only other women who're going to be up there with us and neither is a nurse."

"Anyway, you're jumping the gun a bit, I reckon."

"So you're saying you're not interested in a family now?"

"I didn't say that. It's just that everything's changed. I haven't really thought about it much lately."

"I do, quite a bit."

"Nothing wrong with just thinking, is there?"

CHAPTER 8

As arranged, the truck arrived late in the afternoon and parked in Mannie's driveway to be loaded before dark to save them time the next morning. Everyone pitched in, eager and excited to get everything packed and secured on board before dark. Mannie had told the driver they were keen to be on their way as early as possible.

Everyone was in a positive frame of mind and very excited. It was the start of a completely new life away from the madness and chaos of the city.

The truck was a large one, and they had to pack all their gear with care as they had to leave enough room for nine people as well to fit in the back.

The following morning, Himi, being up and ready to leave by five o'clock, couldn't believe they were actually leaving the city and going to Pokaka. He couldn't stop laughing. Tuku, laughing himself at Himi's mood and optimism, and had to reassure him that they were moving to the country permanently.

It was just after 10:30 AM when the truck pulled into the siding beside the railway line at Pokaka. Mannie was first to disembark and quickly organized everyone into groups with the unloading.

All their supplies and materials were promptly sorted into orderly piles as it came off the truck. Once the truck was fully unloaded and on it's way back to Auckland, everything was taken across the railway line to the start of the main track and stacked out of sight in the bush and then covered with tarpaulins.

Mannie had packed a bundle of twelve, four-metre long bamboo poles, seven centimetres thick, and as they came out, he put them aside with eighteen large empty coal sacks. His idea was to carry everything in on stretchers. The coal sacks had the bottom corners cut off for the four- metre poles to slip through. There were three sacks for each pair of poles. The idea was a very efficient one, as two people could carry more on a stretcher than they could carry individually, and apart from that, it was a lot easier.

Mannie called everyone together. "Okay, listen up. It's a five-hour walk in to where we're going, maybe more with these loads, so pair off, two to a stretcher. It should take approximately three loads each, not counting the materials for the huts. Pack everything nice and tight and secure it onto your stretchers with those," he said, pointing to a box of tie-downs. "With a bit of luck, we'll have most of it up there by the end of the week." He chuckled to himself. "You'll be feeling pretty knackered by then, I can assure you."

Zac broke in, laughing. "We should be pretty fit too by then."

"We need to be fit," Marlene added. "You guys have to hunt to put meat on the table."

"That's what I'm looking forward to," Himi said.

Tuku burst out laughing. "You have to learn how to shoot first before you go out hunting. You couldn't hit a barn door from two paces."

Mannie joined in the repartee. "We got plenty of ammo

for everyone, so don't worry. It won't take long to get used to your rifles. Practice makes perfect."

Nga Rangi was keen to get going and said, "Okay, fellahs. Let's get loaded up, eh?" He tapped Tuku on the shoulder. "You and Himi take one, Marlene and I'll take another. You others sort yourselves into pairs."

Jo gestured to Liana that they would be one pair and they would take one stretcher between them.

After the others paired off and with their stretchers loaded with as much gear as they could carry, they followed Mannie and Manu into the bush. Zac was the odd one out and had a large pack filled with as much as he could carry also.

After five and a half gruelling hours of trudging through the bush with their stretchers and having crossed the river several times with only five rest stops in total, they were finally approaching the long sweeping bend in the river. Mannie pointed out the plateau up the steep face, 120 metres high.

"That's where we're going fellahs. Up there. Home sweet bloody home."

To the right of the plateau but slightly further up the valley the big waterfall stood out like it was in a enchanting display of nature. Nga Rangi and Marlene stopped and put their stretcher down. Nga Rangi watched Marlene's reaction as she gazed around the valley approvingly.

Everyone, mesmerized by the most supremely amazing scenery they had ever seen, all stopped and put down their stretchers and gazed around in wonder.

With the angle of the sunlight, the misty spray from the waterfall had formed a wide glistening double rainbow, and on each side of the falls, the perpendicular rocky face was smothered in lichen and native fauna that glistened in the sunlight.

Further out again and on each side of the waterfall, were small native shrubs, some out in bloom, shining majestically in the misty sun rays, forming a mystical façade of an operatic backdrop on a panoramic stage of nature and, in the centre of it all, the thunderous reverberation of the alluring wall of water plunging into the cavernous hole at the base of the escarpment.

Sensing everyone's happy mood, Mannie said, "Come on. As much as we'd like to, we can't stand around here star gazing all day. You'll have plenty of time for that later."

Mannie took one of the tarpaulins that was on Himi and Tuku's stretcher and unfolded it out on the ground. "We'll stack everything here in the middle of this. We'll wrap everything up in it so nothing gets damp overnight. It'll be dark by the time we get back to the drop-off point by the road. We certainly haven't got time to waste swanning around here."

Jo and Liana were standing beside him. Mannie glances at Liana and asks, "You okay with the stretcher?"

Liana was smiling and stood close to Jo. She pointed to herself first, and with her hand, she put it over Jo's head, and then put her hand over her own head, and then pointed to Jo again.

Mannie looked at her questioningly for a moment, and then suddenly, he guessed what she meant. "Oh, I see. You're saying you're a big girl now, as big as Jo, and that you can handle it?"

Liana smiled and giggled, nodding vigorously.

Tired, hungry, and worn out, they arrived back at the drop-off point beside the railway line a half hour after dark. There was just enough moonlight filtering through the trees for Mannie to find their way.

Mannie looked around at his bedraggled group. "We're going to need some light. Himi, you get a couple of torches out eh? Who's cooking tonight?"

Marlene volunteered. "I will if someone'll give me a hand."

Jo put her hand up. "Yeah. Li and I can help too."

Nga Rangi and Tuku gathered firewood, and in no time they had a blazing fire. With the torches and assisted by the moon and the fire, there was sufficient light for them all to see what they were doing.

Ritchie got out the cooking pots and pans, and Manu went to a nearby spring and filled a large plastic container with water and then went to help the girls with the potatoes and carrots. Pucky and Chappy volunteered to cook the stew with the meat they had brought for that night. Zac went over to the edge of the bush and dug a hole for a temporary long-drop toilet.

Mannie was sorting through some of their gear.

Nga Rangi sidled over to him. "Things seem to be going to plan pretty well."

"We'll soon get used to living by the light of the moon and a fire," Mannie replied cheerfully.

After they had eaten and the dinner dishes washed and put away in their respective boxes, ready for the next day, the mood in the group was inspiring. They sat around the fire talking happily among themselves discussing their new life in the bush.

Tuku was in an especially jovial mood. "This is so great, man. I've never done anything like this before in my life. You know, having to hunt for our meat and all that sort of stuff." He shook his head in disbelief. "Can't believe I'm actually doing it. Gonna take a bit of getting used to." He then pointed to the bush. "And all this open space...! Gee whiz, man."

Mannie smiled as he cast a cheerful eye around the happy faces. "Get a good nights sleep, eh. It's gonna be a big day tomorrow."

Cheerfully, Nga Rangi said, "I'm really glad we decided to come here."

Mannie, flashing his eyebrows, replied, "Yeah. Me too, bro. Jo and I spoke about this for some time before we came around to your place that day. We needed to have the right people. That was the key to the whole idea."

"You can tell by the mood tonight that everyone's really excited to be here. Just getting out of the city was a huge step alone."

"Yeah, mate. Everything's working out fine."

Mannie and Jo rose at daybreak the following morning and woke everyone. "Come on, you buggers. Up you get. Rise and shine. We got heaps to do today."

Liana was already up, getting the fire going. Mannie looked across at her and flashed his eyebrows approvingly. She smiled back.

Nga Rangi rolled over and glanced at his watch but couldn't quite focus. "What's the bloody time?"

Mannie crouched down beside him and grinned. "Four thirty. Come on. Up you get."

Nga Rangi kissed Marlene on the cheek. "You sleep okay?"

Marlene, rubbing the sleep out of her eyes, yawned and replied. "My back's as stiff as a board. I'm not used to sleeping on the ground like this."

"Me too. I'm stiff as a plank too this morning."

Marlene sat up. "I heard you snoring one part of it."

"It wasn't bad, was it?" he asked, thinking he may have kept her awake.

"No. I heard you only a couple of times."

"Hope I didn't keep anyone awake."

"I wouldn't think so. We were all too stuffed."

Everyone was feeling similar to Nga Rangi and Marlene

that first morning. They all had trouble sleeping on the hard ground. Mannie could see everyone had had a lousy night as well as he and Jo. "Tonight, we'll lay a tarpaulin down and put our air beds on that, eh? It should be thick enough to stop anything from puncturing them if we double it over. We had the same problem as you guys."

After a hasty breakfast and the dishes and utensils packed away again, they were getting ready to take another load up to the plateau. Nga Rangi took a moment to survey the surrounding bush. He gazed around, listening to the unfamiliar sound of the birds singing merrily, welcoming in the new day.

"Hey you guys. Listen to all those birds, eh. I never realized it was like this out here in the mornings."

Mannie noticed his gregarious mood. "That's the morning bush chorus in bloody stereo, mate."

They all stopped and listened to the early morning choral group of native birds.

Ritchie was standing there, stretching his back and said, "Don't hear any sub woofers."

Everyone chuckled at his joke. They finished loading their stretchers and then, pairing off again, followed Mannie and Manu along the track through the bush. Jo and Liana carried the last stretcher with Zac coming up in the rear.

Even though they had seen it all the previous day, Marlene was still taken aback when they reached the long sweeping bend in the river, where they could see the plateau and waterfall. She gazed joyfully around at the natural beauty that adorned the small valley. Never before in her life had she experienced such a wonderful feeling of contentment and happiness.

"Wow. I still can't believe we're actually here. What an amazing and wonderful place this is," she said. "It's so beautiful and serene and and picturesque and apart from the waterfall, it's so damn quiet."

"It sure is a great place, all right," Nga Rangi had to agree, smiling at her happy contented face.

Mannie and Jo went over and stood beside Marlene and Nga Rangi. Mannie was interested in Marlene's opinion. "Well...?"

"It's lovely here, Mannie," Marlene said, smiling. "I'm really impressed. It's so quiet and peaceful."

He turned to Jo and Liana. "What do you girls reckon, now that you've seen it for the second time?"

Jo smiled. "It's like Marlene says. It's so quiet and peaceful here. Yeah. I really like it."

Liana nodded with a beaming smile.

It was 7.20 PM when they arrived at the base of the steep face to the plateau with their second load for the day and laid it down with the rest of their gear.

Everyone was gazing up at the lip to the plateau, keen to get up there and explore the place before it was completely dark.

Nga Rangi said cheerfully so everyone could hear, "Hey, you guys. We couldn't have found a better spot if we'd tried. Never in a million years."

"We'll take up as much as we can, including our sleeping gear," Mannie said. "The rest we can get in the morning."

They quickly sorted through their gear, grabbing what they needed for the night and recovered the rest. With Mannie leading, they followed him up the steep climb to the top. At the summit, Mannie paused momentarily to catch his breath.

Tuku punched the air excitedly. "Home sweet bloody home. Yahoo, yeah, man."

Nga Rangi and Marlene stopped beside him and carefully took in the panoramic vista before them. The plateau was 120 metres long and 80 metres wide. On the western side was the bush, going up at a slight angle. To the east were the river and waterfall, with the vertical drop to the valley below, Mount Ruapehu way off in the distance to the north.

The sound of the waterfall cascading down into the valley was only just audible from where they stood. The lip of the plateau was high enough to allow most of the sound to roll over them.

Feeling happy with her new surroundings, Marlene said, "The waterfall will lull us to sleep at night. I like the sound of water."

Conveying his absolute approval Nga Rangi replied, "Even though I was here not so long ago, I still can't believe how beautiful it is."

Cocking one eyebrow, Mannie warned, "It can get bloody cold here in winter though. You might not like it so much then."

"It's a small price to pay for freedom, mate," Nga Rangi admitted. "Perfect for what we want though. Couldn't be better, mate."

Mannie turned to the rest of the group, naturally assuming the role as their leader. "Okay. Listen up." He pointed to Tuku and Manu. "You two, collect some firewood. We need a fire going before it gets dark." He turned to Jo and Liana. "Can you two get some tucker organized?" He saw Pucky and Chappy standing by the edge of the plateau. "Hey, you two. Get some fresh water from the spring up there behind us for the girls, eh? The rest of you do what you can to help."

With the orders given out, everyone began fussing around, getting themselves into some sort of order. In no time at all, Tuku and Manu had a fire blazing away.

While dinner was cooking everyone began to relax and explore their new surroundings. Tuku went over to their gear, and, taking out his guitar, he began strumming and singing an old Beatle song; Nowhere man.

Nga Rangi took one of the tarpaulins and laid it out on the ground. Mannie helped him to double it over, ready for the air beds. Nga Rangi smiled. "I'm glad it's not going to rain for a couple of days. The weather's supposed to be settled for the next week."

"Yeah, mate. It's the right time of year for us to come here. Be a bugger in the autumn. Wet and cold."

"A stroke of luck, really. Not by good planning or management. Just good luck." Mannie laughed at his comment.

"We're going to sleep like a log tonight. We didn't sleep at all well last night."

Tuku and Himi laid out another tarpaulin and began to double it over for the rest of them to put their air beds on.

"I don't think anyone slept at all well last night," Mannie replied, agreeing with him. "I sure as hell will tonight. The ground's too bloody hard for my back."

After dinner, Mannie looked around at the happy assembly sitting around the fire. He smiled, relishing his role as leader, that having been part of his plan from the outset. Everything seemed to be panning out perfectly.

Around the fire that night, they watched the rapidly retreating sun lower itself in a flagrant blaze of glory as it celebrated the end to a busy day. The inexplorable advance of night sapped the volatile brilliance and reposed the fiery tones of fluorescent pink clouds into smoky lavender and then to ashen purple and finally to the sooty, matt black of night.

Both Mannie and Jo rose at daybreak the following morning, having slept well on their new air-bed. After collecting firewood from the bush, Mannie lit the fire so he could make a large pot of tea.

Jo glanced down at Liana, who had been sleeping beside them in a new sleeping bag on her new air bed. "Hey. How's it this morning, Li? You sleep okay?"

Liana nodded with a happy smile and got up to stretch herself.

Nga Rangi and Marlene were sitting up in their sleeping bag on their new air bed. It appeared that they had a good nights sleep and were observing their surroundings. Nga Rangi noticed Mannie by the fire. He slipped out of his sleeping bag and quickly dressed and then went up to join him.

"How'd you sleep?" Nga Rangi asked.

"Good. Better than the night before, I can tell you. How about you guys?"

"Great. I don't think either of us moved all night."

Mannie pointed to the area just behind them. "That's where we'll build our huts, as we discussed when we were here last time. I've decided to stagger them so they're not all in line. Won't be so obvious from the air." He poured two cups of tea then, passing one to Nga Rangi; he went on, "First though, we'll have to build a temporary shelter in case it rains." He pointed at the five large tarpaulins. "That's what two of those are for."

Nga Rangi went over to their gear stacked neatly in the centre of the plateau. He saw the large roll of bird netting for the garden fence. Beside it he noticed a box that was unfamiliar to him. He picked it up, and on the front of the packet it read "Danger, Cyanide." He looked at Mannie quizzically. "What the hell's this for?"

Mannie laughed. "To keep the opossums away from the vegetable garden. There's a small clearing up there in the bush a short distance. Perfect for a garden. It gets plenty of sun and is sheltered enough from the bad weather."

Nga Rangi laughed. "You've thought of absolutely everything."

"Yeah, nothing to it really," Mannie admitted. "First though, while you, me and a couple of others build the shelter, the rest can start digging the garden."

"How did you envisage building the roofs for the huts again?"

"Like in my sketches. Once we get the floors down and the walls standing, we lay the ceiling sections across the top of the walls. Then we'll cut some beams from the bush. You know, small trees all about the same size. We lay them across the centre of the ceiling to form a ridge in the centre. Then we fit the rafters across the top of the beam to give the roof enough fall to run water off the actual roof itself. Then we put others that will angle from the edge of the roof down to the ground, front, and rear. Across everything we lay smaller branches close together with no gaps to support the butynol. Then, giving the Butynol plenty of width on each side, we cut it to length and lay the ends in a trench to run the water away."

"Okay," Nga Rangi replied. "Sounds good so far."

"Before we dig out for the floors though, we turf the grass first and put it off to one side. Then once we have the walls and ceiling up and we have the Butynol in place and pegged down, we'll cover it with the dirt dug out from the floor. That should be roughly fifteen centimetres deep. Then lastly, we lay the turf on top of that, giving it a grass roof." Glancing at Nga Rangi, he asked, "You follow me so far?" Nga Rangi nodded. Mannie continued, "Once they're finished, we hang those camouflage nets over the front of the doorways at about a 130-degree angle with twigs and small branches wound through them."

"It sounds feasible," Nga Rangi agreed.

"It's not only feasible, mate. It'll work."

Tuku, Jo, and Marlene noticed Nga Rangi and Mannie in serious discussion and joined them. Tuku made the tea and poured three cups. He handed one each to Marlene and Jo and then took one himself.

"Man, my new air bed's the best bed I've ever slept in,"

Tuku said, smiling happily. "I don't think I even farted last night. I was so damn tired."

Liana joined Jo and Marlene, and the three were laughing at Tuku's happy mood. Jo pointed with her head to Mannie and Nga Rangi. "Let's go and hear what those two are talking about."

Mannie wandered over to the edge of the plateau. Nga Rangi, Tuku, Jo and Marlene followed; and together, they peered down into the valley below.

By now, the others were all up and curious at what the six were looking at over the edge of the plateau and also joined them.

Mannie pointed out over the bush. "This land once belonged to our tribe." He turned 360-degrees. "All you can see and further. Right across the three mountains and all the surrounding land."

He continued in a sombre tone, "In the late 1800's all this land was given away to the bloody government." He paused, peering down into the valley. "The government threatened to confiscated it, but the paramount chief thought it would be better to gift it rather than let that happen." He turned away, shaking his head angrily. "And you know what? The stupid buggers did. They gave it all away, the lot. Now we own nothing at all up here."

He started walking slowly back toward the fire. "My great grandfather protested against that gift, and they bloody murdered him for it. It was the paramount chief who murdered him." Again, he shook his head. "Can you believe it? He was against gifting the mountains and the land right from the start, and to shut him up, they killed him."

He spoke in a low and bitter tone, his mouth twisted with bitterness. "Today, we take back some of that gift." He looked around at the bush. "Today, we claim back this piece of land from the bloody pakeha." He sniggered sardonically. "This is Maori land once more."

In the warrior tradition, with his knees slightly bent, Mannie poked out his tongue. "Haaaa. We take back our mana." He stood in front of the group, scowling, taking on the stance of a chief. "Society has told us to get stuffed." With nostrils flaring, he punched the air. "Today we tell society to get stuffed."

Apart from Nga Rangi, Marlene, and Jo, the others cheered, punching the air, captivated by Mannie's dramatic and theatrical performance.

Nga Rangi glanced at Marlene and Jo. "What the hell's he doing? He's getting everyone all wound up."

Marlene looked at Nga Rangi and asked, "Did you know he was like this?"

"No, I didn't," Nga Rangi replied dryly, disturbed at the radical connotations. He called out, "Hey, calm down, Mannie. Don't get yourself so worked up."

Jo too was taken aback by Mannie's bitter mood. "Yeah, come on, Mannie. Settle down, eh?"

Liana was somewhat confused and undecided about Mannie's performance. On one side there was cheering and applause for Mannie, on the other there was disapproval and criticism. She was surprised to see that Jo didn't appear to be impressed.

"Of course I'm bloody worked up," Mannie snapped back. "I'm really pissed off, if you must know. I'm sick to death of being dependent on the bloody pakeha." He pointed out over the bush again. "Everything we need is here." Acting like a chief at a hui, he took three steps to his right, the ritual stance of a leader. "Today we are free. What we can't take from this land, we do without." Sneering, he cast his eyes out over the valley. "And God help anyone who tries to fuck with us. Nobody will ever take from us again. Never."

Annoyed with the modus operandi, again Nga Rangi called out, "Do you have to sound so damn angry? I thought this was supposed to be a happy and peaceful place."

Mannie continued, ignoring him. "Here, we are brothers. Here, we are family." He punched the air, calling out, "One big happy family."

Those around him punched the air. "Family."

Nga Rangi had been observing Mannie closely, and the thought crossed his mind that maybe he was schizophrenic. He glanced at Marlene. "Is this guy for real...?"

"Getting a bit carried away if you ask me," Marlene added coldly.

Liana was now convinced that Jo definitely didn't like what Mannie was saying or doing. Then, to add to her confusion and for no apparent reason, Mannie burst out laughing.

Jo interrupted, "Geez, Mannie. Knock it off, will you?"

Mannie completely ignored her and went on. "We can't just eat meat though." He pointed to three very large cardboard boxes among their supplies. "In there we have vegetable plants. We'll grow potatoes, kumara, cabbage, lettuce." Pausing, he grinned. "And corn." He emphasized the word "corn." "Lots of the pirau."

Those around him started laughing at his cultural joke. He walked slowly to the centre of the plateau, speaking in a low, menacing tone. "Today we are free. Free from the oppressor." His mouth twisted with bitterness. "Like a bird escaping the snare. We will call this place Pokaka Pa. We'll keep the temporary shelter as our wharenui."

Taking on the stance of a warrior, Mannie stripped off his T-shirt, poked his tongue out and began a 'haka,' thumping his thighs with his hands, his feet pounding the earth; he shouted in Maori, "Ka mate, ka mate, ka ora, ka ora...."

Taking his lead, the group joined in.

The next three days were taken up getting the rest of their gear up to the plateau. The real work of building the temporary shelter was about to begin.

With the use of a chainsaw, it took them three weeks to

complete all the building work, including the meetinghouse. It would have taken them a lot longer had they not had the chainsaw.

They had built a separate hut for Mannie and Jo, with a separate room off that for Liana, a separate hut for Nga Rangi and Marlene, and two more slightly larger huts for the others. Then to make life simple, Mannie secured a hose in the centre of the spring, which allowed fresh water to gravity feed to a tap screwed to a table leg that was situated just back from the base of the fireplace.

Cuddled up in their air bed one night five weeks later, Marlene and Nga Rangi were evaluating their short time on the plateau.

Marlene said contentedly, "It's lovely up here. I don't think I've ever been so happy for a long time."

Nga Rangi propped himself up on an elbow beside her, and then leaning across, he kissed her cheek. "Yeah. It was a good move coming here. It's a fantastic set up." He looked around their hut, smiling. "It was a good idea of Mannie's to insulate the walls and ceiling. It's going to be quite comfortable in winter. The only down side is only having one window by the door that's under the camouflage net. It doesn't let a lot of light in, but that's okay really, a minor design fault which couldn't be helped."

"Yeah. It's not too bad. We hit the hay pretty early most nights anyway, seeing we're up at sparrows fart in the mornings." She laughed aloud and then kissed him. "That tap's been such a God send too. It makes life so much easier."

"And the garden's coming along fine."

"We'll be eating radishes next week. I can't believe how fast they grow. And the carrots are starting to poke through too. Jo's real good with plants. She's a bit of a green fingers. Liana picks things up real quick too. You only have to tell her something once and she's got it, you know, filed away in her brain. She's a lovely girl. I really like her."

"I'm also mastering the art of butchery," Nga Rangi added. "It's not as easy as it looks. There's a lot to learn, especially if you want to get the most out of a carcass."

"How're the others going at it?"

"Tuku's probably the best. He's got more patience than the others, and he's a real thinker when it comes to butchering. He's a natural at it."

"I wouldn't want to bring children up around here though," Marlene said, suddenly frowning. "How'd we educate them for starters?"

"Let's not dwell on that too much. I'm not at all sure I want to bring kids into this crazy stuffed-up world anyway. It's gone absolutely feral."

"Yeah, maybe you're right." Smiling, she added, and to change the subject, "Have you noticed the way Tuku and Himi have taken on the big brother image with Liana?"

"Yeah, I have," Nga Rangi replied. "They're really good with her. I watched them the other day sitting on the edge of the drop, looking down into the valley below the waterfall. Even though Liana doesn't talk to them, you can see by the look on her face that she enjoys their company."

"Tuku's really protective of her," Marlene told him. "Zac said something about Liana that Tuku didn't like, and boy, did he give Zac a dressing down. He really meant it too. It wasn't just a disagreement."

"It's good Li has someone like them to care for her. It gives her a sense of security."

CHAPTER 9

Andy, Jim, and Phil had arranged a three day deerstalking trip to Pokaka. Andy had been introduced to Pokaka by an old hunting friend of his father's, who had been a deer culler during the late 1960's. In turn, Andy introduced Jim and Phil to the area, two keen but inexperienced hunting friends.

They arrived late Friday afternoon and left their vehicle at the rail siding just before the second bridge past the Makatoki viaduct. It was a two-hour walk in to their camp-site.

Tired and hungry, they arrived at the campsite just on dark. Being too dark to put up their tent they decided to sleep under the stars for the night.

By the light of a torch, Jim collected firewood and lit a fire in the old river-stone fireplace. Phil filled the kettle from the small spring at the rear of the campsite and put it on to boil. Being nominated as cook Jim emptied three large tins of Wattie's beef casserole into an old pot and put it on the fire to heat.

The day had been a taxing one for all three and by nine thirty they slipped into their sleeping bags around the fire.

Andy rose at daybreak the next morning and woke Jim and Phil. "Come on, you buggers. Hands off cocks, feet in socks."

Andy soon resurrected the fire and within five minutes, had a kettle boiling for a hot drink. A light mist hung over the bush, and as they ate a hasty breakfast, Andy noticed a light breeze coming down the valley from the north. "Perfect morning for hunting. Mist'll be gone soon."

"Yeah," Jim agreed and went down to the river to investigate.

Phil joined him and washed his plate. "Let's tidy up and get going, eh? Early bird catches the worm."

"We're not here after worms, mate. Didn't I tell you that?" Phil said teasingly.

Jim replied lightheartedly, "Smart arse."

Andy came down and stood beside them. "Come on, you two. Let's get going, eh? We're not here on a school picnic you know."

"Yes, o fearless leader," Phil laughed, bowing roguishly.

They packed their sleeping bags away in their carry bags and put them in their backpacks. Jim checked his rifle as he made ready to leave.

"It doesn't look like anyone's been around here for a while," Andy noted. "I've got a gut feeling about today."

"We'll stick along the river," Jim announced. "It's easier going, and we'll cover more ground."

Andy gestured north with his head. "Come on. Time to go."

"You lead. We'll be right behind you," Jim replied.

They were well up the river by ten o'clock and hunting the eastern bank of the river. Andy was a little frustrated. "I can't believe we haven't seen any deer sign yet."

"Can't figure it out either," Phil agreed, taking his beanie off to scratch the top of his head. "The last time we were here there was sign all over the place. There was even sign by the camp."

"They do move around quite a bit though. Let's keep moving," Jim said optimistically, pointing north. "We'll cross the river shortly and take that shortcut up to the track that leads to that big flat area by the waterfall."

For another twenty minutes the threesome continued along the riverbank and then crossed the river again and took the steep shortcut that led up to the main western track. They had been heading north at a steady pace, when Jim, who was leading, spotted boot prints on the track. "Hey, look at this...!"

Andy and Phil came forward. Andy went down on one knee to investigate. He said soberly, "Someone else is in here...!" He inspected the prints a little closer. "They're not that old either." He rubbed his chin, deep in thought. "In fact, they're quite fresh." Dubiously, he looked up at his two friends.

"I wonder if it's poachers," Jim replied.

"Hard to say," Phil cut in. "Could be forestry workers, maybe."

Unconvinced, Andy shook his head. "Wouldn't think so, mate. Forestry wouldn't be interested in this place. There's too much rubbish in here." He pointed to one particular print and said quizzically, "Hey, look at these ones. See the size. They're bloody small. Must be a kid."

"There wouldn't be a kid in here," Jim said and then pointed north with his head. "Come on. Let's carry on."

Andy took the lead with Phil and Jim following. Fifteen minutes later, they came to a point on the track where they had a glimpse of the southern corner of the plateau. They watched it for a few minutes and saw nothing untoward.

Jim pointed up the track. With Andy leading, they

continued. Fifty metres further on, they came across more boot prints going in both directions, up into the bush to their left, but also coming out of the bush and going north.

A short distance further on, Andy pointed to more boot prints. He whispered, "Shit...! Look at these! There must be half a dozen of the buggers in here at least."

Guardedly, Phil looked around the immediate area. "What would they be doing way the hell up here? You think it's other hunters?"

Keeping low, Andy crept forward. "Has to be. Let's find out."

Nervous at their precarious situation, Jim said softly, "I think we should go back. This is giving me the creeps."

Andy whispered back, "Where's your sense of adventure?" He started up the main track again. Phil was behind Jim and stepped around him, following Andy.

Reluctantly, Jim followed Phil.

Andy stopped just before the end of the track, where all three had a clear view of the whole plateau. To his left he could see the crudely built meetinghouse. Over by the edge of the vast flat area, he spotted four men and two women looking down into the valley, talking quietly among themselves.

Andy glanced over his shoulder at Phil, and Jim and gestured with his head for them to come forward. They crept up beside him.

Jim pointed at the meetinghouse. "What the hell's that?"

Andy shook his head. "Haven't a clue. Some sort of shed, I expect."

Pointing at the group of six, Phil whispered, "What the hell are they up to?"

"Dunno," Andy replied quietly. "Let's watch for a while and see what happens."

Suddenly, a person appeared as if he had come out of the ground thirty metres to their right at two o'clock. Andy's eyes boggled. "Did you see that...?" he stammered softly. "Did you see that...?"

They were at an angle where they couldn't see the front of the huts, and to them, it appeared as if he had just popped up out of the earth itself.

"What the hell's going on?" Andy whispered. "That's seven we can see."

Then Himi appeared out of the ground from the same spot as Tuku.

"Shit...! There's another one...!" Andy said. "What the hell is this? Some sort of boot camp...? The buggers must be living underground." He looked suspiciously at his two colleagues. "What have we stumbled on?"

"Dunno, but that makes eight. How many more are there?"

Jim whispered nervously, "This is giving me the shits. I think we should bugger off and report this to the cops. I'm sure they'd like to know what's going on here."

Putting a finger to his lips, Andy whispered, "Shut up. Someone'll hear us."

Jim wasn't at all comfortable; a terrible sense of uneasiness enveloped him. "I'm telling you something's not right. This is giving me the shits."

Andy turned to him, annoyed with his wimpish behaviour. "Shut up...! Just shut up, will you! Don't be such a bloody pussy."

"Geez...!" Jim muttered to himself.

Andy grabbed him by the shirt and shook him. "For Christ's sake, shut up. You're starting to piss me off. They'll bloody hear us if you don't shut up."

All three were watching the group on the plateau, when Phil caught sight of two more men coming out of the bush some distance up to the north and started walking down toward the group on the plateau. Pucky was carrying the hind quarters of a red deer on his back, Chappy the fore quarters on his back.

Pointing to them, Phil whispered in Andy's ear, "That makes ten."

Andy whispered back, "Yeah, and no wonder there's no bloody deer around. These bastards are shooting them all."

Jim spun around nervously, having heard a rustle up in the bush behind them. "What was that...?"

Andy glared at him angrily. "Shut up."

Jim said softly, "But I heard something behind us...!" He heard it again and pointed. "There, didn't you hear it? Something or someone's up there behind us I'm tell you!"

"There's nothing behind us, dummy," Phil said, getting impatient. "It's all in your stupid mind."

Jim stood, pointing to the bush behind them. "I'm telling you, someone or something's up there behind us."

Phil was getting angry. "Get down, you dumb prick. Get down. They'll see you."

Jim shuffled uneasily, not knowing whether to go back to camp or stay. He crouched down and looked back at the group of eight, who had gathered around the two men that had just come back from a successful hunt.

* * * *

Jo and Ritchie had been working up at the vegetable garden some distance back from the track in a clearing behind their camp and saw the three men crouched down, suspiciously watching their camp. Jo turned to Ritchie and, pointing at the three strangers, started creeping quietly down toward them through the undergrowth.

They stayed hidden for many minutes, watching and listening. When Jo heard one of them say they were going to report their camp to the police, she signalled to Ritchie that she was going to attack them.

Without warning, Jo and Ritchie charged out of the bush at the three strangers.

Andy, Phil, and Jim had their backs to them. As Jim turned, Jo tackled him around the waist, sending him over on his back onto the damp, slippery soil beside the track.

Ritchie was right behind her and went for Andy. Andy instinctively brought his rifle butt up, hitting him on the side of the head.

Ritchie went down and, with his momentum, slid into the rubbishy scrub just off the track. He scrambled to his feet but again, Andy hit him on the forehead with the butt of his rifle, knocking him unconscious.

Jo was on top of Jim, holding him down, screaming at the top of her voice, "Mannie...! Mannie...! Quick, give us a hand."

Jim tried desperately to topple her off, but Jo had her legs spread wide on either side of him and he couldn't budge her.

Upon seeing Jim's predicament, Andy drove the butt of his rifle into the back of Jo's head.

Stunned by the vicious blow, Jo slumped forward, unconscious on top of Jim. Jim gave her a hefty shove to get her off, and she slid down the short greasy, damp slope head first into the rubbishy scrub below them.

In the rubbishy scrub were two young manuka trees thirty centimetres apart, and Jo's head went between them. Her shoulders prevented her from going any further, but with her momentum on the greasy slope, her lower body swung around and, with her head caught between the two young trees, twisted her neck at an awkward angle.

Both Andy and Phil saw the immediate response to Jo's scream for help. The group of ten began hurrying up toward them.

Andy grabbed Jim's arm and, lifting him to his feet, pushed him to a run down the track. "Get going. They're onto us."

With Jim leading, all three began running down the track the way they had come. Terrified and concerned, Jim kept looking back.

Andy called to him, "Keep running! Don't look back! Just keep running!"

Jim was very nervous and kept glancing back over his shoulder. "I think that girl broke her neck."

"Shut up and run, that's all you have to worry about right now," Andy snapped. "If they catch up with us, we're dog tucker."

"Didn't you hear what I said? I think that girl's neck is broken," Jim repeated soberly.

"Shut up and keep running!" Andy replied angrily. "Just keep running."

"Jim's right though, Andy," Phil cut in fearfully. "Her neck was twisted around at a terrible angle."

"For chrissake, the pair of you. Just keep running."

Jim cast an anxious eye over his shoulder and didn't see the tree root poking out on the side of the track. He tripped, almost losing his balance, and cursed. "Shit...!"

"Geez... Watch where you're bloody going, you stupid bugger!" Andy snapped at him. "Don't keep looking back. Just run!"

CHAPTER 10

Mannie rushed up and saw Jo lying on her back in the rubbishy scrub with her head caught between two small trees, her body twisted at an unnatural angle. He went down on his knees beside her. She was unconscious and not moving. "Jo, Jo...! Bloody hell, girl. Come on, wake up!"

Nga Rangi knelt down on the opposite side to Mannie, and between them, they carefully manoeuvred Jo's body around first and then eased her head out from between the two small trees while, at the same time, trying not to put any unnecessary pressure on her neck. Carefully, they slid her body up onto flat ground.

Marlene went down on her knees beside Mannie and immediately began examining her. She found a weak pulse in her neck.

Distraught, Mannie looked around for the three strangers. "Who the hell were they...?" he shouted. "Who the bloody hell were those pakeha bastards?"

Tuku and Himi were on either side of Ritchie. Tuku was slapping Ritchie gently on his cheek. "Wake up, Ritchie. Wake up. You okay, mate?"

Ritchie shook his head to clear the dizziness and then slowly sat up, holding the side of his head.

"You okay, mate?" Tuku repeated.

Ritchie nodded. "Yeah." He touched the side of his head and cringed at the sharp stab of pain. "Shit...!"

Suddenly, Marlene was frantically searching for a pulse on Jo's neck. Her face went an ashen colour as she tried several spots but to no avail. She looked up at Mannie with tear-filled eyes. "I can't find a pulse. Shit...!" she said, panicking. "She's got no pulse! It was there a moment ago, but it's not there now."

Picking up Jo's hand, Mannie searched for a pulse on her wrist. He found none. "Shit, Jo. Come on, girl." He gently patted her face, desperately wanting her to wake up. "Come on, sweetheart." In desperation and with both his palms placed firmly on her chest, he started CPR, counting, "One... two... three... four... five... six...." He counted to thirty and then leaned down and blew two short breaths into her mouth.

He continued CPR for another fifteen minutes without any response at all from Jo. He picked up her hand. It was totally limp. He lifted an eyelid and saw her eyes were glazed, lifeless.

Gently, Marlene put her hand on Mannie's shoulder. "She's not responding, Mannie. She's just not responding."

He continued CPR, his dilated eyes exhibiting extreme fear with tears streaming down his cheeks. "I can't stop now. She's not going to die. I won't let her."

For another five minutes, he kept up CPR, pounding her chest, and then, realizing his efforts was ineffectual, he slowed and then eventually stopped. Sobbing painfully, he put his head on Jo's chest and cuddled her.

Nga Rangi and the others felt completely useless and moved back out of the way. Wrapping both arms around Mannie's shoulders, Marlene tried to console him. He looked up at her, tears pouring down his face. Nga Rangi helped him to his feet, and the three stood there together, hugging each other.

In absolute despair, Mannie threw back his head and screamed at the top of his voice. "Nooooooo...! Nooooooo!" He knelt down beside Jo again, cradling her head on his lap and frantically tried to find a pulse in her neck but found none. Totally shattered, he threw his head back and cried out at the top of his voice. "Joooo...! Joooo...!"

Liana had been standing behind them all, watching in horror and silence with her hands covering her mouth, not wanting to witness what was happening; but she couldn't drag her eyes away from Jo's peaceful face. To her, she looked like she was just asleep. Her worst fears were materializing right in front of her, and she couldn't help herself when Mannie screamed out Jo's name. She slowly shuffled down and stood beside Marlene, tears streaming down her face.

Everyone had been so engrossed with Jo's sad demise they had not noticed her. She couldn't believe what she was witnessing. Her nightmare memories came flooding back. First, she had lost her wonderful, loving mother, whom she adored; and now she had lost Jo.

At the time of her mother's death, her grief had been unbearable, so utterly crushing it had almost suffocated her; and now, here it was again rearing it's ugly head.

Jo had been so good to her. She never once tried to replace her mother, but she was always there, so caring and understanding and full of joy and hope.

Without even realizing and to everyone's astonishment, Liana let out a piercing, blood-curdling scream, and she screamed and screamed. Dumbfounded, everyone looked at her. It was the first sound she had uttered for three years.

Mannie still had Jo's head cradled on his lap, and he turned and put his hand out to take Liana in his arms, but she unintentionally pushed his hand away, distraught at the gesture when the hellish memories of her father assaulted her fragile mind. She wanted to get away and was about to run off, when Marlene took her in her arms and, cuddling her, helped her down to kneel down beside Jo, both sobbing sorrowfully and hugging each other.

Then, to everyone's surprise, Ritchie knelt down beside Liana. He was totally shattered, and he gently picked up Jo's hand and held it for a moment, and then with tears silently running down his face, he kissed Jo's hand. "Come on Jo. Please wake up. Jo, wake up." He looked at Mannie, then back at Jo, whispering quietly to himself, "Come on, Jo. Don't leave us now. Your my very best friend." He looked up at Mannie. "We were just hiding up there, watching the bastards. What got Jo mad was when one of them said they were going to report our camp to the cops. That's when she decided to attack the buggers."

Mannie could see the pain in Ritchie's face, and he gently eased Jo's head back to ground, his face creased with pain and grief.

Then shaking like an enraged animal, he leaped to his feet. Wiping his tears with the back of his hand, he turned to Pucky and Chappy, shouting hysterically, "Get our rifles! Get our bloody rifles! No one's going to report us to the cops."

With tears still streaming down his face, he peered at Liana, Marlene, and Ritchie kneeing bedside Jo, all sobbing. Again, he flung his head back and screamed, "Nooooo. Jooooo...! Yaaaaaahhhh...!"

Moments later, Pucky rushed up carrying two rifles and handed Mannie his 30-06. "She's got a full magazine. Here're some spare bullets to put in your pocket if you need some more," he said and handed Mannie a half-empty packet of ammunition.

Mannie snatched the rifle, drove a bullet into the breech and then began raving hysterically to himself in a low bitter tone. "Fuckin' pakehas! Always taking from us. Take, take, fuckin' take! I've had a fuckin' enough! This is the last bloody straw!" He glanced down at Jo, tears pouring down his face, and then turned to Marlene. "Take care of her for me, will you, please, until I get back."

Marlene saw the pain in his eyes and, reading what he had on his mind, said softly, "You stay and help me with her, eh, Mannie?"

"I got a score to settle first," he sobbed, eyes glazed black with his hatred. He glared down the western track. "I got business to take care of. Those bloody pakehas don't kill my Jo and get away with it. No way. Not my Jo. Fuckin' white maggots! They just can't do that and get away with it." He shook his head, his agony engraved deep on his tattooed face. "No way."

Nga Rangi grabbed him firmly by the arm, concerned at what he might do. "You can't go after them in your state, mate. You'll kill them if you catch up with them."

Nga Rangi saw a spark explode in Mannie's eyes as he shouted into his face. "That's exactly what I'm gonna do." He turned to Pucky and Chappy, pointing with his head. "Come on. We got a score to settle with those pakeha bastards."

Nervous and unsure what to do, Chappy and Pucky turned to Nga Rangi, their eyes filled with indecision.

Sensing their reluctance, Mannie said menacingly. "Come on. We can't stand around here all bloody day. They'll get away." He turned, pointing his rifle across the plateau. "It'll be quicker if we take the shortcut over the edge."

Wiping tears, Mannie charged across the plateau.

Nga Rangi took a few steps after him, shouting at the top of his voice, "Mannie...! Mannie...! Don't do this. Come back here."

Ignoring him, Mannie jumped over the edge onto the small ledge and started sliding down the steep face on his backside.

Mannie made it to the river's edge, followed closely by Pucky and Chappy. Looking downstream, he saw three men, two running ahead of the other.

Nga Rangi rushed back up to Jo. Marlene and Liana were still kneeling beside her body, crying softly, Liana holding Jo's hand. Mortified at Jo's sudden death, the others crowded around. Tuku and Ritchie had tears in their eyes, unsure what to do. They looked sadly at Nga Rangi for direction.

Nga Rangi put his hand on Marlene's shoulder, and then slowly helped her to her feet. "We'll lay her out on her bed, eh? We can't leave her here. Come on, Li. Help us lay her out on her bed, eh?"

Sobbing mournfully, Marlene put her arms around him. "She was my best friend." She looked down at Jo, totally devastated. "Oh, Jo. How could this happen?"

Nga Rangi held her for a moment and then, looking at Tuku and Himi, said, "Give us a hand, please. We'll lay Jo on her bed and wait until Mannie gets back."

Tuku looked nervously at Nga Rangi. "I hate to think what he's going to do if he catches up with those buggers?"

"Your guess is as good as mine," Nga Rangi said nervously.

"I hope he doesn't do anything too drastic," Himi added fearfully.

Ritchie, who was still sobbing, sitting on his heels beside Liana cut in angrily, "Those bastards shouldn't have been snooping around like bloody thieves. They deserve everything they get if you ask me. Bloody arseholes. Look what they did to Jo."

Overwhelmed at the tragic turn of events, Nga Rangi put his hand on Ritchie's shoulder in an attempt to pacify him. "I'm sure they didn't do it intentionally. It would have been an accident."

Ritchie glared at Nga Rangi through narrowed tearful eyes and then, clenching his fists, shouted, "Accident my arse! They shouldn't have been snooping around in the first place. That guy smashed her in the head with his rifle butt." Overcome with grief, he turned away, self-conscious for crying in front of the others. He wiped his tears with the bottom of his shirt. "Stuff those pakeha bastards. Jo was my friend. She was the only person who ever really liked me."

Understanding his unhappy background and his feelings for Jo, Marlene put her arms around him and hugged him. "I know how you felt about Jo, Ritchie. But there's still me. I'm not going anywhere. We're good mates, you and me, aren't we?"

Ritchie broke free from Marlene's arms. "She was like a mother to me." He couldn't hold back his tears and, embarrassed for showing weakness in front of the others, hurried off into the bush and went up to the garden that he, Jo, Liana, and Marlene had lovingly nurtured.

$*$ $*$ $*$ $*$ $*$

Andy led Phil and Jim down the track as fast as he could. Upon reaching the narrow shortcut they had come up earlier, Andy looked back for a second to see if they were being followed. Upon seeing no one, he turned left and rushed down the narrow slippery track.

The three burst out onto the riverbank. Andy and Phil carried on at a steady pace. Jim had to stop for a moment to catch his breath. Andy called back, "Jim, don't stop now. Come on. Get a move on."

Jim was bent over with his hands on his thighs, breathing heavily. Phil was now running beside Andy and looked back over his shoulder just as Mannie burst out onto the riverbank two hundred metres upstream toward the waterfall.

"Shit...! There's three of them after us," Phil stammered and then cupped his hands and yelled, "Jim! Look behind you! They're after us!"

Jim started jogging, thinking they just wanted him to hurry.

Phil yelled again, pointing upstream, "Run, Jim! Run! They're behind you!"

Jim shot a glance over his shoulder and saw three men running toward him. Shocked, he began running downstream as fast as he could.

Andy and Phil came to the spot on the river where they had crossed earlier that morning. They both leaped in and quickly picked their way across the rocky bottom. Jim was still eighty metres behind them.

Jim glanced back. The three men chasing him were gaining on him.

Andy clambered up the riverbank and called back. "Come on, Jim! Hurry up! Get a move on!"

Jim leaped into the river and began picking his way across the current. He stumbled on the rocky bottom and went down on his knees, dropping his rifle, and in the panic to get away, he left it behind.

Andy noticed the man leading the pursuing group stop and go down on one knee, shouldering his rifle. Horror struck him like a mallet. He screamed at the top of his voice, "Run, Jim! Come on, mate! Run, run, run!"

Boom! The thunderous echo of Mannie's powerful 30-06 reverberated through the valley. Instantaneously, a huge waterspout erupted out of the river fifteen metres ahead but slightly to Jim's left.

Jim screamed, panic threatening to devour him. "Yaaahh...! Yaaahh...!"

Andy and Phil were horror-struck. "They're shooting at him...!" Phil stuttered. "The mad bastards are shooting at him...!"

Boom! A second shot rang out. Again, water exploded out of the river less than twenty centimetres from Jim's left leg. Stunned and in a panic, he stumbled on the uneven rocky riverbed and, again, went down on his knees.

Andy and Phil were screaming at him. "Come on Jim! Run, mate, run!"

Boom! A third shot rang out.

The bullet hit Jim just above the knee in the back of his leg, sending a shock wave through his whole body like a runaway concrete truck, so insanely powerful that it whipped his leg out from under him and he went over sideways in the river.

Horrified and in a state of disbelief, he instinctively tried to stand, but his shattered femur in his upper leg wouldn't respond. There was no pain, just a terrible pulsing numbness. Again, he tried to stand and forced himself up with his hands and right leg.

As he drew himself up, he noticed a thick stream of red flowing away in the current. Not wanting to look down at his wound for fear of what he might discover and hearing Andy and Phil shouting at him, he tried hopping, picking his way carefully across the current.

Jim didn't hear the fourth shot as it echoed through the valley like a thunderclap directly overhead. It struck him in the back with the force of a runaway train. The soft-nosed projectile mushroomed on bone, shattering it, and then exploded his heart out through his chest, showering the river with a crimson gelatinous tissue. He was hurtled forward, his arms wind-milling in the air; and he went down, face first in the river, his limbs thrashing involuntarily in the water.

Andy and Phil watched the horrendous scene in utter horror. "Shit...!" Andy screamed. "Shit...!"

Andy, wanting to help Jim, leaped into the river, and began stumbling his way across the rocky bottom.

Boom! A fifth shot rang out.

A huge waterspout exploded out of the river beside him. Terrified and panicking, he turned back and stumbled towards the riverbank. The three men pursuing them were less than 150 metres away and closing fast.

Phil was screaming at the top of his voice, "Murdering bastards! You murdering bloody bastards!"

Andy glanced back at his friend, lying face down in the river, his head completely submerged, the water red with his blood in the current.

Two more shots rang out. Dirt and silty soil exploded out of the riverbank just behind Phil as Andy, trembling like a leaf, stumbled up the riverbank.

Phil grabbed him by the arm, helping him the final metre. In horror, he glanced back at Jim. He knew there was nothing either of them could do now to help. "Let's get the hell outta here!"

After firing a shot each at the approaching men, they started running, keeping close to the bush, using it as cover whenever they could.

They were approaching a short bend in the river 130 metres ahead. Once around it, they would be out of view from their pursuers for a short time. Andy hesitated as they reached the bend and fired two quick shots at their pursuers, slowing their advance.

Breathing heavily and suffering from stitch, they managed to keep ahead of their pursers for the next hour.

Phil pointed to a shallow section in the river where they had crossed earlier on their way upstream. Phil charged into the river with Andy fifteen metres behind him.

They were almost across when - Boom! A shot rang out. Phil was thrown to his left with the impact, hit high in the back, and went down on one knee in the river.

Andy was behind him and grabbed him by the shirt and lifted him to his feet and then, putting his left arm around his waist, helped him up the riverbank.

Boom! A huge water spout burst out of the river just behind Andy. "Shit...!" Andy yelled, urging Phil on. "Come on, mate. We're almost there," he said, trying to sound calm, dragging Phil up the riverbank. Andy swung around and fired single-handedly from the hip at the advancing men. Then with his arm still around Phil's waist, he half carried him into the bush.

Phil was bleeding profusely, his gaping wound needing immediate attention. He involuntarily slowed, his body beginning to shake in obvious shock. Andy chanced a look behind and saw the three men less than a eighty metres away; one man was down on one knee.

Boom! A branch just above Andy's head shattered and fell to the ground. Phil's head had flopped forward on his chest, his breathing laboured and weak. Andy dragged him to a tree and propped him against it and then turned to face their attackers.

He bellowed across the river at the pursuing group. "Come on, you murdering bastards! Come on!"

Boom! Andy took the shot in his left collarbone, catapulting him backwards into a tree. With a massive effort, he slowly slid his back up the tree trunk, using it as support. Then staggering, he bravely took a step towards the river to face the three advancing men.

One man leaped into the river, running straight at him. With his right arm, Andy swung his rifle up and pulled the trigger. Click! His magazine was empty.

The man came up the riverbank and fired. Hit in the chest, Andy was thrown violently backward from the impact. He crashed into a birch tree, and dazed and winded, he slowly slid down it, smearing a thick line of blood on the trunk.

For Andy, time stood still. Knowing his pursuers were close, he shook his head, trying to focus; but his vision was clouded and blurred. His rifle was on the ground at his feet; his arms and legs were like lead and wouldn't move. A shiver ran down his shattered spine. He began to feel incredibly cold; numbness cloaked him like a massive blanket, slowly seeping over his body, threatening to suffocate him.

Mannie, going down on one knee in front of him, looked into his eyes. "You see me, pakeha? You see me?"

Andy could hear someone talking to him, seemingly way off in the distance, but couldn't quite make out the words. Straining his eyes through the haze, he made out the shape of a face in a blurry cloud. Slowly his vision began to clear and focused on Mannie's tattooed face, trying to understand what he was saying. He wanted to speak, but the words wouldn't form on his dry lips.

Mannie watched Andy's eyes as they slowly focused on him. "You can see me now, eh, pakeha?" His face was twisted with anger and grief. "You bastards took my ancestral land." He picked up a handful of dirt and threw it in Andy's face. "This land." His nostrils flared as his anger grew. "Then you took my job, tried to stop us from fishing." He grabbed Andy's shirt and shook him, pulling his upper body forward. "Then you wanted to kick me out of my fuckin' house." He threw Andy back against the tree trunk with a thud that it took his breath for a few seconds. "Then the last straw was when you took my woman, my beautiful Jo."

In his mind's eye, he could see Jo's smiling face. Tears began streaming down his cheeks. "What hurt the most was when you took my woman." He started to sob uncontrollably. "Fuck all you bloody pakehas to hell."

Chappy came in from the riverbank and stood behind him. "What are we going to do now?"

Mannie shook himself, his face drenched with sweat, tears, and grief. Throwing his head back, he screamed at the top of his voice. "Yaaaaa...!" In sheer rage, he took hold of Andy's head and, snapping it to the left, broke his neck.

Mannie stood there for several long agonizing minutes, glaring down at the two dead hunters. The loss of Jo was devastating, and killing these two hunters didn't make him feel any better.

"What we gonna do with them?" Pucky asked soberly.

"We'll bury the bastards across the river in the bush somewhere."

"They'll have a vehicle parked close by somewhere too," Pucky added. "We'll have to get rid of that as well."

"It'll probably be parked back somewhere around the siding by the railway line. But before we do anything though, we'll come back tomorrow with a couple of shovels and dispose of the bodies first."

Reluctantly, Chappy and Pucky went through Andy and Phil's pockets. Pucky found a set of keys and held them up. "Here's the car keys."

"Good," Mannie replied, taking them. "Come on. Let's get back to camp." He put the car keys in his pocket and then stood momentarily, looking down at Andy. "I can't believe Jo's not going to be with us any more." In a rage, he kicked Andy's body. "Fuckin' pakeha. Always fuckin' taking. Stinking white bastards."

With a sense of emptiness and in complete silence, Pucky and Chappy followed Mannie back to camp. Marlene, Nga Rangi, and Liana had Jo laid out in her best clothes on her and Mannie's air bed. Marlene was sitting beside her body cuddling Liana and crying when Mannie entered his hut. He knelt down beside Jo, the pain of his loss etched on his face. His eyes were lined with dark rings, giving him the appearance that he hadn't slept for a week. He looked at Liana. He didn't know what to say. She was just as devastated as he was, and there was nothing he could do to comfort her.

Upon seeing the three come back into camp, Nga Rangi took Pucky aside and asked quietly, "What happened?"

Glancing first at Mannie, who was in his hut, to make sure he wouldn't hear what he had to say, and then at Nga Rangi, Pucky sadly looked down at his feet. "He shot them."

"All three...? They're all dead?"

Pucky nodded and then followed Chappy to their hut.

Nga Rangi had a loath sense of indifference for the three hunters, and to him it was purely an accident but there was no way he could convince Mannie otherwise. He went into Mannie's hut and put his hand on Mannie's shoulder. "I know there's no words that can comfort you at the moment for what you must be feeling for Jo, but did you have to kill them? I mean, did they all have to die?"

Mannie's face was screwed up with bitterness and grief; his eyes were dilated with his hate for the three hunters. He glared at Nga Rangi. "Bloody pakeha. All they've done is take from us, you included." He looked painfully down at Jo's body. "That was no accident. Not to me. She was my soul mate. We had been together since fifth form. Those bloody white bastards took her from me." Mannie's loss was immeasurable, and he burst into tears.

Not wanting a confrontation, Nga Rangi left it at that. He could understand where Mannie was coming from, but he felt there was no reason to kill all three hunters. It was going to take Mannie a long time to come to terms with Jo's death. She and Mannie had had a good, caring, loving relationship. The next few weeks were going to be very hard for him, and there was nothing anyone could do but support him in any way they could.

Feeling totally deflated and taking Marlene's hand, Nga Rangi helped her to her feet and took her for a walk up past the waterfall toward the mountain. Marlene was in tears and very upset.

"Do you think those hunters deserved to die?" he asked her quietly.

Marlene looked up through tear-drenched eyes and shook her head. "No. No one deserved to die. Not like that. The whole thing was a terrible accident."

"I don't know what's going to happen now," Nga Rangi said, totally overwhelmed with the whole travesty. "I don't know what to think any more either. I can feel for Mannie, having lost Jo like that, but shit...! That's going a bit too far."

"My feelings are for Li," Marlene told him. "She feels like she's lost her mother all over again." She glanced back at their camp. "Ritchie's absolutely shattered too," Marlene went on. "He really looked up to Jo."

"Yeah, I know. He also looked up to you too, but I think Jo was his favourite. She really was like a mother figure."

"What's going to happen when those three hunters don't go home?" Marlene said anxiously. "I mean, the cops'll come looking for them. What then?"

Shaking his head, Nga Rangi replied, "It all depends. We'll have to find out if they camped in here somewhere last night. That's the first thing we have to find out. If that's the case, which I'm assuming it is, we'll have to put everything back in their car and dump it somewhere away from here."

The following day, they buried Jo overlooking the vegetable garden in the sunny clearing, the place they all knew she would have liked to be laid to rest.

It was after lunch when Mannie, Nga Rangi, Pucky, and Chappy went down the river and buried Jim in the bush across the river from where he had died; Andy and Phil were buried together in the bush opposite where they had died. Following that, they found the hunters' camping gear at the original campsite and took it back to the rail siding where they found Andy's car. Putting everything inside, Mannie and Pucky drove the car along to the next bridge, south, toward Horopito, another two kilometres away. They pushed it the final few metres into the deep narrow ravine and it plunged down into the river below.

Over the next day, everyone in camp were very subdued. They all shared Mannie's loss. Now that Jo was no longer with them and with her absence, they realized how much Jo's presence was felt in camp. She gave them all a real sense of belonging, and her sense of humour was unmistakeable.

Even when Mannie was annoyed and upset, she could calm him and have him laughing in minutes.

Liana was devastated and felt totally abandoned. She was in a vacuum of grief and loss. She spent most of her day up at Jo's grave sitting there, utterly depressed. She began mumbling incoherently as she had the day after her mother had died.

Marlene was really concerned for her well-being and went up and sat with her, but Liana was unaware anyone was with her. When Marlene left her an hour later, she was sitting on her feet, rocking back and forth, as if she had shut out her existence.

Mannie, feeling sorry for himself, went up and sat with her and tried speaking to her; but again, Liana was unaware of his presence. She had shut herself off completely from the rest of the world. He was beginning to worry about her and tried talking to her again but with no response. After thirty minutes he left her and went back to his hut.

Marlene took dinner up to her and nudged her, asking her to eat, but still, there was no response. Marlene knelt down in front of her and took her face gently in her hands. "Li," she said, trying to get her to focus. "Li. Eat something, will you, please. You have to eat or you'll get sick." No response. Poor girl, she thought sadly. I have to try and help her somehow. Show her I care and that I'm here for her when she needs a friend to talk to.

It was almost dark, and everyone was sitting around a fire. Liana had not come back from the grave site. Mannie decided to go up and bring her down before she got cold. Thirty seconds later, they all heard him scream at the top of his voice. "Yaaaaahhh! Give me a hand! Help! Someone, please!"

Tuku was the first to respond with Nga Rangi close on his heels. The first thing they saw was Mannie trying to lift Liana by her legs to take the weight of her body off the noose around her neck. She had hung herself. "Help me, please!" Mannie was screaming, tears running down his upturned face. "We can't lose her as well."

Nga Rangi quickly grabbed her knees, and with their combined strength, they took the weight while Tuku cut the rope with his hunting knife.

Immediately, they lay her down on her back and Mannie started CPR but when Tuku showed them the rope with a crude but effective 'hangman's' knot tied in it, they knew any efforts would be futile. Somehow she had tied a crude hangman's knot in the rope. Needless to say, Mannie kept up CPR for five minutes but, deep down, he knew it was too late to save her. Nga Rangi estimated that she must have been hanging there for a good fifteen minutes before they discovered her.

The rest of the group had crowded around. No one spoke. They all knew with Jo dying the way she did, Liana's grief had been just too much for her fragile mind to cope with. Both Tuku and Himi were distraught and couldn't hold back their tears.

Mannie was kneeling, thumping the ground with his fists, screaming at the top of his voice. "Yaaaahhh....! Why Li...! Yaaaahhh....! She was so young...! Why...! Yaaaahhh....!" He began to shake and then broke down and sobbed uncontrollably. Marlene knelt down beside him and hugged him to try and console him. She too was crying, and when she looked around, the rest of the group was crying with them.

For many weeks after, Mannie spent a lot of his time alone up by Jo and Liana's graves. He went out hunting by himself, and even when he was in camp, his time was spent away from the others, in his hut. At times he was heard mumbling to himself, consumed with hatred. Everyone could understand his grieving for Jo and Liana, and they all sympathized with him. But Nga Rangi knew, deep down, that something had snapped in Mannie's mind. Liana's death, together with Jo's death, only two days before, had a dramatic effect on him psychologically. Mannie was not Mannie any more.

CHAPTER 11

John Amohia and Tui Paloa had recently returned from their third tour of duty in East Timor. Having been to a debriefing camp north of Auckland on the Whangaparoa Peninsula with the eight other members of their squad, they were flying back to the Papakura Military Base in an army Iroquois helicopter along the coastline of East Coast Bays in the Auckland Province.

Seated beside the open cockpit door, Tui peered down at the affluent display of capitalism below. He cast a pondering eye at John. "You know, mate, it's amazing how little these people down there appreciate what we have here in New Zealand."

John replied musingly, "You're not wrong there, Tui. Compared to where we've just come from, this is absolute paradise." He was totally engrossed in his thoughts for a second or two. "We got leave due in a week. I've been thinking."

"Yeah. Been thinking about that myself. Be nice to get away somewhere for a few days," Tui responded.

"I'm heading home for a couple of days to see the family,

but after that I'm free. I wouldn't mind heading off into the bush somewhere for a bit of deer stalking."

"Yeah."

"What say we give Brian and Dave a call after we get back to barracks? Maybe they'd like to join us."

"There's plenty of places to go. What about Pokaka? That's as good a place as any. We could go there."

"Now you're talkin'."

At the Papakura Military Base, they headed for their barracks to clean up and unpack. While Tui was in the shower, John rang their friends.

Brian and Dave were delighted with the idea and were looking forward to spending four days with John and Tui, keen to hear about their overseas exploits in East Timor.

John arranged for he and Tui to pick them up in Tui's four-wheel-drive Toyota Landcruiser on their way.

John was busy unpacking his kitbag, when Tui came in from the shower with his towel wrapped around his waist. "You get hold of them?"

"Yeah. They're keen as, mate. We'll pick them up on the way through."

"Good one. Should be a good few days then. It's been a while since we've seen those two."

* * * * *

It was mid afternoon when Tui's Landcruiser pulled into the siding beside the railway line at Pokaka. Tui parked out of sight behind the stock pile of crushed gravel among the scrub and weeds.

Brian, who had been talking nineteen to the dozen, was the first out and opened the rear doors of the four-wheel-drive. Full of enthusiasm, and as he put on his backpack, he commented, "Didn't take long to get here, eh? Must've been all that yappin' we were doing."

John smiled and, glancing at Dave and Tui, said with a chuckle, "We...? You've been a right bloody motor-mouth since we left Dave's. Man, no one could get a word in edgeways."

They all laughed at the light humour. John took out his rifle. Dave smiled teasingly at the sight of John's military British SLR rifle.

"See you've still got that old military cannon."

John grinned as Tui took out his American M16 military weapon and interrupted before Dave could comment.

"Yeah, and I've still got my bloody machine gun."

Everyone was in a jovial mood. John put on his backpack, jumped up and down a couple of times to get it comfortable, and then slung his rifle over his shoulder. He glanced at his wristwatch.

"It's three-forty. Should be at camp by five forty. Be enough time for an evening shoot."

Tui flashed his eyebrows cheekily. "You buggers ready yet? You been mucking around here for ages. Come on. Get a bloody move on, eh?"

Dave and Brian laughed and, knowing he was mocking them, took it in the manner in which it was intended. Dave looked across at the opening in the bush to the start of the track. They were reasonably familiar with the terrain, having hunted there before with John and Tui.

The four headed off, eager to get away from the normal humdrum of life and relax in the tranquillity of the bush. The long-range weather forecast was good for the next five days, and they were keen to take advantage of it.

Once they reached the river, it was an easy walk with only a slight incline in a northerly direction toward the mountain. On either side of the river there was a three to four metre wide clear strip most of the way apart from one short section on the western side. It took them just under two hours to reach the old campsite.

John pushed through the thin line of scrub bordering the small but natural grassy area fifteen metres in diameter. It was the perfect camping spot, providing shelter from the wind off the river and a small fresh water spring in one corner.

Smiling, John dropped his backpack and rifle on the ground and gazed around. "Hasn't changed at all since we were here last. Doesn't look like there's been anyone here for some time."

"That's good," Tui agreed. "The place won't be shot out then."

Dave felt a slight breeze coming off the river. "Perfect conditions for hunting."

Tui, with a hunter's eye, glanced upstream. "Yeah, mate. That's the way we like it. Breeze on the nose."

John, unzipping his backpack, took out a cup and scooped a cupful of water from the spring. He drank it in one gulp, savouring the taste. "Mmmmm. Beautiful fresh New Zealand spring water. Nothing like it, eh."

Brian was keen to get out hunting. "We won't have a meal before we go out. We'll cook up a big feed when we get back."

"Yeah," Tui agreed, looking out toward the river. "Come on. Let's get going."

John, flashing his eyebrows, glanced at his wristwatch. "We'll split up into pairs, eh? Brian, you go with Dave. Tui and I'll stick together."

"That's fine," Brian agreed. "We'll even hunt the other side if you like." Dave cocked his rifle and applied the safety catch. Brian followed suit.

Smiling, Tui rolled a joking eye at Dave, patting his M16. "Fair enough. We'll stick to this side then."

Dave shook his head at Tui's antics. "Geez, man. You're a bloody nut-case." Tui laughed and then kissed his M16.

Shaking his head disdainfully, Dave cast a cautionary eye at John. "Is he always like this?"

John nodded, smiling. "Yeah. Pretty much."

Brian pointed towards the river with his head. "Come on. Enough of this bullshit. It'll be dark in a few hours."

Brian took the lead. John and Tui waited on the riverbank while Brian and Dave crossed. On the opposing riverbank, Dave called out, "See you back here just before dark, eh?"

Patting his rifle, Tui called back, "Yep. We'll have the big one."

Again, Dave shook his head, trying not to grin. "You talk a lotta crap, mate."

Brian smiled, putting his thumb in the air. "We'll have the big one. You'll probably get some smelly old goat."

"We'll see, mate. We'll see," Tui replied, grinning cheekily.

John pointed up behind the camp. "We'll do a sweep up behind here first, eh? Could get lucky. You never know."

"Led on, maestro," Tui said, waving John forward.

＊　　＊　　＊　　＊　　＊

Dave and Brian headed off upstream along the riverbank and had been stalking for half an hour, when Dave spotted fresh deer prints coming out of the river and went off into the bush. He pointed, whispering, "Let's follow up here. See where they lead."

Brian nodded excitedly.

They had only gone twenty metres when suddenly, crashing off to their right up a short gulley above them, they spotted a young hind as it disappeared over the edge.

Dave cursed, glancing back at Brian. "Bummer...! Bugger must've got our scent."

Brian, observing the wind direction, nodded. "Yeah. Wind's swirling in here at the moment. Bugger it."

"Bloody young hind too."

Brian pointed with his rifle. "Come on. Let's keep going. Keep your eyes peeled."

Dave spotted another short ridge to the north and turned to Brian, pointing with his head. "Let's get up on top of that. Get a better view and the breeze's on the nose."

Brian agreed, and together, they stalked up the ridge. "Keep low," Dave whispered. "Don't wanna silhouette ourselves on the horizon."

At the top of the ridge they laid down behind a small clump of brush and fern to observe the valley below. For several minutes they watched and waited.

Looking casually north, Brian was surprised at what he saw. "Hey, look," he whispered, pointing. "Smoke...! Someone must be camped up by the waterfall."

Puckering an brow, Dave replied. "I thought you said there wasn't supposed to be anyone else in here?"

"That's right," Brian said reflectively. "When I got the permit, the bloke at the DoC Office said there hadn't been any permits issued for this area for quite some time."

"That's strange," Dave said curiously. "Then what's that bastard doing up there now."

Lost in his thoughts for a moment, Brian added, "In fact, the DoC guy said three hunters came in here last year and disappeared without a trace. They found their car in the river below that bridge before Horopito but no bodies."

Lifting an eyebrow, Dave said, "What...?"

"That's what he said," Brian replied dubiously. "I didn't take much notice at the time. It all sounded a bit far-fetched, but the guy was real serious."

Dave looked at him with a critical eye. "No trace at all...?"

"That's what he said."

"That's a bit hard to swallow."

"He showed me the computer screen."

"Nah, mate. Somethin' must've been wrong."

"Well, that's what he said, and I saw it myself on the computer screen," Brian said, trying to sound convincing.

Dismissing the issue, Dave said, "Nah. Wouldn't believe that. They've got their wires crossed somewhere." He gestured toward the track. "Let's head back down where we spooked that hind. Could be a stag hangin' around in there. You never know."

Brian nodded and they started making their way slowly back down the ridge. Judging they were close to the spot where they had spooked the young hind, Dave pointed with his head. "Come on. In here."

Cautiously, they edged their way down into an area that was thick with supplejack, rubbishy scrub and vines. Brian was leading and glanced over his shoulder at Dave. "Too bloody thick in here. We'll have to detour around it."

Dave nodded and started backtracking.

Brian followed Dave down a narrow animal track, where large clumps of damp soil had been freshly turned over. Excitedly, he whispered to Dave, "Pig rooting!"

Dave's face lit up like a lamp. "Not little buggers either."

"They certainly rip the ground up, eh?"

They slowly made their way down to a small clearing that had pig rooting all through it. Brian stalked around the perimeter, rifle at the ready in anticipation of a quick shot.

An object caught his eye on the edge of the clearing among the recently disturbed soil. He went over to it and was stunned at what he saw. "Hey, Dave. Come here. Take a look at this!"

Dave looked back curiously. "What is it?"

"Human skull."

Hurrying over to Brian, Dave peered down at the partially uncovered skull. "Must be a grave."

"Way out here...?" Brian replied warily. He bent down and began scraping the soft soil away from the skull with his hands. Then, with face aghast, he stood up. "It's a whole bloody skeleton."

Dave leaned over, observing the partially uncovered skeleton. "Shit...!"

"Why would someone bury a body way the hell out here?"

Brian shook his head. "Somethin' strange here, mate. Let's leave it and come back in the morning with the John and Tui, eh?"

"Yeah," Dave agreed and then glanced at his watch. "Better start back shortly anyway. Be dark soon."

"I can't figure it out," Brian said, looking a little confused. "Why would some bugger bury a body up here? If it was an old hunter, wouldn't they have a headstone or a sign, you know, something to mark his grave?"

Dave looked down at the skeleton undecidedly. "Got me stumped, mate."

CHAPTER 12

John and Tui did a sweep up behind the camp in a north westerly direction, Tui leading. With all their military training in bush and jungle warfare, Tui had developed an acute awareness of his surroundings. They had been gone forty minutes when he suddenly put his hand up to stop.

"What's up?" John asked.

"You hear that?"

"Hear what? Don't hear anything."

"That's just it, mate," Tui said and then squatted down, observing the area carefully. "The sound of silence."

John squatted down beside him.

Tui put his finger to his lips. "Listen."

John strained his eyes through the thick bush. Then a twig cracked, fifty metres ahead at eleven o'clock. Tui pointed in the general direction, then there was another crack. John turned to Tui, grinning. They strained their eyes through the dense undergrowth but couldn't pin-point anything. Moments later, there was another crack at twelve o'clock. Tui pointed and then, there was another crack at one o'clock.

Tui signalled with his head to get closer. "Whatever it is, it's heading for the river." Keeping low, he darted across to a tree, and then to another. He gestured for John to follow.

Tui ran to another tree while John ran to the tree Tui had just left and then ducked quickly to another. Tui dashed to another and then signalled to John to join him. Half way across, John accidentally stood on a dry twig. Crack.

"Shit...!"

Tui waved him forward. John rushed over and squatted down. Tui pointed to the soft soil in front of him. "Whatta you make of that?"

John looked down at the fresh boot prints in the soft damp soil.

"Another bloody hunter," he whispered, surprised.

Tui nodded and then pointed to the soil again. "Going by the boot pattern, he's aware we're in here too. See how they step back and forth over each other in the same spot?" Tui said, looking warily at John. "He's lookin' out for us."

"He's heading toward our camp too," John said, pointing with his rifle.

"Let's cut the bugger off."

They followed the fresh boot prints for another fifty metres and then lost them. John pointed toward the river.

Fifteen minutes later they came out on the riverbank without making contact. They looked upstream, and then downstream. John frowned, confused, and then turned to Tui. "Bastard! Wonder who it is?"

"Whoever he is, he shouldn't be here," Tui replied irritably. "When Brian got the permit he said we had the whole place to ourselves."

"Yeah. I remember him saying that. Maybe we should carry on upstream."

"I think we should wait here for a few minutes," Tui suggested. "Bastard might come out on the riverbank."

It was only three minutes later when John noticed a movement beside the bush a short distance to the north. He jumped to his feet, pointing. "There he is."

Tui saw a man 150 metres upstream. Having obviously

seen them, the man started jogging north, hugging the bush, trying to make himself less visible.

Tui was about to give chase when John called to him. "Waste of time, mate. He'll lose us in the bush."

"And the bugger'll scare everything for bloody miles as well," Tui said and kicked a small rock into the river. "Stuff the bastard."

*   *   *   *   *

Aware there had been pigs in the area recently, Nga Rangi was slowly stalking through the bush when he heard something or someone coming slowly towards him. Guessing it was a hunter, he decided to head back to the river. He hadn't gone far when he realized that, who or whatever it was, it was stalking him. He immediately did a ninety-degree turn and headed due north. When he had gone a short distance, he changed direction again, going east, and made his way down to the riverbank.

As he stepped out of the bush onto the grassy verge of the riverbank, he noticed two men downstream, one sitting on a large rock beside the river. He saw one man leap to his feet and cursed silently to himself for not checking that the riverbank was clear first before stepping out of the bush.

Immediately, Nga Rangi headed north, jogging along the edge of the bush. After he had gone fifty metres he glanced back and noticed the men downstream were not giving chase.

Wanting to stay out of sight, he stepped into the bush, having decided to observe the two hunters for a few minutes. He had his old binoculars tucked inside his shirt and, upon taking them out, focused on the taller of the two men first. He couldn't recollect where he had seen him, but the person seemed a little familiar. He thought for a second and then refocused. Suddenly, it dawned on him.

* * * * *

Tui shook his head, disappointed, and, out of sheer frustration, kicked a small branch lying on the riverbank into the water. "Bastard. I wonder what that bugger's doing up here?"

John replied, puzzled and upset, "Seems strange that he ran like that. Why would he run?"

"Because he probably doesn't have a permit, I'd say at a guess." Tui pointed downstream with his head. "Come on, mate. Might as well head back to camp. There'll be nothing around for bloody miles now."

"Yeah," John agreed and, disappointed with their effort, started walking back to camp. "Can't understand why he ran though. Doesn't make sense."

"Buggered if I know. Most hunters are sociable buggers normally. Might catch up with him tomorrow with any sort of luck," Tui said optimistically. "I'd like to give him a bit of the ol' biffo."

Back at camp, John gathered dry twigs and lit a fire. They knew Dave and Brian would be on their way back. Tui decided to get dinner started and took out a large packet of pork sausages from his backpack and emptied them into a frying pan.

John peeled some potatoes and put them on to boil. He then emptied a packet of mixed vegetables in with the potatoes.

"I'm gonna curry these sausages," Tui said, smiling.

"Fine, mate," John replied with a chuckle and then added, "I'll be sleeping up wind from you tonight."

After the fire had built up, Tui scraped some of the hot embers to one side and placed the frying pan in them.

John had been keeping a close watch on the riverbank. He called out, "Here come Dave and Brian. Wonder how they got on?"

Glancing across the river through the thin line of scrub, Tui grinned and said, "They're not carrying anything. About as lucky as us I'd say."

Upon crossing the river, Dave and Brian came in through the thin line of scrub into camp. "So where's the big one?" Brian asked sarcastically.

"Was so big we couldn't carry it," Tui said jokingly.

"Yeah, right," Brian replied. "You didn't see any goats then?"

John laughed at the snide remark. "Cheeky bugger. Where's your big one if you're such a good hunter?"

Smiling, Dave replied, "Same place as yours."

CHAPTER 13

Nga Rangi hurried into camp and squatted down beside the fire to catch his breath.

Mannie was standing outside his hut and noticed Nga Rangi come into camp. He was winded from hurrying, that was obvious, but what really caught his eye was the fact that he was acting rather strangely.

Curious, he went over to him. "What's up? You look like you've seen a ghost."

Nga Rangi looked up, not knowing whether to tell Mannie about the two hunters or not. He didn't approve with what had happened the previous year to the three hunters, but he understood how Mannie felt about Jo and the way she had died. Then with Liana's death on top of all that. He'd had a lot to deal with mentally. It had taken him many months to get over the tragedy and his grieving.

Mannie had changed dramatically since then. He was physically fine, but mentally, he wasn't the same person. He spoke about the land now as if he owned it personally, especially now with Jo and Liana buried up there overlooking the vegetable garden that they had both so lovingly nurtured and cared for. It had been Jo's pet project, and she had been so proud of what Liana had achieved helping her. Jo had mentioned to Mannie several times that the garden was good for Liana. She had been as happy as they had seen her, and, Jo thought confidently, it would only be a matter of time before she would speak again.

Mannie's hatred for the government and any European was so obviously clear. To him, this small piece of land was Maori land, and if anyone tried to hunt or occupy it in any form or try and evict them off it, he would fight to the death if necessary before relinquishing it.

He had drawn an invisible line across the river up from where the three hunters had camped that night before Jo's death, and he was adamant that nobody, but nobody, other than themselves had any right to hunt there.

Nga Rangi had expressed his objection openly, on several occasions, to Mannie about the killing of the three hunters. Mannie had accepted his viewpoint, but at the time, he was so enraged over losing Jo, he wasn't in a sane frame of mind. Nga Rangi understood that and had made allowances, but even still, he wasn't happy with the way Mannie was acting.

Mannie saw that same look in Nga Rangi's eyes, the one he had seen when he expressed himself about the killing of the three hunters. He guessed instantly that there was a problem. Nga Rangi's apprehensive behaviour had betrayed him. Again, Mannie asked, "What's wrong? Something's up, I can tell."

Ignoring the question, Nga Rangi sat there, looking into the fire, and in his minds eye, he was mesmerized by the image of John Amohia's face in the flames.

Mannie cocked his head to one side as if he had read his mind. "You've seen hunters down below, haven't you?"

Nga Rangi looked out over the side of the plateau for a second, weighing up his options. There was no point in trying to hide it. Sooner or later, Mannie would find out.

Against his better judgement, he decided to tell him. "I was down in the bush not far from that old campsite where those others camped last year," he said, glancing warily at Mannie. "There were two of them." He took a deep breath. "Lucky for me I had my binoculars. I recognized one of them."

"You recognized one...? Who was it?" Mannie demanded impatiently.

"You remember that day in the pub before we came here when you and I went for a drink? You got into an argument with a tall guy. You said his father was a paramount chief."

Mannie recollected the incident. "Yeah. John Amohia. I remember."

"I think one of them was him."

Mannie's eyes boggled. "What...?"

Nga Rangi kept looking into the fire.

"John Amohia," Mannie scowled, rubbing his neck. "That arsehole's great-grandfather murdered my great-grandfather way back in the old days." He frowned, turning away. "You remember me saying that?"

Nga Rangi nodded, knowing Mannie's hatred for John Amohia was deep-rooted.

Agitated, Mannie rubbed the side of his face. "I'm going to keep an eye on him tomorrow. Make sure he doesn't come up any further."

"Mannie," Nga Rangi said, picking his words carefully. "He was hunting in the bush by the camp. They may not come up this way."

"He'd better not," Mannie replied heatedly. "He'd better bloody not."

Tuku noticed Nga Rangi and Mannie in serious discussion. He went over and stood with them. Mannie began pacing, mulling things over in his mind, and then went to his hut.

"What's up?" Tuku asked quietly. Sensing Mannie's unpredictable mood, he glanced back to make sure he wasn't in earshot.

"Hunters down below," Nga Rangi whispered.

"Shit...! Does he wanna go after them?"

"If they come up this way, yeah," Nga Rangi replied in a sombre tone.

Tuku glanced over his shoulder at Mannie's hut. "Shit. I've had a feeling since last year that, sooner or later, someone was bound to come in here."

"We were damn lucky to get away with those three last year," Nga Rangi admitted soberly. "We may not be so lucky next time."

Marlene joined Nga Rangi and Tuku by the fire. "Whatta you two looking so down in the mouth for? What's going on?"

Disgruntled, Nga Rangi looked up. "Two hunters down below."

"Oh, shit. I see," she replied uneasily. "So what's gonna happen?"

"Mannie'll go after them if they come any further than that old campsite." He shook his head anxiously. "And that's not all," he continued, looking into the fire. "I think one of them was John Amohia."

"The one whose father's the paramount chief...?"

Nga Rangi nodded.

"Of all the people to come in here hunting. Holy moly. What can we do?"

"What can we do...? This is a public domain. Mannie won't take any notice of us. He hates this guy." Again, he shook his head. "Things aren't the same since Jo and Li died. He's so obsessed with this land thing. It's like he's had a whole personality change."

"You know this Amohia?" Tuku asked.

"No. Just know his father's the big chief."

*   *   *   *   *

Dave decided to tell John and Tui about their discovery. "We came across a grave over the other side."

"A grave...?" Tui replied. "You mean a fair-dinkum grave like the ones they bury people in...?"

"Yeah, stupid. It wasn't very deep either. In fact, when I think about it now, it was real shallow."

"Who'd bury someone up here?" John asked skeptically.

Puzzled, Brian added, "Dunno, but when I got the permit the other day, the bloke at DoC said three hunters came in here last year and disappeared without a trace."

Tui looked at Brian in disbelief and said dolefully. "Without a trace...?"

"That's what he said," Brian told him adamantly. "Wonder if there's a link. He said they found their car down in the river below the bridge just before Horopito, but there were no bodies."

"Geez, mate, that's getting a bit carried away isn't it?" Tui criticized.

"Well, what do you think then?" Brian asked, a little disgruntled. "There could be a link, you know."

"Wouldn't think so," John interrupted. "That's pure speculation, Brian."

"We'll go over there in the morning. You can see for yourself," Dave said. "See what you make of it."

Tui thought about their afternoon. "Just to change the subject, we came across another hunter."

"You mean someone else is in here?" Dave asked.

"Yeah. The bugger took off when he saw us too."

"So much for having the place to ourselves," John said agitatedly. "I'd like to know who the bugger is."

"We saw smoke up by the waterfall," Brian added. "Could be the same guy."

John glanced at Tui. "We'll take a look tomorrow, eh?"

They were up at the crack of dawn the next morning and

ate a hasty breakfast. "Okay you guys. Let's get goin' eh?" John said as he put his web belt on.

Both he and Tui had army web belts with shoulder straps. Water bottles were attached to their belts, but on John's left shoulder strap he had a sheath attached upside down. The sheath housed a surgically sharpened stainless steel SAS survival knife. He snapped the survival knife into the sheath.

"Shit," Brian said, casting a curious eye at the knife. "That's a bloody knife and a half, isn't it!"

Grinning and partially ignoring Brian's comment, John said, "Okay, let's get going, eh? You guys lead."

"We won't need our backpacks today, will we?" Brian asked quizzically.

"Nah," Tui replied. "We'll be back by lunchtime. We'll cook up a feed then."

Walking at a steady pace, it took them thirty-five minutes to reach the small clearing where they found the grave. Standing side by side, they peered down at the half-uncovered skeleton.

Dave cast a probing eye at John and Tui. "Well! Whatta you make of that then?"

"Phew. I must admit, I didn't believe you guys at first," Tui said dryly. "I thought you were just exaggerating things just a wee bit."

Brian was a little peeved. "Why would we bullshit you about something like this?"

Feeling a touch disloyal, Tui quickly apologized, "Sorry, mate. But you must admit, it did sound a bit ridiculous at the time."

Tui knelt down beside the skeleton and started scraping soil back with his hands.

"What are you doing...?" Dave asked. "You don't want to disturb anything."

"I'll be careful, mate. Don't worry."

Tui scraped back sufficient soil to allow them a better view of the skeleton. John knelt down on the opposite side to examine it. He carefully brushed loose soil away with his fingers and was shocked at what he discovered. "Bloody hell...!"

Dave knelt down beside him. "What is it?"

"Look at that shoulder blade," John said, pointing at the shattered bone. "It's completely smashed."

Tui took a closer look. "Shit...!"

With a stern face, John said, "This poor bugger must have been in agony when he died. That could only have been done with a high-powered bullet."

Dave knelt down beside Tui. "Here. Take a break. Give me a go."

Tui moved back to give Dave room. Three minutes later, Dave glanced tersely at Tui. "Hey. Look at this. There's another hand down here." He dug down deeper. "There's another whole body...! Bloody hell...! One's buried on top of the other." He looked up dubiously. "What's been goin' on here...?"

Stunned at Dave's discovery, John knelt down and began brushing loose soil away from the shoulder and chest bones. Seconds later, he looked up. "Look at the collar bone of that second body." He leaned down even closer. "It's totally smashed and...," he hesitated, pointing, "look at the spinal cord. The neck's been broken."

John stood, looking gravely at his friends. "These guys have been murdered. There's no doubt about it. It's murder."

Tui shook his head in disbelief. "Shit a brick, mate. We gotta report this."

John looked at Dave and Brian. He could see they were shocked by the discovery, but nonetheless, he himself didn't want to leave immediately.

"I agree. We do have to report this, but I don't wanna bugger off just yet," he admitted. "We've come all this way.

I say we stay today and go out tomorrow morning. And I'd like to see whose making that smoke up by the waterfall. And on the plus side, I wouldn't mind getting a deer while we're here."

Pondering the suggestion, Tui looked at Dave and Brian for their opinion. "You guys comfortable with that?"

Brian shuffled uneasily, not at all happy; but before he could voice his opinion, Dave broke in.

"So long as we go out tomorrow morning, I'm happy with that. How about you, Brian?"

"I'm not comfortable with any of it," Brian confessed. "Not one little bit. I'd prefer to go out today."

Tui wasn't happy with leaving. He was in favour of doing some hunting before they left. "These skeletons aren't going anywhere. They'll still be here tomorrow, and it's not as if they've been shot yesterday. I go along with John."

Knowing he was out voted, Brian reluctantly gave in. "Okay. We stay today, but we definitely leave tomorrow morning. No later. Agreed?"

"It's agreed," John replied. "We leave tomorrow morning."

"Yeah. That's fine."

Looking north, John slung his SLR over his shoulder. "Now, there's that smoke you guys saw up by the waterfall, and that fellah we saw yesterday. I wanna see who it is."

"There could be more than one person," Brian added.

"We'll soon find out," John said.

"Pity we don't have a camera," Dave cut in. "It would've been good to get a photo of the grave to show the police."

Tui shook his head. "It is a pity but we haven't."

"I'll be glad to just get out of here," Brian said soberly.

"Don't worry, mate," John told him, trying to sound convincing. "As soon as we see who's up there and figure out what they're doing, we'll head back to camp."

CHAPTER 14

With John leading, they made their way back to the river and began stalking north.

Tui pointed across the river. "Why don't you and I cross over? Dave and Brian can cover this side. We'll cover the other."

"You're right," John replied. "We'll stalk the other bank until we reach that shitty bit then we'll come back over here. There's a lotta good country we're not covering."

"Yeah. That's fine," Dave agreed. "Might as well make the most of it while we're here. Stay in view though, eh."

For the next hour and a half, the four hunters stalked both sides of the river, making sure to stay in view of each other.

John and Tui crossed back over to Brian and Dave's side when they reached the rough section of supplejack, vines, and rubbishy scrub that was too thick and dense to get through.

As he stepped out of the river, John noticed Brian's solemn face and, guessing what was bothering him, patted him on the shoulder. "Don't worry about it, mate. We'll head back once we've seen whose up by the waterfall."

"I know I'm being a little paranoid," Brian confessed. "I just want to do what's right."

Trying to sound positive, John said, "We'll be okay, mate. Don't you worry. Okay?"

Brian nodded. "Yeah, I know. I'm just being silly."

*   *   *   *   *

Mannie came out of his hut just as day broke. He went up by the meetinghouse and peered out over the bush.

Nga Rangi and Marlene were up as well and had been discussing the two hunters. Nga Rangi didn't sleep well and had been on edge most of the night. He and Marlene noticed Mannie up by the meetinghouse and decided to have a talk with him.

Mannie sensed their concern. "What's up? The pair of you look worried as hell."

"There's been some pigs hanging around that area where we buried those two hunters last year," Nga Rangi said sombrely. "I'm a bit worried they might uncover the bodies with their rooting. We should've buried them deeper." He cast a concerned eye at Marlene. "We might go down and check just to make sure. We wouldn't want those hunters finding them. The cops'd be all over us in a flash."

Mannie thought about their suggestion for a few seconds and then nodded. "Yeah. Not a bad idea. If that Amohia bastard comes any further though, I want him. He's after our meat, thieving arsehole."

Mannie started pacing, formulating a plan. "Take Manu with you as well and go down that track on the other side," he said, pointing across the river past the waterfall.

Tuku and Himi joined Nga Rangi and Marlene. "What's going on?" Tuku asked inquiringly.

"These two and Manu are going down to where we buried those buggers last year to check on the grave," Mannie replied sternly. "There's been some pigs hanging around that area.

We don't want them uncovering the bodies now do we?" He paused, deep in thought, and then pointed behind the meetinghouse. "You two go down the track behind us here. Wait down there opposite the grave but stay on this side of the river. I'm going down the river itself to make sure Amohia doesn't come any further."

"Whatta you planning?" Nga Rangi asked fearfully.

Mannie scowled, "If they come any further, I want the bastards. They're not coming in here stealing our meat. It's time someone put a stop to this once and for all."

"You're not gonna kill them, are you?" Tuku asked nervously.

Mannie eyed him skeptically and said, "If they come up here, there's gonna be bloody trouble. Whatta you think I should do with thieves, eh? Just let them come in here and take our meat?"

Tuku shuffled nervously.

Mannie snapped, sensing his disapproval. "Look, you bugger's. Amohia's ancestors gave away this land, and no bloody government is going to trick us out of what is rightfully ours. That Amohia's just like his bloody ancestors. This is Maori land. Always was, always will be. Simple as that. Nothing has changed." Mannie cast a scrutinizing eye at everyone. "If he comes up here there's gonna be trouble." Mannie then put his face up close to Tuku's and shouted, "Okay?"

Tuku turned away, afraid of Mannie's unpredictable mood swings.

Mannie turned to Nga Rangi and Marlene. "Okay then. Grab your rifles and get going. Stay wide on the track. We don't want them seeing you on the way down if they come up the river." He hesitated for a second. "If I see them and I need you to come up the river, I'll fire three quick shots in the air."

Distrustfully, Nga Rangi looked Mannie directly in the eye. "This Amohia's one of us. We can't kill our own people."

"Now you listen to me. It was his ancestors that gave away this bloody land. He's no better than them and those thieving fuckin' pakehas."

Nga Rangi replied hesitantly, not at all comfortable with the plan, "Geez, Mannie." He shook his head. "I don't like this, not if you're so hell-bent on killing them."

"Amohia's not one of us. I'm not in favour of killing anyone either, but if he finds out we're up here, he'll have us evicted. You can bet your life on it. Now go get your rifles and get going."

Knowing it was fruitless to argue, Nga Rangi and Marlene headed off to their hut. Nga Rangi glanced over her shoulder at Mannie. "I just hope things don't get out of hand today. Once he gets his mind made up about something, he's impossible to talk to."

Marlene added sadly. "Things would have been different if Jo was still with us. He's obsessed with this land thing, especially now, with Jo and Li buried up here. If only he could see himself the way we see him. He's gone completely feral."

Mannie called out to Tuku and Himi, "Stay on this side of the river when you get there and wait. Nga Rangi and Marlene'll be on the other side."

Mannie then called to Nga Rangi and Marlene just as they reached their hut. "You got two hours to get there before Ritchie and I come down the river. If we meet up and haven't seen them, that'll mean they haven't come any further, and we'll come back here. Is that fair enough?" Nga Rangi nodded, and he and Marlene went into their hut.

Manu came out of his hut just as Nga Rangi and Marlene came out of theirs. "You're coming with us. Grab your rifle."

"What's going on?" Manu asked, looking half asleep.

"We'll tell you on the way."

Manu rushed back into his hut.

Nga Rangi unenthusiastically led Marlene and Manu across the river above the waterfall to the eastern track.

The rest of the group had now gathered by the meetinghouse. Mannie was organizing them into groups and issuing orders.

He pointed at Pucky and Chappy. "You two. Over by the edge and keep a sharp eye out." Then pointing at Ritchie, he said, "You're coming with me down the river, but we're not going for a couple of hours yet."

Mannie called out to Zac as he came out of his hut, "Zac. You stick with Pucky and Chappy, okay?"

Ritchie looked around at the others, smiling. Mannie was his mentor since Jo had died, and he enjoyed pleasing him in any way he could. "We gonna waste the bastards?"

"Only if they come up this far."

"Cher, bro."

After getting their rifles, Pucky and Chappy hurried over to the edge of the plateau to keep watch on the valley.

Pucky was a little anxious about the day's activities. "Sounds like there's gonna be some excitement around here today."

"Yeah," Chappy agreed, peering over his shoulder at Mannie. "Should take away some of the boredom for a while."

"You get bored up here?"

"Yeah, sometimes. I often wonder what life would be like if we had've stayed in the city."

Pucky shook his head dispassionately. "I never want to go back there, mate. No way. Give me this place any day."

"Even when it's boring?"

"There's no contest as far as I'm concerned."

"Don't you want to get married some day and have a coupla kids?"

"You are joking...?"

"What...?"

"You're not serious about getting married and bringing kids into this crazy fucked up world are you? Geez, man...! Get a grip. That's the last thing I'd want to do."

"Why? What's wrong with that?"

"I wouldn't be so cruel. What could possibly be good about introducing kids to life on this stinkin' planet? It's nothing but a shithole."

"It's okay, I reckon."

"Not good for children for a start. How'd you educate them?"

"Don't need to. We could teach them how to survive on their own."

"Yeah, right. You just don't get it, do you?"

"Get what?"

"Geez, man. You can be so bloody thick at times."

* * * * *

John, Tui, Dave, and Brian were slowly stalking their way upstream. Tui had been observing the opposite riverbank and could see they were well clear of the rough patch. "We should head back across the river. It's clear there now."

John glanced across. "Yeah. And it's not that far to the shortcut up to the main track." He turned to Dave and Brian. "We're crossing back over. I'll give you a wave from the plateau when we get there, eh?"

"We'll stick to the river then," Dave replied. "Catch you later."

John and Tui stalked their way along to the shortcut track that went up to the main western track that would take them directly to the plateau. With Tui leading, they quickly reached the main western track and headed north.

Ten minutes later, Tui suddenly cocked his head to one side

and then put his hand up to stop. He stood there, listening. They could hear voices in the distance coming down towards them. John ducked behind short scrub and ferns on the right of the track; Tui slipped in behind a stand of punga trees on his left and waited. Tui gave John the signal to 'take them' by running his thumb across his throat. John acknowledged with a nod.

Two minutes later and with their rifles slung over their shoulders, Tuku and Himi came walking casually down the track. As they drew parallel, Tui stepped out onto the track in front of them.

Himi, startled at the sudden appearance of the stranger, instinctively aimed a punch at Tui's head. Tui blocked, and then taking hold of Himi's right hand, he flipped him onto his back, all in one swift move. It was done so swiftly that Himi didn't have time to react.

John stepped out and, taking Tuku by the right arm, turned and swung him over his hip onto his back, partially winding him.

Taken completely by surprise and with John standing menacingly over him, Tuku decided to stay down.

Tui stood over Himi, glaring down at him and was about to speak, when Himi lashed out with such force at Tui's right leg, kicking it out from under him, sending him crashing to the ground.

Both men leaped to their feet but before Himi could react again, Tui gave him a round-house kick to the head, sending him reeling over backward onto his back.

Tui eyed the two men up angrily. "What the hell're you two buggers doin' up here? We know you don't have a permit."

Neither Himi or Tuku uttered a word.

Tui glanced at John. "Lost their bloody tongues, eh?"

John grabbed Tuku by the shirt. "We'll ask you again. Whatta you doin' up here?"

Again, neither man spoke.

Tui was beginning to lose his composure. "You're starting to really piss me off. I'm going to ask you just once more. What the hell're you doin' up here? We know you don't have a permit, so you're obviously poaching."

Tuku put his hands up in a gesture that he didn't want any trouble. "Look. We're just after meat. Somethin' wrong with that?"

"You weren't hunting," John said, matter-of-factly. "No one hunts the way you buggers were, talking your heads off. You've scared everything for bloody miles. You think we're stupid? I saw one of you buggers yesterday when you ran off."

Himi jumped up and shouted, "Why don't you bastards fuck off and leave us alone!"

Tui shoved him in the chest, sending him staggering backward into a patch of scrub. "We got the permit," he said angrily. "Why should we fuck off? You're the poachers. Not us."

Himi lunged at Tui, but Tui grabbed his hand and applied a wristlock. In the same move, he kicked Himi's feet out from under him, sending him falling flat on his face and stomach.

"You still wanna argue?" Tui snapped and then let Himi's wrist go and stood back. "Take off your boots and knife belts," he commanded sternly.

Both Himi and Tuku sat up and slowly started taking off their boots. Tui shouted impatiently, "Come on! We haven't got all bloody day!"

John gathered their rifles, boots, and hunting knives.

Tui said in a low serious tone, "Now get the hell outta here and don't come back unless you have a permit. You can pick up your gear at the National Park Police Station in a couple of days. Got it?"

Tuku nodded despondently.

"Now piss off."

Himi and Tuku slowly got to their feet and began walking down the track. Tuku glanced back. Tui waved him away dismissively and shouted, "Go on. Piss off and don't come back."

Fifty metres down the track, Tuku glanced back again to make sure they were out of sight of the two strangers. He said nervously, "You notice their clothes?"

"What do you mean?" Himi said, a little agitated.

"They looked like army dudes to me. Did you notice that?"

"Yeah, but I didn't think anything of it."

"They definitely looked like army fellahs."

"What if they were?"

"Dunno. Just thought I'd mention it."

John took the rifles, hunting knives, and boots and hid them in the bush.

Tui was summing up the sudden appearance of the two men. "They said they were hunting for meat. They weren't hunting. They were making too much noise for that."

John scratched the top of his head. "It doesn't make any sense."

Tui pointed up the track. "Come on. Let's take a look at where the smoke was coming from yesterday."

*　　*　　*　　*　　*

Two hours after leaving camp, Nga Rangi, Marlene, and Manu arrived down at the grave site. Marlene was the first into the small clearing and discovered the partially uncovered skeletons. She stood there, frozen to the spot, in absolute shock. "Holy bloody shit...! They've found the grave...!"

Manu rushed over beside Marlene. Nga Rangi looked

nervously around at the bush to make sure they weren't being observed.

Marlene crouched down to study the boot prints. "Hey, you guys, look at this," she said, showing extreme concern. "There's been more than two hunters in here." Pointing to the boot patterns, she said ruefully, "Look at this. See those prints? They're mine. Worn soles." She then pointed to the other prints. "Look at those, and those, and there. They're all newer with a lot more tread. And each one has a different pattern."

Nga Rangi eyed her nervously. "You mean, we're after four hunters, not two? Is that what you're saying?"

Marlene nodded.

"Shit a bloody brick...!"

Manu looked suspiciously around the small clearing. "Shit, mate. What's goin' on here?"

"Dunno, but one of us has to go back and tell Mannie," Nga Rangi replied. "I don't like this at all. There's definitely gonna be bloody trouble now. You can count on it."

Looking down at the strangers' boot prints, Manu said dryly, "I'll go. Mannie'll be along the river by now. Should be easy to see him from the track."

"Okay," Nga Rangi agreed. "You get going and don't muck around."

Manu nodded and quickly disappeared into the bush.

Nga Rangi, looking very dejected, turned to Marlene. "Geez, girl, I don't like this one bloody bit. I hope this doesn't get outta hand."

"Mannie's getting too big for his own boots if you ask me," Marlene said nervously. "He'll be the downfall of us all, you wait and see."

"We came here to get away from this crap," Nga Rangi said and then pointed towards the river. "Come on. Let's keep an eye out along the river. We'll get a better view down there. I haven't a clue where these buggers are right now."

Cautiously, they made their way down to the river and hid in thick scrub, where they had a clear view upstream.

"I wonder where they are?" Marlene said, a touch anxious.

Nga Rangi replied pessimistically, "Dunno. They could be anywhere."

CHAPTER 15

Manu was half way back to the plateau along the eastern track, when he noticed two strangers down on the riverbank, stalking slowly upstream. He decided to stop and observe them for a few minutes while he caught his breath.

* * * * *

John and Tui were almost at the top of the western track. Tui was leading and suddenly caught a glimpse of the plateau through the trees. He spotted smoke from a dying fire. "Shit...! Look at that!" he whispered to John. "Is this a camp...?"

John quickly studied the scene. "Buggered if I know, mate. Hard to say from here."

Tui was watching one man in particular over by the edge of the plateau. He had his back to them, looking down into the valley. The man then turned and walked over to a group of young men gathered in the centre of the large flat area.

Startled, he turned to John. "Hey...! Look at that fellah over by the edge. His face's tattooed to buggery."

John was studying the man's tattooed face when, out of the corner of his eye, a man appeared as if he had popped out of the ground itself. "Hey. Did you see that?" John said, pointing. "Call me a nutcase, mate, but this looks just like some sort of rebel camp from where I'm standing."

Tui cast John a suspicious look. "Yeah. I can't believe it though. Who would do something like this?"

John, wanting to get higher up in the bush, pointed with his head. "Come on. Let's get a better view. I'd like to have a real good look at this place."

They crept higher, to a point in the bush where they had an unobstructed view of the camp just above Mannie's meetinghouse. John surveyed the area up behind them and saw, a short distance away, a vegetable garden in a small clearing with a wire netting fence around it. "Hey! Look at that. They've even got a garden growing here."

Tui glanced over his shoulder. "These buggers are too well organized for my liking."

John studied the crudely built meetinghouse. "And what the hell's this?"

Tui shook his head. "No idea."

John refocused on the man with the tattooed face. He seemed to be vaguely familiar. His mind suddenly went back to a day in South Auckland, when he was in a public bar with two friends. It came to him. "I know him, that bugger with the tats," he whispered. "Mannie Te Ngongo." John quickly assessed everyone on the plateau, not at all happy with what he was seeing. "Another thing. Have you noticed everyone's got a rifle?"

Tui cocked a wary eye at John. "You know this bugger?"

The man who had come out of the underground hut hurried over to Mannie, and then, after a short discussion, he and Mannie disappeared over the edge.

John nodded, looking very worried. "Yeah. I know him all right. He got tats since I last saw him but it's him all right. He's nothing but trouble. I'll tell you about him later." He hesitated, looking around suspiciously. "Right now, I think we should get back to Dave and Brian and get the hell outta here. That tattooed bugger has just gone over the edge with another guy. They're heading for the river." John pointed with his head. "Come on. Let's get outta here. Brian and Dave are down there."

∗   ∗   ∗   ∗   ∗

Brian and Dave were on the riverbank, slowly stalking their way upstream. Brian, for no apparent reason, glanced back up along the ridge. To his surprise, he saw a man crouched down, silhouetted against the skyline. Shaken and suddenly anxious, he turned away, not wanting the man to realize he had been spotted.

To be certain he wasn't seeing things, he cast his eye back along the ridge again. The man suddenly ducked down lower but not quite out of sight.

Brian's heart missed a beat. He called softly to Dave, "Don't look now, but someone's up on the ridge watching us."

Dave stopped dead in his tracks. He turned to Brian. "What...? What did you say?"

Trying to appear as normal as possible, Brian kept on walking. "Don't stop now," he said nervously. "There's a guy up on the ridge at four o'clock watching us. Keep walking as if we haven't noticed him."

"You sure...?" Dave said, catching up with Brian.

"Positive. Just keep walking."

Dave felt suddenly edgy. It didn't add up. The fact that someone was watching them did seem a little adverse. In his mind's eye, he saw the grave they had unearthed. John and Tui were a little blasé about the whole thing and didn't appear to be at all phased by the discovery.

∗   ∗   ∗   ∗   ∗

After making their way down the steep face, Mannie and Ritchie began jogging south along the riverbank.

"Keep your eyes peeled," Mannie said. "I don't want anyone discovering our camp."

Ritchie smiled excitedly, his eyes searching along the bush line on both sides of the river. They were 150 metres from the long sweeping bend, when Mannie pointed at the river.

"Come on. We'll cross over here."

They quickly crossed and continued jogging south along the eastern riverbank.

*   *   *   *   *

Nga Rangi was pacing restlessly back and forth behind the scrub that hid them from view along the river. Marlene, also tense, was sitting on a large rock, chewing her fingernails when suddenly, out to their left, they heard splashing in the river. Someone was crossing downstream from them. Alarmed, they turned towards the sound, but from where they were positioned, that section of the river was obscured from sight by the thick scrub.

Ducking down low and in a panicky voice, Marlene said, "Whatta we do...? Shit...!"

Nga Rangi, crouching down beside her, put his finger to his lips, his signal to be quiet and to listen. Then they heard footsteps coming towards them.

A voice called out softly, "Where are you?"

Nga Rangi recognized the voice and gave a low whistle. Seconds later, Tuku and Himi appeared through the scrub.

Nga Rangi let out a sigh of relief. "Shit. Am I glad to see you two."

Marlene drew in a sharp breath. "Whatta you doin' here? Aren't you supposed to stay on the other side?"

Tuku replied nervously, "Yeah, we were but...."

Nga Rangi interrupted when he noticed they were both bare feet. "Where's your boots...? And... where's your rifles?"

Both Tuku and Himi looked around uneasily. "A couple of dudes jumped us on the way down," Tuku replied, rather embarrassed. "They looked like army fellahs to me."

Himi shuffled restlessly, glancing around at the bush. "They made us give them our rifles and hunting knives then made us take off our boots."

Nga Rangi, sensing their nervousness, rubbed the back of his neck, unsure what to do. "Whoever they were, they found the bloody grave."

Himi's eyes boggled in disbelief. "They found the grave...?"

"Yeah, and that's not all either. There's not just two of them, there's four of the buggers."

"Four...? Four...?" Tuku repeated, taken aback, his eyes bulging.

"So where's the other two then?" Himi asked anxiously.

"We don't know," Marlene told them. "They've gotta be along the river somewhere."

"We've sent Manu back to tell Mannie," Nga Rangi said and started pacing again.

Tuku, shaking his head, gazed around the bush. "Geez, man. This is turning to shit."

"Proper bloody balls up, if you ask me," Marlene added.

*   *   *   *   *

Dave and Brian were eighty metres from the long sweeping bend. Both were very nervous and unwittingly slowed their pace.

Brian cast a cautious eye back along the ridge but couldn't see anyone. "That bugger's not up there any more," he said to Dave, who also glanced back at the ridge. "What do we do?"

*　　*　　*　　*　　*

Hugging the bush and jogging at a steady pace, Mannie and Ritchie slowed their pace as they approached the long sweeping bend in the river.

Then Mannie heard a sound behind them and spun around with his rifle at the ready. Manu appeared out of the undergrowth. "What the hell...!"

Manu threw his hands in the air, shocked at Mannie's reaction. "It's only me. Take it easy, man. Steady on."

"What the hell're you doin' here?" Mannie demanded.

"Keep your voices down. There's some hunters coming up the river," Manu told him. "They're just around that bend."

Mannie crept to the bend, and to his dismay, two strangers were walking along the riverbank towards them.

Manu pointed at the two hunters. "That's the buggers I'm telling you about. They've found the grave."

"What...?" Mannie snapped, his eyes bulging.

"Yeah, and that's not all," Manu continued. "There's four of the bastards, not two."

Mannie's mouth twisted viciously. "Four...?"

"Yeah," Manu replied.

"Where's the other buggers then?"

"Dunno, but they're in here somewhere."

Mannie settled in a spot where he had a good view along the riverbank and looked out at the two hunters. "These fellahs are pakehas...! Thievin' bloody pakehas." Confused, he scratched his head. "If they've seen the grave and they get out of here, there's gonna be bloody cops crawling all over the place."

Ready for action and wanting to impress Mannie with his enthusiasm, Ritchie asked excitedly, "You wanna drop the bastards right there?"

Mannie shook his head. "Nah. I wanna have a good look at them first. We'll wait till they get closer."

*   *   *   *   *

The bush was deathly quiet. Other than the river, not a sound could be heard in any direction. Dave cast a nervous eye around the immediate area. "Somethin's not right here. Let's stop for a minute, eh?"

Brian stopped beside Dave and glanced back along the ridge but saw no one.

*   *   *   *   *

Mannie was watching the two hunters, getting impatient at their slow progress; their body language conveyed their nervousness. He began muttering to himself, Keep comin', come on.

"You wanna waste the buggers now?" Ritchie asked.

Again, Mannie shook his head. "Nah, not just yet. Wait till they get a little closer."

Mannie sensed the two hunters' unease. "Shit...!" His eyes narrowed as he watched them disappear out of view. "They know somethin's up." Turning back to Ritchie, he growled, "Bastards've disappeared into the bush."

"They'll come out again. Don't worry," Manu said reassuringly.

"Hope you're right," Mannie replied, glancing cautiously along the bush line.

*   *   *   *   *

Dave and Brian were standing beside the bush, where

168

they could still see in both directions. Dave was feeling very nervous. He beckoned with his head toward the bush. "Let's get outta sight."

Cautiously, they moved into the bush. "This is bloody nerve-wracking, mate. Something's definitely not right here."

"Yeah. I got a gut feeling about this too."

"I think we should head back to camp. We'll wait for John and Tui there."

Brian beckoned with his rifle. "Come on. This is giving me the creeps. It's too quiet."

Stepping back out onto the riverbank again, they started heading south along the edge of the bush.

$$* \quad * \quad * \quad * \quad *$$

Mannie was outraged when he saw the two hunters come out of the bush and head downstream. "The bastards are buggering off...! They know something's up."

Wanting to take them by surprise and impress Mannie at the same time, Ritchie rushed out onto the riverbank and went down on one knee. He shouldered his rifle and aimed at Brian as Brian turned to look upstream and saw him.

"Shit...! Behind us...!" Brian shouted fearfully.

Dave spun around and saw Ritchie just as Ritchie fired.

The bullet narrowly missed Brian as he darted for the confines of the bush. In a panic they began running downstream inside the bush.

Mannie rushed out and cuffed Ritchie across the side of the head with his open palm. "What the fuck you do that for? Now they know we're after 'em, you stupid fuckwit," he said, looking at where Brian and Dave had disappeared. He waved his arm forward. "Come on. Can't let them get away now."

CHAPTER 16

John and Tui were racing down the main track and hesitated at the shortcut to the river. John pointed with his rifle. "Down here."

They quickly made their way to the river and were jogging along the riverbank, when they heard a shot ring out. Tui looked over his shoulder at John. "Who's doing the shooting? There's no sign of the two that went over the edge of the plateau."

John, anxious, cast a fearful eye at Tui. "Dunno. Whoever it is, you can guarantee it won't be at deer."

Tui took a quick glance back at the plateau. "Let's cross now. Stuff those buggers up on top."

John nodded and together, they leaped into the river, crossing as quickly as they could and then continued racing south on the eastern side, hugging the bush as they went.

Another shot rang out just as they reached the long sweeping bend. John glanced at Tui, his face serious with concern. To stay out of sight, they ducked into the bush and continued at a steady pace.

* * * * *

Pucky and Chappy were watching the valley from the edge of the plateau. They saw John and Tui cross the river and continue south for a short distance along the opposite bank before disappearing into the bush.

Pucky's eyebrows shot up, mystified at the sudden appearance of the two strangers. "Who the hell're they and where'd they come from...? Mannie's way past there!"

Zac, who had been stacking firewood he'd collected from the bush, heard Pucky's startled comment and rushed over. "What's goin' on? What's happening?"

Pucky pointed to the two strangers, who had crossed the river and were heading south along the riverbank before disappearing into the bush.

Chappy looked at Pucky, confused. "Whose Mannie shooting at then? Maybe we should go down?"

Pucky shook his head. "Mannie said to stay here."

"I know, but somethin's wrong. Who the hell's he shooting at then if he's not shooting at those two buggers we just saw?"

"If you buggers go down, I'm bloody well goin' too," Zac said anxiously. "I'm not stayin' up here on my own. No bloody way, man."

Pucky began pacing along the edge of the plateau, looking down suspiciously at the big sweeping bend. With a terrible feeling of apprehension, he turned to Chappy, pointing to the river with his head. "I'm going down," he said and leaped over the edge.

Not wanting to be left behind on their own, Chappy and Zac leaped over and followed Pucky down the steep descent to the river.

*   *   *   *   *

Mannie, Ritchie, and Manu were racing along the riverbank;

Dave and Brian racing through the trees. Mannie called to Ritchie, who had pulled out in front of them.

"Ritchie, you carry on downstream and cut the bastards off. We'll go into the bush after them."

Brian could hear Ritchie running parallel with them on the riverbank, slowly gaining the advantage. Panicking, he called out to Dave, "He's trying to get ahead of us. We'll be trapped."

Dave pointed up to the main eastern track. "Get up on the ridge. We might have a chance up there."

Mannie saw Dave race across a small grassy clearing. He shouldered his rifle, but before he could fire, Dave disappeared into the bush. Brian was behind Dave, and as he rushed across the small grassy clearing, Mannie caught him in his sights and squeezed the trigger. Boom!

Brian was hit high in the back and, with the impact of the high-powered projectile, was flung to the ground in a sprawling heap.

At the sound of the second shot, Dave glanced back as Brian went down. Afraid and knowing Brian was badly wounded, he froze in his tracks for just a second. Brian slowly came up onto his hands and knees. Dave was about to rush back to help him, when another shot rang out.

In utter horror, Dave saw the second bullet strike Brian in the ribs, just below his outstretched arm. Brian collapsed face down in the grass.

Knowing Brian could not have survived that second bullet and in desperation, Dave dove into a small stand of pungas. Shock and horror struck him like a thunderbolt. His worst nightmare was materializing as he peered out at Brian, lying deathly still in the grass. Shaking with terror, he searched for any sign of movement but saw none. His only option, he thought, was to get up onto the eastern track above them; but these people were so close, it would be suicide to make an attempt.

Dave could not believe the situation he was in and, again, looked out at Brian, lying face down in the grass, dead, shot in the back; and he himself was now the hunted. He couldn't help himself and began to shake uncontrollably as he searched desperately for an escape route.

Manu, having gone into the bush at a ninety-degree angle from the riverbank, was on his hands and knees, quietly creeping through the undergrowth toward the main eastern track, where he could get a better vantage point to pin-point the second hunter and get a clean shot at him. He knew he was somewhere near.

Movement inside the punga stand caught his eye. Grinning, he muttered to himself, Aha. So there you are. Say your prayers pakeha. He lay against an old fallen tree and shouldered his rifle.

Dave heard a voice shout from the riverbank. "Ritchie! Get back here! I've wasted one of them. The other bugger's in here somewhere."

Dave moved cautiously in the pungas, trying to locate the position of the man who was shouting. Wherever he was, it wasn't far, and he wasn't prepared to risk being shot by attempting to get to the track above him along the ridge.

Suddenly - Boom! The punga tree next to his head exploded with the instantaneous sound of a rifle shot. He instinctively flattened himself on the ground, shaking uncontrollably, like a tree in a tornado.

*   *   *   *   *

John and Tui were racing down the eastern track. It was obviously clear their friends were in mortal danger, and it was up to them to help them out. With the element of surprise, it was crucial they take full advantage of it.

As they came over a rise on the narrow track, a shot rang out just ahead of them. John saw the faint puff of cordite and spotted Manu leaning against the fallen tree, his rifle shouldered and aiming below him. He knew he had to be firing at either Brian or Dave. There would have been nothing else there. Any game in the area would have been long gone.

Tui was close behind John and said softly, "See him?" John nodded and, slowing his pace, passed his rifle back to Tui.

Manu was preoccupied with getting another shot at Dave, and it wasn't until he heard faint footsteps on the track directly above him that he saw John out of the corner of his eye. Panicking, he swung his rifle around as John launched himself into the air.

John landed firmly with both feet together beside Manu. Instantaneously, he grabbed the butt of Manu's rifle with his left hand, the barrel with his right and, pulling it out away from Manu's body with all his strength, drove the butt up into Manu's nose, snapping the bridge cleanly. The blow was so powerful that it forced the shattered bone back into his brain, killing him instantly.

Manu dropped to the ground and rolled down the slippery slope a short distance.

Tui landed, both feet together, beside John. "Shit mate," Tui said, shaken by John's narrow escape. "That was bloody close. Another second and he'd have shot you."

Shaken also, John was searching the immediate area for anyone else. "These bastards are trying to kill us. Why...?"

Upon handing back John's rifle, Tui caught a movement among the pungas below them. He recognized the colour of Dave's shirt.

Pointing, Tui said, "There's Dave. Cover me."

John brought his British SLR rifle up to the firing position and swept it across the area.

Tui raced down to the small stand of pungas and took up a defensive position beside Dave. He signalled for John to join them.

"Where's Brian?" Tui asked anxiously as his eyes combed the surrounding bush.

Dave pointed to Brian, lying face down thirty metres away. "He's ... been ... shot," Dave stuttered.

"He's dead...?" Tui asked, dumbfounded. He turned to Dave and saw he was visibly shaking with fear.

Dave nodded remorsefully. "He was right behind me. I heard the shot and saw him go down." Because of his fear, he had to stop and take a sharp breath before continuing. "They shot him twice."

"Where'd you last see them?" Tui asked. "Did one have a tattooed face?"

"What...? Tattoos...?" Dave replied, confused and still shaking. "Ah, shit...! I'm not sure."

Dave pointed to where he had last seen Mannie.

John tapped Tui on the shoulder. "Cover me."

Keeping low, John raced out to Brian and went down on one knee beside him. Frothy blood was congealing on Brian's back. He knew immediately it had been a fatal lung shot, and then he saw where the second shot had hit him in his ribcage below the armpit.

With emotional rage and a fierce surge of adrenaline, John's eyes searched the immediate area for any movement. Then he heard footsteps running towards them along the riverbank. A voice called out somewhere in the bush ahead.

"In here, Ritchie. In here."

Tui called quietly to John, "We got company."

John nodded and, keeping low, ran backwards to Tui and Dave, his rifle sweeping the bush as he went.

"He's dead?" Tui asked gravely.

"Yeah," John replied. "Shot in the bloody back. The bastards." He turned to Dave. "You okay?"

Dave nodded, still visibly shaking and in such a state where he could hardly talk.

John knew it was fatal to remain in the pungas. He pointed up the steep face. "Cover me. I'll get up on the track and cover you two when you make a run for it. Okay?" Tui nodded and shouldered his M16.

John raced up the slope, and upon taking up a defensive position behind the fallen tree, he gave Tui the thumbs up.

Tui turned to Dave, pointing up at John. "Time to go."

Dave followed Tui out of the pungas and began running up the slope toward John.

Ritchie stepped out from behind a tree and fired from the hip. John fired twice. He wasn't shooting to kill, but shooting just close enough to put the man off his aim. Both bullets tore bark off the tree beside Ritchie. Ritchie quickly ducked back out of sight.

The ground exploded around Tui and Dave as Mannie fired, showering them with dirt, twigs, and dead leaves.

John couldn't see Mannie through the dense bush, but he fired two quick shots in the general direction. In sheer panic, Dave turned and rushed back to the temporary safety of the punga grove. Tui carried on up the slope and dove over the old fallen tree, landing beside John.

Fuming with rage, Mannie fired several shots into the pungas.

Punga dust and splinters exploded all around Dave, but, miraculously, he wasn't hit. He was lying flat on his stomach in the dirt with his hands over his head, shaking with fear.

Tui and John returned fire, but Mannie kept moving through the undergrowth, firing as he went, making himself hard to pinpoint.

*   *   *   *   *

Nga Rangi looked at Tuku and Himi nervously. "Hear those rifles? Two of them are semi-automatics."

"There's a bloody war going on up there," Tuku admonished.

"Maybe we should get up there," Himi suggested.

"Let the bastard fight his own war," Marlene cut in. "Stuff him."

Anxious and undecided, Nga Rangi started pacing back and forth, listening to the rifle shots as they echoed down the valley, and then, with a pang of guilt, he pointed with his head. "I think Himi's right. We should get up there."

Shaking her head, Marlene grabbed his arm and said, "I'm not happy. None of us came here for this. This is a bloody war we're in. You could get your damn head blown off. What good would you be to me then, eh? I don't want to be here without you. I've nowhere else to go."

Nga Rangi hesitated for a moment. "I think this time we need to get up there."

Marlene nodded with a shrug and followed Nga Rangi, Tuku, and Himi up the riverbank.

*　　*　　*　　*　　*

Tui took off his magazine and reloaded while John covered the area below them. Tui slammed his full magazine into his rifle and, upon recocking his weapon, gave John the thumbs up. John reloaded while Tui covered.

Tui signalled to Dave to get ready. Swallowing hard, Dave nodded.

Tui called out as he and John came up firing in Mannie's general direction. "Now, Dave. Now."

Dave dashed out of the pungas, running as fast as he could up the slope toward them.

Mannie saw him make a dash for the slope and started

firing wildly. Dirt and twigs erupted out of the earth all around him.

Tui kept calling, "Come on, Dave. Keep going. Keep going."

They concentrated their fire in the general direction, but Mannie kept moving, firing wildly.

With bullets thumping into the ground all around him, dirt, twigs, and dead leaves filled the air. With forty metres still to go Dave glanced up the steep slope at Tui, who was calling to him; but with the thunderous sound of gunfire, he couldn't hear him.

Out of the corner of his eye, he caught sight of Mannie firing at him. Overwhelmed with sheer terror and fear, he faltered and then turned back and made a dive for the pungas again. In utter horror, a punga beside his left shoulder exploded into a thousand splinters, and covering his head with his arms, he rolled himself up into a ball, screaming at the top of his voice.

John glanced at Tui, frustrated at Dave's faltering courage, and said, "Shit...! Why the hell did he stop running?" John's magazine was low on ammunition.

Dave's petrified face looked up at them through the pungas. His eyes were dilated and black with fear. Tui signalled for him to get ready. Seconds later, he gave Dave the thumbs up. Dave swallowed hard and waved, acknowledging the signal.

Glancing at John, Tui said, "Poor bugger's shitting himself."

John was concerned for Dave's safety. "If he doesn't get outta there soon, he'll die there." With that, they both came up firing.

Tui shouted, "Come on Dave. Get the hell outta there!"

Dave made another dash for the slope, Tui encouraging him. "Keep going, Dave. Keep going."

Keeping out of sight and because of the heavy fire from

John and Tui, Mannie couldn't get a clean shot and fired at Dave from the hip.

Dave was running as fast as he could, screaming at the top of his voice. He leaped over the fallen tree beside Tui, breathless from panic and fear.

"You okay?" John asked.

Speechless and breathless, Dave nodded. John patted him on the shoulder and then pointed behind them with his head. "Go with Tui and get up the track behind us. I'll cover you both."

Tui and Dave made ready for their dash up the track. Tui tapped John on the shoulder. "Ready." John came up firing.

Suddenly, footsteps could be heard running toward them and a voice called out, "Mannie. Mannie. Where the hell are you?"

Mannie darted to another tree as Tui and Dave made a dash up the track. Firing from the hip, he darted to another tree.

"In here," Mannie called back. "In here. They're above me."

Tui fired several shots into the bush from the hip as he ran, followed closely by Dave. They made it to the top of the ridge and took up a defensive position.

Tui signalled a thumbs up. John reloaded and made ready to rush up the track to them. As Tui came up firing, John leapt to his feet and raced past them and then took up a defensive position further up the track.

John signalled a thumbs up. Tui and Dave raced up the track while John gave covering fire. Then, keeping low, John followed them to another defensive position further up in the bush.

All around Mannie, bullets thumped into the ground and ricocheted off trees; dirt and bark chips filled the air. He flew into a rage at not being able to get a clean shot and screamed at the top of his lungs when he saw John disappear out of sight up the track. "Fuck you, Amohia. Your days are fuckin' numbered, arsehole."

The bush was deathly quiet, the air filled with the smell of cordite. John, Tui, and Dave ran a short distance up the track and then ducked off into a patch of thick scrub and rubbishy fern and waited.

Below them, they heard running along the riverbank as Pucky, Chappy, and Zac came down to join Mannie.

"That's the rest coming in for the kill," John said watching them through the trees.

Puckering an eyebrow quizzically, Tui asked, "That bastard called out your name!"

"Yeah. I knew it was him all right," John replied. "Remember me saying when we were up by the plateau? He's bad news, that one." Tui nodded. "We can't talk now. I'll tell you later. Come on. Let's keep moving."

"What we need is a diversion," Tui suggested, deep in thought. "With everyone down here, we should burn their camp. It'll alert the forestry. With any sort of luck, they might even send a spotter plane in to investigate."

Dave was still in a state of shock and couldn't comprehend what Tui was saying. In disbelief, he said, "You're thinking of burning their camp...! Are you guys completely mad...?"

"No we're not. It's a good idea," John said, and, trying to sound positive, he patted Dave on the shoulder. "But we do have to keep moving."

Dave looked up, his face showing absolute horror. "You said they gotta camp up there?"

"Yeah. Big one too. On the plateau," Tui replied. "Come on. Let's get up there. They won't be expecting that."

Cautiously and quietly, they made their way up to the main eastern track again and headed north toward the waterfall.

*　　*　　*　　*　　*

Nga Rangi, Tuku, Himi, and Marlene rushed into the grassy clearing from the southern end. Mannie saw them and stepped out from behind a tree. Pucky and Chappy came rushing into the clearing from the northern end.

"What the hell's happening? It sounded like a bloody war goin' on," Pucky asked.

"Bastards got away," Mannie replied angrily.

"Where's Manu?" Chappy asked, looking around for his friend.

"Dunno," Mannie said and then pointed up towards the eastern track. "He was up there somewhere last time I saw him."

Cautiously, Pucky and Chappy crept through the bush up toward the main track. They found Manu's body half way down the slope lying in the undergrowth.

Chappy called to Mannie, "Manu's here. He's dead."

"Stuff those bastards," Mannie said, cursing, and then noticed Tuku and Himi were bare feet and without their rifles. "Where's your boots and rifles?"

Himi sensed Tuku's reluctance to say anything about what had happened earlier that morning and decided he would tell Mannie himself. "These two fellahs took Tuku and me by surprise on our way down this morning. To cut a long story short, they took our boots, rifles, and ammo belts."

Infuriated, Mannie roared at them, "They took your fuckin' boots and rifles...?" He started pacing, rubbing his chin impatiently. "Fuck...!"

Not wanting Himi to take all the blame, Tuku cut in, "They jumped us when we were goin' down. They were goin' up."

Mannie was quickly losing his self-control and shoved Tuku in the chest, almost knocking him over. "Dumb bastards. Fuck..! What's wrong with you buggers...?"

Nga Rangi stepped between him and Tuku. "Enough of

this shit. Manu's dead." He then pointed to Brian. "And he's dead." Nga Rangi stood his ground, rebelliously, his eyes dilated with anger. "How many more have to die before you're satisfied?"

Mannie's face twisted with bitterness. He pointed at the ground. "This is Maori land. They're stealing our meat." He glared at Nga Rangi, breathing heavily. "Now lighten up. We don't have time to debate this shit. We've got to go after them." He pointed to Himi. "You, get Manu's boots and rifle." And then pointing to Tuku, he said, "And you get that pakeha's boots and rifle."

Nga Rangi stood there defiantly. "You're obsessed with this Maori land thing. Get real, man. This isn't Maori land. It's not ours. We don't own it."

Mannie sneered, stabbing a finger at the ground again. "We have taken this land back. What the hell's up with you?"

Observing Mannie's obsessive behaviour, Marlene could see serious trouble was about to erupt. She stepped between Mannie and Nga Rangi. "Come on, you guys. Let's not start fighting among ourselves, eh. We're in enough trouble as it is. Can't you see that, Mannie?"

Mannie took advantage of the interruption. "She's right." He hesitated for a second, weighing up their options. "But if those bastards get outta here, there'll be cops swarming all over the bloody place like fleas on a mangy dog. We've got to stop them." Then he shouted in Nga Rangi face, "Okay?"

Not wanting another confrontation, Nga Rangi felt despair flood over him like a dark heavy cloak. Mannie was out of control. He turned away, disgusted. Nothing anyone said or did brought him to his senses. There was so much anger and hatred built up inside him since Jo's death. It was like he was a man possessed by a demon.

*   *   *   *   *

From across the valley at the top of the eastern track, John, Tui, and Dave observed the camp on the plateau for a good ten minutes. There was no sign of movement.

"Doesn't look like anyone's there," Tui said.

"Come on," John replied, pointing to the river above the waterfall. "Let's get over there before someone comes back."

They quickly crossed the river and, keeping low, cautiously but quickly approached the camp.

"Find anything that's flammable," Tui said as they rushed into the camp. "Anything that'll burn."

As they drew closer, Tui saw the entrances to the huts. "It's like a rebel camp all right. These huts are well camouflaged." He ducked into one. "They're not big but certainly quite comfortable. They've been here for some time." He ducked into another hut. "And everyone's got an air bed. These guys are well set up."

"We haven't got time to hang around and debate it," John replied, surveying the area.

John and Dave searched the huts while Tui rushed up to Mannie's communal meetinghouse.

John went into one of the huts. Surprised, he called to Tui. "There's enough bloody ammo here to fight a small war."

The meetinghouse was built of manuka tree trunks, all approximately ten centimetre thick and to his surprise, Tui found a chainsaw and six fuel containers inside; three were still full. It was obvious they had used the chainsaw to build the meetinghouse and later, for firewood.

"Perfect," he muttered to himself then called to John, "Bring the ammo over here and stack it against the wall. I've found some chainsaw fuel. This should get someone's attention."

John and Dave gathered all the ammunition they could find. They hurriedly took it over to the meetinghouse and stacked it against the wall. John noticed a stack of firewood by the fireplace. With Dave helping, they carried it over and began stacking it around the ammunition.

Picking up two of the full fuel containers, Tui ran through the huts, pouring petrol over the beds, open home made shelves, walls, anything that would burn. In one of the huts, he found a shirt and wound it onto a stick. He soaked the shirt with petrol then poured the remainder over the ammunition. He lit the shirt as John and Dave finished stacking the last of the firewood on top of the ammunition. "You guys get over the edge while I set this lot on fire."

Tui set fire to the camp, and then, looking back to make sure everything was ablaze, he set fire to the firewood around the ammunition. Grinning, he rushed to the edge, where John and Dave were patiently waiting. "That should get someone's attention."

John took one last look and then pointed with his rifle down the steep face. "Let's get the hell outta here."

They quickly made their way to the rivers edge and, hugging the bush, they ran downstream a short distance to where the river was shallow enough to cross.

The first of the ammunition started to explode. Tui looked up at the thick smoke billowing high into the sky. Box after box, the ammunition exploded as it overheated and ignited in thunderous blasts that echoed through the valley with bullets whining and whistling in every direction. It was like the Fourth of July in Arizona.

"Should cross here," John suggested, pointing at the river. "Don't wanna get too far down."

"I'll cover. Take Dave across with you."

CHAPTER 17

Mannie and his disheartened group spent an hour and a half searching the bush, slowly making their way upstream. There was not a single trace of the three hunters anywhere.

Mannie was still angry with Nga Rangi for questioning his authority earlier. They were just below the big bend in the river.

Pucky, looking upstream, saw the massive cloud of billowing smoke high above the plateau. "Hey. Look up there." Pointing, he shouted, "That's our camp. It's on fire!"

It was then that the first of the ammunition started to explode with a thunderous boom. Mannie's eyes bulged, his face went red with rage. He threw his arms in the air, screaming, "Fuck. They've set fire to our bloody camp...! Fuck those bloody bastards. Shit...!" He paced around cursing and kicking at the ground. "They burned our fuckin' home. Stuff the bastards!"

He stood there, dumbfounded, watching the billowing smoke, listening to the horrendous echo of their ammunition exploding. His eyes narrowed, his nostrils flared. "If it's war they want, they've fuckin' got one," he bellowed. "They may be laughing today, but it'll be our turn tomorrow. You wait and see."

Himi was saddened and upset at the sight of their camp burning. "Whatta we gonna do now...?"

Looking up at the smoke, Mannie snarled, "These buggers think they're fuckin' clever. They expect us to go rushing off up there. That's when they'll make a break for it and try to get away." He hesitated, formulating a plan. "We stay right here. Those bastards can come to us."

Upset at seeing what he considered the only real home where he felt he belonged, Tuku looked up sadly. "All our gear'll be gone. Even my guitar'll be toast."

With his face full of fury, Mannie charged at him and shoved him in the chest. "Is that all you're bloody worried about, you fuckin' wanker? You and your bloody guitar."

Angry and shaking his head, Mannie walked down by the water's edge, kicking at anything on the ground that got in his way. He turned to his group. "We'll go back and wait this side of the old campsite. When they don't see us up there at our camp, they might think we've given up."

"You don't think they're that stupid, do you?" Nga Rangi cut in.

Mannie, thinking of their earlier confrontation, glared at him. "Well, that's what we're gonna do anyway, so let's get goin'."

*   *   *   *   *

John, Tui, and Dave made it across the river and hurried into the bush. Tui looked up at the sky. "It'll be dark soon. We should rest up for the night and make a break at first light."

John nodded. "Yeah. Not much choice, mate."

Cautiously, they made their way up to the main eastern track and found a spot on the opposite side of the ridge among a stand of pungas, ferns, and rubbishy scrub. It was dusty and dry inside the pungas and it smelled of mould and fungi, but it offered a temporary refuge for the time being.

Dave was beginning to calm down even though he was still having trouble coming to grips with their predicament. He was exhausted, tired, and hungry.

Tui gave him his water bottle to wash the foul taste from his throat. "We should be okay here for the night. Try and get some sleep if you can, eh."

"Thanks," Dave said, taking a drink. "What a bloody day."

"Yeah, mate. You're not wrong there," Tui agreed.

"Can't believe Brian's dead," Dave said, handing the water bottle back to Tui. "Those buggers are absolutely mad. I don't understand why they want us dead!"

"'Fanatics' is the optimum word, Dave," John cut in. "Bloody Maori fanatics."

"What are they trying to achieve?" Dave asked. "I mean, why do they want us dead?"

"I have a feeling it's something to do with this land. Let me explain a bit here. Way back in the 1880s a lot of land was confiscated from many tribes, our tribe being one of them. My great grandfather decided to gift the land instead of losing it through confiscation. A few in the tribe disagreed, and to cut a long story short, there was a fight in which his great grandfather was killed and his family blamed my family."

"So how do you know this tattooed bugger then?" Tui asked inquiringly.

"I was in a pub a while back with a couple of friends. He was there in the same pub, and somehow, he recognized me. That's when he brought all that old nonsense up. He got real angry, and we had a bit of a scuffle. What did come out though was that he really hates pakehas, and that's his problem."

"I wonder if there's any link with those other hunters who disappeared up here last year then," Tui asked.

"I'd say there's every likelihood after what we've just been through," John replied solemnly.

The sound of a light plane engine coming towards them caught their attention. Tui looked to the sky, wanting to rush out and wave but decided against it, as it could compromise their position.

"Plane's on the other side of the ridge. Too low to see. Could be the forestry."

"Let's hope so," John said. "They would've seen the smoke. We might get some help up here tomorrow with any luck."

"I hope so," Dave cut in. "We might even get outta here alive."

"We'll get out of here alive, Dave," Tui assured him. "The trick is not to panic."

"It's all right for you guys," Dave said worriedly. "You guys have been trained for this sort of thing. Me, I'm just a plumber."

John looked at him sympathetically. "We'll get out of here, don't worry, mate. Just keep your cool and don't panic."

*   *   *   *   *

Following the river south, the old Piper Super Cruiser flew over the waterfall and then swooped down into the valley. In the passenger's seat was Senior Sergeant Peter Smith from the National Park Police Station, a middle-aged meticulous person nick-named Smithy.

"There's the fire," Smithy said, pointing down. "There's one hell of a lot of smoke."

They followed down the river a short distance. The pilot was about to make a turn and fly back over the plateau, when Smithy noticed several young men hurriedly ducking into the bush. "Hey, look down there," he said to the pilot, pointing. "Did that look suspicious to you?"

"Yeah, sure did," the pilot replied.

"They all had rifles," Smithy said, a little bemused.

"They might've had rifles, but they certainly didn't look like they were hunting," the pilot said. "Bet my life on it."

"I wouldn't go that far," Smithy replied and then pointed behind them with his thumb. "Fly back over the plateau again. I noticed smoke coming out of the ground." He looked at the pilot skeptically. "Did you see that?"

"Yeah. I did."

The pilot banked the small plane around over the bush and flew back along the same flight path, following the river north. The young men who had ducked for cover earlier had come back out onto the riverbank, and again, when they heard the plane returning, they made another dash for the bush.

Frowning, Smithy glanced across at the pilot. "Something's not right down there," he confessed. "They're acting damn suspicious in my estimation."

The pilot let the speed drop off as the plane did a sweep up over the plateau and he banked to the left. Smoke was still coming out of what appeared to be several large holes in the ground and from the smouldering remnants of the meetinghouse.

"I wonder what the hell those holes were," he said, pondering the scene for a moment, "and that other smouldering mess at some time may have been some sort of trampers hut."

Smithy cast an analytical eye over the scene below. "Those holes in the ground are quite big. It was definitely smoke and not steaming pot holes, wouldn't you agree?"

The pilot nodded. "Yeah. That was definitely smoke."

Smithy looked back over his shoulder as they flew past. "Pity we can't land. I'll have to come in by foot tomorrow morning. Bugger," he cursed, slapping the dashboard. "I saw enough of the lower reaches of that place last year looking for those three hunters who disappeared."

"When was that, Smithy?" the pilot asked.

"March last year. Three hunters disappeared in this area," he replied, looking rather puzzled. "We found their car over in the ravine below the bridge just before Horopito. They were supposed to have been hunting in here but we couldn't find any trace of them anywhere."

"Really?"

"Yeah. It was quite strange at the time. We never ever found anything anywhere. Not a single thing. Most of their camping gear like pots, pans, clothing, and stuff were still in the car but nothing else. No trace of the three hunters. Real strange."

* * * * *

The following morning, Smithy and Constable Ernie Colhoun pulled into the siding beside the railway line at Pokaka. Smithy pulled in beside the Toyota Landcruiser parked there out of sight. "Get the registration number of that vehicle before we leave, Ernie."

Taking a small notepad from his pocket, Ernie wrote down the registration number, the make, model, and colour of the vehicle and then smiled as he gazed across the railway line to the start of the track. "Shouldn't get lost in here Smithy. Not after that fiasco last year, looking for those three hunters."

"You're not wrong there, Ernie," Smithy replied, not at all happy with the long walk ahead of them. "Could do without this today."

* * * * *

Rising at daybreak, John, Tui, and Dave were making ready to leave their overnight hiding place. Dave was nervous, his face an ashen colour with dark rings around his eyes.

John, sensing his unease, patted him on the shoulder. "We'll be okay, Dave," he said, trying to be reassuring. "Don't panic. That's the worst thing you can do. Understand?"

"Yeah," Dave replied.

Tui gave him a drink from his water bottle and then took a swig himself. "Time to move out."

"You lead, Tui," John said and then turned to Dave. "You follow Tui. I'll take the rear. There's no need to rush. We got all day, so let's be as quiet as we can, okay?"

Nodding, Dave followed Tui up onto the track.

They had been on the eastern track, heading south for an hour and a half, when Tui put his hand up to stop.

"That's about where we crossed the second time yesterday," he whispered, pointing down at the river. "You wanna take a look?"

John nodded. Tui led them down a narrow animal track and stopped just inside the bush line. Cautiously, he looked upstream and then downstream. "No bugger in sight."

"We'll carry on along here, but be careful. Take your time, eh," John whispered and then noticed Dave's face was pale with fear. "You okay?" Dave nodded. "We're gonna get outta this, don't you worry."

Staying inside the bush line and picking each footstep carefully, making sure not to step on any dry twigs, and with Tui leading, they cautiously carried on.

Suddenly, after twenty long drawn-out minutes, Tui put his hand up to stop, beckoning John forward.

John came up and whispered, "What's up?"

"Someone's ahead."

They squatted down and listened. Every minute or so they could hear faint voices ahead. John beckoned for them to retreat back to the main track and go around. Unintentionally, Dave stepped on a dry twig. It made a loud crack as it broke under his weight.

Dave froze, cursing to himself. His eyes dilated as panic began to set in. Without saying a word, John took him by the shoulders and shook him.

Dave saw the look in John's eyes and knew exactly what he meant. Dave nodded and took three deep breaths. John put his finger up to his lips and then pointed at the ground, meaning be careful. Again, Dave nodded and took another deep breath.

Tui then heard footsteps coming slowly towards them. He pointed behind them with his head. John drew his thumb across his throat, the sign to take him. Tui handed John his rifle and then crept out to the edge of the bush and waited.

Himi came slowly along the riverbank, sticking close to edge of the bush, cautiously searching.

Tui crouched down low behind a thick fern, and as Himi drew parallel to him, he stepped out and karate chopped him in the throat to stop him from calling out a warning. Before Himi could react, Tui grabbed him by both shoulders, pulled him into the bush, and then head butted him in the temple.

With Himi now unconscious, Tui dragged him further into the bush and laid him down in the undergrowth. John and Dave were beside him and were about to carry on back the way they had come when they heard a low voice call out.

"You okay, Himi?"

John looked at Tui, his face flashing alarm. Tui called back softly, trying to fool the caller. "Just an opossum." Then pointing to the eastern track, they quietly retreated to the top of the ridge.

When Himi didn't return, Nga Rangi and Marlene came slowly forward. Marlene noticed a boot in the undergrowth and went to investigate. Startled, she waved nervously to Nga Rangi. Putting her hands to her face, she whispered, "Shit...! It's Himi. He's out cold, unconscious."

Nga Rangi quickly accessed the situation and rushed out onto the riverbank. "Himi's down," he shouted across the river. "He's been knocked out!"

At the top of the ridge, John, Tui, and Dave heard splashing in the river, a stumble, cursing, footsteps running along the riverbank, then stopping where they had left Himi. John hurriedly turned around and started walking backward, making it appear as if someone had walked up the track. He beckoned with his hand for Tui and Dave to follow suit.

They had just gone around a bend in the track a short distance, when they heard footsteps rushing up the track they had just come up.

John saw another narrow animal track on a steep, slippery, muddy face that went down seventy metres to the riverbank. He pointed at the narrow opening and went down. Half way down, on the left, was a thick stand of rubbishy pungas and ferns.

John grabbed a punga as he slid down and pulled himself inside a punga grove. He put his hand out to catch Dave as he came down and pulled him in, and then caught Tui's hand as he came down and helped him in.

Being the first up to the eastern track, Mannie quickly studied the boot prints. Some prints came up the way he had come, others came up the main track toward him, but none led away. To him, the prints coming up the track were too close together for someone walking forward.

As the others gathered around him, he sneered angrily, "Cunning bastards. They think we're bloody stupid." He then pointed at the boot prints on the track. "I think the bastards are walking backward."

He followed the boot prints and stopped abruptly where they left the track. He pointed down the narrow muddy face for the others to follow, but he remained at the top for a few seconds.

Suspiciously, he peered around at the bush but saw nothing untoward. The others had gone down the narrow face and were waiting for him on the riverbank.

John crouched just inside the pungas, out of sight, but at a point where he had a view of the start of the narrow muddy face. He watched as Nga Rangi and the others slid down past them, but noticed that Mannie had not come down yet.

Cautiously, he looked out through a gap in the pungas as Mannie started his descent. At what he guessed was the right moment, John threw his left arm out to catch Mannie around the neck as he drew parallel with the intention of getting him in a sleeper hold.

Mannie saw the arm suddenly shoot out from the punga grove and instinctively ducked. John was a split second too premature and managed to only get a minor grip around Mannie's forehead, and with his momentum and weight, Mannie slipped out of his grip.

Mannie lost his balance at the sudden attack and slid backward into a tree trunk on the side of the track with a heavy thump. He sat up, partially winded, propped against the tree, two and a half metres away from the punga grove.

John was about to rush over to him, but Tui grabbed his arm and held him back. He whispered disconcertedly. "Whatta you doing?"

"I'm gonna break his arm," John replied, trying to shrug Tui's hand away. "Just wanna slow the bastard down a bit."

"You'll give away our position."

Winded and using the tree trunk for support, Mannie slowly rose to a half-standing position and looked across at John. "Amohia," he croaked, his voice hardly audible.

John's face glowed with anger and then, supporting himself with the outside punga, he leaned out and kicked

Mannie in the face as hard as he could and then withdrew back inside the pungas out of sight.

With the force of John's kick, Mannie's head slammed back hard into the tree trunk. He rolled over and lay there unconscious, his backside against the tree.

Mannie had dropped his rifle on the side of the track near where John was standing inside the pungas. John quickly picked it up and, with the expertise of his army training, quietly but swiftly opened the breech, ejecting a bullet in the process, took out the bolt, and wound off the end, exposing the firing pin. He drew his survival knife. The back of the survival knife blade had teeth that were multi functional. He put the firing pin between two teeth and snapped it off.

Tui whispered into his ear impatiently. "What the hell're you doin'...?"

Ignoring him, John quickly put the bolt back together, slipped it back into the breech, and laid it back where he found it.

Then turning to Tui, he whispered, "Let's get outta here."

Tui led Dave and John up the slippery face to the main track undetected and then quietly but quickly, headed south, treading on the moss that lined both sides of the narrow path.

Mannie gained consciousness and tried to sit up, but with the thumping headache, he had difficulty maintaining his balance and accidentally rolled another metre down the slippery face.

Nga Rangi, standing with the others on the riverbank, wondered what was keeping Mannie. A couple of sounds in the bush by the slippery face caught his attention. He walked to the start of the slippery track and called out, "Whatta you doin'? You okay?"

Hearing Nga Rangi's voice just below him, Mannie called back, "Give me a hand."

Nga Rangi rushed up and found Mannie sitting awkwardly on the side of the slippery track, rubbing the side of his head. He had blood running down the back of his head from where his head slammed into the trunk, and on his cheek, he had a small cut where John had kicked him.

"What the hell happened...?" Nga Rangi asked, speculating that he had misjudged the track and slipped.

Scowling, Mannie shook his head to clear the dizziness. "Amohia. Arsehole was hiding in the pungas."

Nga Rangi spun around, pointing his rifle.

"He's gone now," Mannie snapped, and then stood, shaking his head to clear his vision and said in an angry tone, "Bastard kicked me in the face." Again, he shook his head and then pointed to the riverbank. "Get the others."

Staggering uneasily, Mannie went up to where he had dropped his rifle. He spotted a cartridge lying in the dirt and upon a closer inspection, he recognized it as one of his own. He picked it up and, not understanding how it got there, peered suspiciously at the surrounding bush. Bastard, he cursed to himself. I'm gonna get you Amohia. You can count on it.

* * * * *

Tui, leading at a steady pace down the eastern track, pointed across the river. "That's where our camp is. Wanna cross here?"

Not wanting to risk being seen along the river, John shook his head. "No. We'll cross further down. Be a lot safer."

* * * * *

Nga Rangi rushed out onto the riverbank, where the others were waiting restlessly.

"Come on you guys," he ordered. "Amohia's in here somewhere. He just whacked Mannie."

"He whacked Mannie...?" Tuku replied, and then with a wry grin, he asked sarcastically. "I hope he isn't hurt?"

Shaking his head, Nga Rangi pointed up the narrow, muddy track. "Come on."

Marlene looked at Tuku, frowning. "Only hurt his stupid pride. What a pity."

CHAPTER 18

Mannie was studying the boot prints, waiting on the eastern track. He wiped blood from his cheek with the back of his hand. "If Amohia and his mates get away we'll have cops charging all over this place like bloody ants." He looked back down the slippery face, formulating a plan. "We'll head back along the riverbank and cross by their camp. If I know Amohia, he won't leave without his gear."

Mannie led down the steep slippery face. It took them just over an hour to reach the old camp-site. He rushed in and found everything was still there. With a malicious grin, he pointed upstream. "They haven't got this far yet. We'll wait for them up there along the riverbank."

He led them back upstream a hundred metres. "Okay. Spread out and keep your eyes peeled. They want to play cat and mouse. We can play too."

*   *   *   *   *

Tui led John and Dave another three hundred metres past their camp but still on the eastern track, when John called softly to him. "This is far enough downstream. Let's cross here, eh? They won't be able to see us here. I'll cross first."

They made their way quietly to the edge of the bush and peered upstream for several seconds. John glanced at Tui. "Cover me."

Tui took up a defensive position on the edge of the bush, where he had a clear view upstream. John quickly crossed and then took up a defensive position on the far bank.

Tui turned to Dave, pointing across the river. "Way you go. John's got you covered and I'll be right behind you."

With Dave and Tui safely across, John followed Tui and Dave into the bush, heading west toward the main track that would take them back to Tui's Landcruiser.

It took them ten minutes to reach it, where they hesitated, momentarily, listening. The track meandered through the bush, making it difficult to see any further than twenty metres. Tui suddenly heard voices coming toward them from the south. John signalled for him to take cover on one side of the track; he and Dave would take cover on the other.

The footsteps grew louder and then Sergeant John Smith and Constable Ernie Colhoun appeared on the track, walking casually, talking quietly. John recognized the uniforms and gave Tui the signal that they were friendly. John stepped out, holding up his hand for the two policemen to stop.

Startled by John's sudden appearance out of nowhere, both policemen stopped dead in their tracks. "What the hell're you doing?" Smithy snapped in a demanding tone.

Tui and Dave stepped out of the bush and stood beside John, and for a moment, both groups eye-balled each other.

Again, Smithy repeated his demand. "What the heck's going on?"

Introducing himself, Tui, and Dave, John explained who they were and what they were doing. "We weren't sure if anyone would come, but I can tell you, we're real glad to see you two."

He then went on to explain the events that had taken place over the last twenty-four hours. At first, neither of the policemen believed them. Their story did sound rather bizarre. Smithy noticed Dave kept glancing nervously north along the track. He slowly began to realize that maybe there could be some truth in what they were saying.

"These buggers aren't far behind us," Tui said, getting a touch impatient. "We can't stand here yapping all day. Look, I'm telling you, these people are deadly serious. They're trying to stop us getting out and going to the police. That's what we're trying to explain to you. Don't you understand?"

Smithy glanced at Ernie and then at John and Tui. "You know how ridiculous this all sounds?"

"Ridiculous or not, it's the truth," John told them, trying to sound as convincing as he could.

Ernie noticed the two military rifles and frowned, a little suspicious. "They're both category 'E' rifles. Do you have a license for them?"

"Yes," Tui assured him. "We're military, SAS soldiers. Is that enough for you?"

Dave was standing beside Smithy. "Those people out there shot our friend Brian in the back. He didn't die with the first shot, so they put another one in him."

Smithy cast a scrutinizing eye over the three men. He still wasn't fully convinced they were genuine. "How many more are with you? I saw eight or so people up the river when I flew over here yesterday."

"It wasn't us you saw," John replied. "That would've been the people we're telling you about."

To Smithy, as outrageous as their story sounded, Dave did appear to be genuinely very distressed and very nervous.

"It was us that set that fire on the plateau," Tui told him. "We were hoping it would alert the forestry or the police."

Smithy interrupted him. "So it was you three? You lit the fire?"

"Yeah," John replied. "Didn't have much option. We needed to alert someone about the trouble up here."

"You deliberately lit the fire?" Smithy asked, ignoring John. "How did you get here? I mean, where's your vehicle?"

"We came in my Toyota Landcruiser," Tui replied, getting short on patience. "It's parked behind that stock pile of metal by the railway tracks just before the second bridge past the Makatoki viaduct."

Frustrated, John cut in, "Listen. There's about eight or nine guys trying to kill us. They've already killed one of our friends. I actually killed one of them in self-defense. He tried to shoot me."

"You've killed one of them...?" Ernie asked apprehensively.

"Yes, in self-defense," John admitted soberly. "He was trying to shoot me, for chrissake."

Dave interrupted, getting worried. "Listen to me, please. These people shot my friend and then tried to shoot me. We had split up into pairs. Brian and me were hunting the eastern side of the river. John and Tui were up on the western side. They were heading for a large flat area further up the river when they heard shooting. They figured something was wrong and came to help. If it hadn't been for them, I'd be dead myself. If John and Tui hadn't found me when they did, that bloke John killed would have shot me."

For several seconds, Smithy looked them up and down, summing up the scenario. "What are you suggesting then?"

John eyed him sternly, trying to convey the seriousness of their position. "For starters, you guys are going to need backup. There's no way the two of you will apprehend them on your own. Dave could go out and get help. We'll stay here with you until help arrives."

"We don't need your help," Smithy replied sternly. "This is police business. We can handle it, Ernie and myself. We've been in worse situations than this before."

"Trust me," Tui said, trying to convince them. "You're gonna need all the help you can get. Have you any weapons?"

"Yes. Ernie's got a pistol," he replied. "They wouldn't fire on police."

"Don't kid yourself. These guys think it's the Maori wars all over again," John said firmly. He turned to Dave. "Give Smithy your rifle and ammo."

Smithy cast an unappreciative eye at Dave and pushed his rifle away. "I don't need that. What do you guys think we are? Boy Scouts."

"Take it and be thankful you've got something to protect yourself with," Tui told him unsympathetically. "You can always give it back later."

Smithy rubbed his chin attentively. "Okay. I'll take your word for it. Dave, you go back to my vehicle. It's parked by the Landcruiser. Use the radio-telephone and call for backup." He cast a cautious eye at John and Tui. "If you guys aren't telling the truth, there'll be serious consequences for you all, believe me."

Frustrated, John replied, "Why would we go to all this trouble and stop you if this was just a prank? We could've just let you go past but we didn't. Have you thought about that?"

"Okay, okay." Smithy put up his hand submissively. "You two stay behind us, understand?" He pointed a finger at both John and Tui. "I don't want you guys getting in the way once we catch up with these people. Do I have your word on that?"

"Yeah, whatever. We're here purely as support."

Dave interrupted nervously, "What do I do once I've called for backup?"

John cut in before Smithy could answer, "Take Tui's Landcruiser and go to the National Park Police Station. You can wait for us there. You know where the keys are?"

Smithy explained to Dave where the keys to the police Toyota Hilux utility were and how to use the radio-telephone. To John and Tui, he said, "Right. Let's get going. But stay behind us. Okay?"

John put his hand on Dave's shoulder. "You be careful and we'll see you back at the police station."

Dave waved good-bye and headed off up the track.

Smithy pointed along the track, and they headed north, Smithy and Ernie leading.

"Forty minutes later they were approaching the campsite. John tapped Smithy's shoulder. "Our camp's just up here."

Smithy slowed his pace and then stopped at the thin line of scrub when John tapped his shoulder.

John went in to check on their gear. "Everything's still here," he said, looking around their immediate surroundings. Smithy cautiously carried on, and ten minutes later, they came out into a small clearing beside the river, where they spotted two men.

Smithy called out, "Police. Stay where you are."

Shocked at the sudden appearance of the two policemen, the two men ducked for cover. Smithy called again, "Police. Stay where you are. I want a word with you two."

Smithy was standing out in the open. John grabbed his arm and tried to entice him back to take cover. Cautiously, Tui directed Ernie back to the edge of the bush.

Smithy shrugged John's arm away and turned back to where the two men had disappeared. He was about to take a step forward when John grabbed him by the arm again and physically pulled him back as Mannie appeared on the riverbank.

Smithy turned to him, scowling angrily, trying to shrug him off. "What the hell do you think you're doing...?"

John pointed to Mannie as he rushed to get a better vantage point. "See that bugger over there. He'll have your guts for garters if you're not careful." Then John saw Marlene briefly cowering on the riverbank. "Shit...!" he said, glancing over his shoulder at Tui. "There's a woman here as well."

A shot rang out, barely missing Smithy's head. The concussion of the bullet buffeted his ears and the realization struck him like a sledge hammer. Everything John and Tui had told him were true.

Smithy ducked behind a tree and called out, "Police. Lay down your weapons. I repeat, lay down your weapons."

Then another shot rang out but from a different direction. Bark and wood chips exploded from the tree trunk next to Smithy's face. He retreated back further and got behind another tree, shocked at the negative response. "Geez...!"

John called to Tui, pointing behind him. "Take them further into the bush. I'll cover you."

Boom! Bark exploded from a tree next to Ernie. Horrified, Ernie and Smithy retreated with Tui. John was running backward, firing as he went.

Mannie waved his men forward. John knew he was preparing for a frontal attack. Zac darted across open ground, firing at them as he went.

Tui, not wanting to kill anyone, fired low, hitting Zac high in the thigh. Zac went down, screaming, rolling on the ground.

Ritchie stepped out from behind a tree, grabbed Zac's arm, and dragged him back into cover. Ritchie then fired wildly at Tui, sending bark and splinters exploding from the tree next to Tui's left shoulder.

Tui returned fire, hitting Ritchie in the forearm. Unintentionally, Ritchie dropped his rifle and, crying out in pain, leaped back behind the tree.

Mannie and his men were slowly closing in. Tui called to John, concerned for their safety. "They're trying to surround us."

Tui took the two policemen deeper into the bush, John covering.

Suddenly, Chappy stepped out from behind a tree and fired, hitting Ernie in the centre of his chest.

With the impact, Ernie was tossed backward, knocking

Smithy completely over onto his side. Chappy fired again. Dirt and dead leaves flew up around Smithy's head.

Smithy scrambled to his feet and ducked behind a small tree. He looked across at Ernie, who was rolling around on the ground, clutching at his chest. He put his hand out for Ernie to grab.

A shot rang out. Ernie arched his back as the second bullet found its mark. He slumped forward and lay very still, his eyes wide open, staring into oblivion.

Smithy looked at him in disbelief.

Tui grabbed Smithy by the shirt, snapping him back to reality, encouraging him to follow further into the bush.

Smithy was in a state of shock. For a moment, he just knelt there behind the tree, staring at Ernie.

John rushed back and grabbed Smithy under the arm, lifted him to his feet, and together, they retreated. Tui fired two short automatic bursts then followed.

Physically shaken by the sudden attack, Smithy glanced over his shoulder. "Ernie...!"

"Gotta keep going, Smithy," Tui whispered soberly. "Gotta keep moving."

"Can't leave Ernie like that," he said, confused and disorientated.

"We'll come back for him later," John replied gravely. "Can't afford to hang around or we'll be next. Come on. Keep moving."

Taking up a defensive position, Tui said, pointing behind him, "You two keep going. I'll cover." John jumped into an old dried creek bed and headed north.

Smithy hesitated, pointing south. "The vehicle's that way," he said, desperation echoing in his voice.

"They'll expect that," John told him. "We go this way."

Smithy didn't understand John's tactic, but he wasn't going to argue. He could see John and Tui were well-trained soldiers and followed them up the old dried creek bed. Tui fired another quick burst and rushed up behind them.

*   *   *   *   *

Upon hearing the shooting and fearing for the safety of his friends, Dave ran as fast as he could. An hour later, he reached the top of the track and staggered across the railway tracks to the police Toyota Hilux utility parked beside Tui's Landcruiser exhausted. He stopped and bent over with his hands on his knees, winded, trying to get his breath. He found the keys under the front bumper. Unlocking the door, he sat there on the driver's seat, taking deep breaths, trying to stem his breathing.

After twenty seconds he switched on the radiotelephone and picked up the microphone. "National Park Police. National Park Police. Do you copy? Over."

The radiotelephone burst into life immediately.

"National Park Police here. Identify yourself. Over."

"My name's Dave. I'm calling from Smithy's Hilux. I've been with him and Ernie in the bush at Pokaka. There's been some trouble, and they need help urgently. Do you hear me? Over."

"Hey. Slow down a bit, will you? Now tell me, what sort of trouble are you talking about? Over."

"They're being shot at by these crazy people. One of my friend's is dead, shot yesterday. They're in serious trouble and need all the help you can get. Over."

"How many are in there? I mean, are Smithy and Ernie on their own? Over."

"No. Two of my friends are with them. They're army, SAS, but they're outnumbered. Over."

"Do you have transport? Over."

"Yes. Smithy told me once I've notified you he needed help, I'm to go to the police station and wait there. Over."

"Okay. Get yourself in here as soon as you can. Do you know where we are? Over."

"No, over."

The officer explained where the police station was. "You get all that? Over."

"Yeah, I think so. Give me about thirty minutes. Out."

✳   ✳   ✳   ✳   ✳

Dave pulled up outside the National Park Police Station twenty-five minutes later on Buddo Street in National Park. He rushed in through the front door. The constable in charge, Jim, offered him a cup of tea.

"Sugar?" Jim asked.

"Yeah, thanks."

Jim, sensing his anxiety, handed him the cup of tea. "Sit down. I'm Jim. Okay. Now tell me what's happened."

Dave explained in detail the events that had taken place. How they found the grave purely by accident first, about the smoke up on the plateau, being attacked, Brian's death, his escape with John and Tui's help, and then coming across Smithy and Ernie.

Jim sat back in his chair with a staid expression, rubbing the stubble on top of his almost-bald head. "We've got one problem. I can't get any help for at least twelve hours."

Dave's head jerked back, shocked. "They could all be dead by then." He sat there, deep in thought, staring at Jim. Suddenly, he had a thought. "What about the army? John and Tui are SAS. Surely they'll offer some help?"

Jim picked up the telephone directory. "I'll ring and find out. They could be worth a call."

Jim rang the army headquarters at the Waiouru Military

Base. A duty officer answered. Jim explained the situation in depth for several minutes, and then, smiling wanly, he put the receiver down. "He'll call us back in a few minutes. He's going to talk to his superiors. It made a difference when it's a couple of their own, especially under the circumstances when we can't get any other help."

Dave sat back, letting out a sigh of relief and waited. It took twenty-five long agonizing minutes for the duty officer to phone back.

"We've got regular army volunteers preparing to leave in fifteen minutes," the duty officer said. "They'll be going in by helicopter. Do you have the exact location of your men?"

"Yes. Just a minute," Jim replied and went to the drawer, where they stored the topographical maps. Dave helped him search for the correct one and went back to the phone. Dave pointed out the exact spot while Jim relayed the grid references of the location to the duty officer. "Okay. Got that."

The duty officer then gave Jim the VHF radio frequency channel in case the helicopter needed to communicate with them.

"Thanks. That's one we owe you," Jim replied.

"Glad to help out. It'll give our boys something constructive to do."

Jim switched on the VHF radio and waited.

Fifteen minutes later, the VHF burst into life. "Eagle One is in the air. Do you copy? Over."

The duty officer responded instantly. "That's affirmative, Eagle One. Over."

"National Park Police. This is Eagle One. Do you copy? Over."

Jim picked up the microphone. "Affirmative, Eagle One. Go ahead. Over."

"We'll be over the target area in approximately twenty minutes. You have a person with you that's been in the area. Ask him to standby in case we need to talk to him. Over."

"Affirmative. He is standing by. Over."

CHAPTER 19

Mannie was furious at seeing the presence of the two policemen. He rushed over to Zac to check on his wound. Zac was in serious pain and in no state to walk. Mannie ordered Chappy and Pucky to carry him down to the riverbank. Zac took his shirt and singlet off and, using his singlet as a bandage, wrapped it tightly around his thigh.

Ritchie was bleeding steadily from the wound on his left forearm. Luckily, the bullet had gone right through. Pucky tore the bottom off his shirt and wrapped it around Ritchie's forearm to help stem the bleeding.

Mannie cast a cautious eye around the bush. "That Amohia's in here somewhere. He's gonna pay for this."

Himi, concerned at seeing the two policemen, turned to Tuku and said, "How'd those bloody cops get in here...?"

"Dunno, but there's gonna be bloody trouble now, you can guarantee that," Tuku replied ruefully.

Mannie looked back toward the river, where Chappy and Pucky had taken Zac and Ritchie. "There's no bloody medical kit either. Burned in the bloody fire. They'll have to wait here till we get this over and done with."

"Zac's leg's pretty bad," Himi said nervously.

"I know that, dick brain," Mannie snapped. "There's

nothing we can do about it for the moment. We've got to get after those bastards again."

"They've got automatic rifles," Tuku broke in.

"We can take them out," Mannie shouted.

"Why'd you have to shoot those three last year anyway?" Tuku asked. "If you hadn't done that, none of this would be happening."

Angry at his negative attitude, Mannie grabbed Tuku by the shirt and bellowed into his face, "They killed Jo!" He shoved Tuku back, and then, at the mention of Jo's name, he hesitated, his voice momentarily losing its venom. "They killed my Jo." A nerve twitched on his cheek; his brown eyes turned dark with anger again. Frustrated, he looked around at everyone. "We shoot to kill." He stabbed a finger at Tuku. "If it was left up to you, the bloody pakeha would have all our land. Not just some of it."

Marlene had been observing Mannie's schizophrenic behaviour, angry at the way he was treating everyone. She stormed up to him and yelled into his face. "We've killed a bloody cop and one of them pakehas! Whatta you thinks gonna happen now?"

Nga Rangi stepped between them, knowing that Mannie wouldn't allow her to talk to him like that in front of everyone and get away with it.

He pointed a finger at Mannie. "You know as well as I do there's gonna be serious trouble. We're in it up to our eyeballs now whether we like it or not."

Mannie glared at him. "No good crying over spilt milk. What's done is done, so let's get on with it."

He raced off in the direction John, Tui, and Smithy had disappeared, followed by Pucky, Chappy, Himi, and Tuku.

Nga Rangi and Marlene followed at a walking pace.

Marlene shook her head. I'm really sick of this. I feel like a damn yo-yo, running back and forth through the bush and for what? It's crazy!"

I'm sick of it too, girl. But what can we do?" Nga Rangi said. "Where could we go, especially now? We're all in so much bloody shit."

*　*　*　*　*

Tui came across a tree that had fallen over in a storm. He stopped beside it, glancing along its trunk. He turned to John, pointing with his head. Tui leaped up on the trunk and walked carefully along to the tip and jumped off on the opposite side. John and Smithy followed and then raced off behind Tui back toward the river again.

Four minutes later, Mannie was in pursuit and halted forty metres past the fallen tree. He peered around at the bush, unsure what direction to go. There were no fresh boot prints to follow.

"Bastard," he said. "Backtrack and see if we can find which way they went. Fan out." Cursing, he wiped his cheek with the back of his hand.

Spreading out in a line, they began searching for anything that would give them some indication of the direction the two soldiers and the policeman had gone.

Pucky slowly searched his way back to the fallen tree and noticed the bark along the trunk had been recently disturbed. Peering along the trunk, he saw specks of fresh mud and even more bark disturbed.

Excited, he called out, "Hey, Mannie. Look over here."

Mannie rushed over to him. "What is it?"

Pucky pointed out the disturbed bark and the fresh mud along the tree trunk and then worked his way along the trunk to the tip. Glancing over the opposite side of the trunk, he saw deep fresh boot prints where Tui, John, and Smithy had jumped off.

Mannie patted Pucky on the shoulder, sneering bitterly.

"Well done. Cunning bastards, eh. They're heading back to the bloody river. Come on."

The small group followed Mannie back through the bush toward the river.

∗　∗　∗　∗　∗

Smithy followed close behind Tui and John as they hurried back toward the riverbank. As they reached the edge of the bush, John heard Zac on the riverbank cry out at the pain in his thigh. They quietly backtracked.

Then hearing footsteps charging through the bush toward them, Tui quickly looked around for somewhere to hide and spotted a tree that had fallen over in a storm. Its branches had embedded themselves in the soft river soil, suspending the trunk sixty centimetres above the ground. A lot of foliage had grown up around the embedded branches, giving some concealment under the fallen tree.

Tui pointed to it and quickly helped Smithy under, followed hastily by John. When he slid under himself, he dragged extra foliage with him to conceal them even more.

Seconds later, Mannie and his men dashed past and went out to the two wounded men on the riverbank. Mannie asked Ritchie impatiently, "You seen anyone come past here in the last couple of minutes?"

"Nah," Ritchie replied and then looked over at Zac, who shook his head. He was in too much pain to have noticed anything.

Tuku was feeling very uneasy and said, "They look like army dudes to me."

Ignoring him, Mannie scanned the bush. "They must be close."

"The next thing we'll know is the bloody army'll be in here," Tuku went on.

Mannie spun on his heel and shouted in his face, "Shut up! Fuck you! You're starting to really piss me off with your whining."

Standing his ground, Tuku lifted his chin defiantly. "What if the army does send in troops?"

"So what if they fuckin' do?" Mannie snapped back. "Fuck the army."

Tuku stood there, staring at Mannie rebelliously. By now, Mannie was in such a rage at Tuku he couldn't contain his temper any longer. He needed to vent his anger on someone, and Tuku gave him the prime excuse.

Mannie went down low and spun 360 degrees, doing a sweeper move. With his right leg, he caught Tuku just above the ankles with such force it whipped his feet out from under him, sending him crashing to the ground on his back.

Mannie straddled him, pinning his arms to the ground with his knees and then, drawing his hunting knife, put the blade to Tuku's throat.

Breathing heavily, nostrils flaring, eyes fierce with rage, Mannie screamed, "I should slit your fuckin' throat, you bloody coward!"

Nga Rangi leaped forward, grabbing Mannie's right wrist, which was holding the knife, and tried to pull it away from Tuku's throat; but Mannie strained against him.

"Mannie...! Mannie!" Nga Rangi shouted, trying desperately to break the grip. "Calm down. Geez, man. Calm down, will you?"

With eyes dilated black with rage, Mannie glared down at Tuku. He slowly relaxed and stood.

He turned to his group, his face twisted with bitterness. "We shoot to kill. There's no option but to kill the bastards." He glared at everyone, shouting, "Understand?"

Tuku rolled over onto his hands and knees and then stood there for a moment, trembling. He slowly retreated and stood beside Himi and whispered, "We're stuffed, mate. Up shit creek without a bloody paddle, well and truly."

Then in the distance to the south, they heard thumping on the air. Mannie lifted his head toward the sky, listening. The sound seemed to be growing nearer. Fearfully, the others looked up at the sky.

*   *   *   *   *

Only too familiar with the sound and in his confined hiding place, Tui glanced back at John. It was the sound of an army Iroquois helicopter and knew it would be distracting Mannie and his followers.

Tui pointed with his head toward the bush.

Nodding, John turned to Smithy and whispered, "We're gonna sneak up into the bush. You make your way back to the vehicle when the coasts clear. Okay. That's an army Iroquois. Let's hope they're coming in to help us."

Smithy acknowledged with a nod.

John and Tui cautiously crept out from under the fallen tree and slipped quietly into the bush undetected.

*   *   *   *   *

The Iroquois helicopter was coming in from the south at speed, following the course of the river. With its side doors wide open, it flashed past Mannie and his men standing on the riverbank. They couldn't help but see the M60 machine gun in the open doorway. The big war bird carried on upstream half a kilometre and then turned, facing them, and hovered above the river.

Mannie watched the army helicopter for several seconds and then shouted, "Pucky, you and Chappy go for the tail rotor when it comes back down, okay? Go for the tail rotor."

Then to the remainder of his group, he ordered, "The rest of you, go for the turbine. Aim for the turbine behind the cockpit. That might bring the bitch down." He turned back to the helicopter hovering upstream. "But don't fire until I tell you. Wait for my signal."

Nervously, Himi was watching the helicopter and cut in, "Did you see the clothes those guys were wearing?" He looked around at everyone. "They're the same clothes as these guys we're chasing. Tuku said they were army. Now, do you believe him."

Tuku had a terrible churning sensation in his stomach and added fearfully, "And did you see the size of that bloody machine gun? They'll cut us to bloody shreds."

Mannie shoved both him and Himi in the chest. "Shut up... Shut up the pair of you! We haven't got time for this bullshit." He glared around at everyone. "Go for the tail rotor and the turbine. We can bring that bitch down." He turned back to the helicopter. "Fuck these bastards. The day's not over yet."

Ritchie came in and stood beside Pucky. "You okay?" Mannie asked.

"Yeah. I can still use my rifle."

"Good," Mannie said smiling. "You go for the turbine, eh."

Ritchie nodded.

The Iroquois started moving, coming slowly down toward them.

*   *   *   *   *

Dave's nerves were shattered. He received a tremendous fright and jumped as the VHF radio burst into life. He and Jim sat forward in their chairs, listening to the pilot's voice.

"We have contact. I repeat, we have contact. There's eight

men on the riverbank that I can see, possibly more. All are armed."

*   *   *   *   *

The helicopter was approximately one hundred metres upstream from Mannie and his group on the riverbank, moving slowly down toward them. The pilot switched on the external speakers.

"Put down your weapons. I repeat, put down your weapons."

Mannie, standing defiantly on the riverbank, waiting for the opportune moment, watched the helicopter slowly approach. As it drew parallel he screamed above the sound of the helicopter. "Fire! Fire!"

Underestimating the group's resolve, the soldiers in the helicopter were caught completely by surprise. They naturally expected the group on the riverbank to lay down their weapons and give themselves up. One soldier was standing casually in the open doorway beside the M60 machine gun.

Bullets reined into the helicopter, slamming into the turbine and the fuselage. The soldier standing next to the M60 machine gun was hit in the chest, the force of the projectile catapulting him backward out through the opposite cockpit door, and he fell into the river.

Mannie aimed at the helicopter turbine and pulled the trigger. Click! "Fuck. Bloody old ammo." He dropped his rifle on the riverbank and leaped into the river and quickly searched the soldier's body for weapons but found none. "Keep firing!" he screamed at the top of his voice. "Keep firing!"

Not anticipating such a negative response from the riverbank and as the helicopter surged forward to avoid the shower of bullets, the soldiers momentarily lost their balance and aim.

Another soldier grabbed the M60 machine gun, cocked it, and fired. The edge of the riverbank exploded in a shower of gravel, dirt, and silty dust. Miraculously, no one was hit.

Mannie rushed up the riverbank, snatched up his rifle, and ejected what he thought was a dud bullet and drove another into the breech. Before he could fire, the helicopter banked out over the bush out of sight. "Fuck." He glanced at Pucky and saw he was reloading. "Gave them a bit of their own medicine, eh? See how they like that."

Fearing for everyone's safety, Tuku called out, "We have to give ourselves up. They'll chop us to mincemeat with that machine gun when they come back."

Mannie pushed him violently, knocking him over onto his back. "I should have slit your fuckin' throat when I had the opportunity."

Tuku slowly stood. Mannie grabbed Tuku's rifle by the barrel. Instantly, he noticed how cold the barrel was. He snatched it out of Tuku's hands and then tossed it to the ground, screaming, "You fuckin' coward," then he turned to the others. "He hasn't even fired a single shot. Barrel's still cold." He backhanded Tuku across the face. "Fuck you, you useless bloody arsehole."

Incensed with Mannie's behaviour, Nga Rangi stepped between him and Tuku. "Calm down, will you! Bloody hell. Look at yourself! You're going absolutely crazy, man. Tuku's right. We're in deep shit, which ever way you look at it. It'll be suicide to take these guys on."

Mannie cut him short, "Not you too...? Fuck man...! You're all turnin' dog on me. What's fuckin' wrong with you lot?"

It was then that they heard the abrupt change in the rhythm of the helicopter's engine. They looked up, shielding their eyes from the sun rays with their hands. The sound became even more pronounced as it banked wide over the bush. They had a quick glimpse of it over the tree tops and saw a mist of smoke trailing it.

Then the mist turned to a distinctive smoky blue colour. The rear tail rotor blades had suffered serious damage; the turbine had been hit twice putting it out of balance. The helicopter began to shake and vibrate. The engine started to lose power as the helicopter came back into view.

Triumphantly, Mannie punched the air, and then, turning to Nga Rangi, he gave him an unexpected shove in the shoulder, sending him into Tuku and Himi.

With a victorious evil smile, he shouted, "Didn't I tell you bastards? Didn't I say we could bring the bitch down?"

For several seconds they all stood there, aghast, their mouths wide open in disbelief. The helicopter began to yore and wallow erratically. Pucky punched the air, cheering.

* * * * *

The sound of rifle fire on the riverbank was horrendous. John and Tui heard the helicopter bank out over the bush, heading in a northerly direction. They began racing north, ducking and weaving their way through the bush to find a clearing where they could signal to it.

They were horrified when they heard the distinct change in the rhythm of the engine and were even more horrified when it became more pronounced. As the helicopter passed overhead, they glanced up and saw the blue smoke trailing.

"Shit...!" Tui said as they raced through the bush trying desperately to find a clearing. "They're in big trouble."

The way the helicopter was flying, they could see it was almost out of control. The vibrations grew louder as the turbine slowly but surely began to destroy itself.

*   *   *   *   *

The lights on the dashboard flashed red as the pilot struggled with the controls. The mighty war bird was shaking violently, losing altitude rapidly. The pilot's only option was to put it down as quickly as he could, the river offering his best choice.

Then suddenly, the helicopter took on a mind of its own as the tail rotor started to disintegrate. The helicopter started to side swing to the left, drop two metres, gain power momentarily, and then side swing again, blue smoke pouring from the exhaust.

The pilot snatched the microphone as they began to descend at an ever-increasing rate. "Losing power and altitude." He then dropped the microphone, struggling with all his strength and skill to maintain his course. He made another grab at the microphone again.

"Mayday, mayday, mayday. Going down. I repeat, we're going down. Mayday. Mayday. Goi---."

The helicopter crashed at a forty-five-degree angle into the river. Only the pilot and two soldiers survived the impact. Two other soldiers were catapulted out through the open cockpit door into the rocky riverbed and died instantly.

Like a dying dinosaur, the helicopter slowly rolled over on its side in the river. Still turning, the main rotors exploded into a thousand pieces as they ploughed into the rocky river bottom, sending lethal fragments flying into the bush in every direction. There was a horrific explosion as the cold water poured into the upturned shattered hull and drowned the hot engine.

*   *   *   *   *

Back in the National Park Police Station, Jim jumped to his

feet, his face aghast with shock. Dave was speechless, lost for words. Neither could believe what they were hearing. The VHF radio went dead, only a loud hiss audible.

Jim was standing, frozen to the spot, his mouth agape. "D... did you hear that...? Th.. they've gone d.. down...!" he stuttered then turned to Dave. "Shit...! What the hell's go... going on up there?"

*   *   *   *   *

John and Tui, upon hearing the horrendous crash, ran as fast as they could to get to the crash site. They drew parallel with the downed helicopter on its side in the river. Smoke and fumes were pouring out of the upturned hull. A soldier leaped up onto its side through the open cockpit door, shook his head to clear it, and then helped another soldier up onto the side of the cockpit and then the pilot.

The pilot had severely injured his legs. One soldier leaped into the river while the other lowered the pilot down to him, and, then he, too, jumped into the river. Taking a side each, they carried the injured pilot toward the rivers edge. Then the helicopter fuel exploded. Boom!

From the concussion, all three were blown over in the river. Instantly, the two soldiers stcrambled to their feet and, lifting the injured pilot, they headed for the riverbank.

Mannie, Pucky, and Chappy cheered as they watched the smoke streaming out of the upturned hull. To their surprise, they saw two soldiers help the pilot out of the downed helicopter into the river just before it exploded.

Pucky and Chappy opened fire. The first soldier went down on the edge of the river. Jamie, the second soldier, took the weight of the pilot as another volley was fired at them.

Jamie felt the thud as the pilot took a bullet in the back.

The pilot's head flipped back then forward with the impact and then went limp.

John and Tui reached the edge of the bush. They, too, were blown over onto their backs with the concussion of the explosion. They quickly leaped back onto their feet and saw one soldier go down, but the other, supporting the pilot, kept coming. John recognized the soldier supporting the pilot and called to him, "Jamie. Up here, mate."

Jamie managed to drag the pilot up into the bush. John and Tui rushed to help Jamie lower the pilot to the ground. Tui put his forefinger to the pilot's neck, searching for a pulse. There was none.

"He's gone. Shit...!"

John glanced downstream and saw Mannie and his men charging up toward them. He pointed to the bush. "We'll have to leave him. Come on."

They picked up the pilot's body and carried him into the undergrowth where they laid him down out of sight. Tui then led them at a run into the bush.

They had gone a short distance when Tui stopped, pointing to his right. "We'll change direction and go north for a bit then we'll head back to the river. That should stuff them up for a while."

John grabbed Jamie by the arm. "You okay?"

Jamie nodded and followed Tui and John into the bush.

* * * * *

In the National Park Police Station, Dave and Jim were in a dilemma as to what they could do next.

"What the hell do we do now?" Dave shouted, panicking. "Geez, bloody hell...!"

Jim picked up the phone and rang the Waiouru Military Base. "What the hell happens now?"

"We have another Iroquois fuelling up as we speak," the duty officer came back. "They should be ready to leave in approximately ten minutes."

"Thank God for that," Jim replied, relieved. "There's a bloody war going on up there."

"Keep your VHF radio tuned in. We'll keep you informed. They'll be ready for them this time. These boys are SAS."

"Thanks for that," Jim said and hung up. He looked at Dave. "They're sending in the SAS."

* * * * *

Smithy made it to his vehicle but was completely out of breath. He quickly found the keys, opened the Hilux, and picked up the microphone.

"Number one to base. Number one to base. Do you copy? Over."

Jim immediately recognized the voice. "Base here. That you, Smithy? Over."

"Yeah. I'm at the Hilux at Pokaka. I need someone to come and pick me up. I'll leave the vehicle here for the other two if they make it out. Over."

Dave immediately volunteered to go and pick him up. "Wait there, Smithy. Dave's on his way. He'll be there shortly. Over."

"Jim. Ernie didn't make it. He's been shot. Over."

"You mean he's dead...? Over."

"Afraid so. Over."

"You okay? I mean, you're not injured yourself, are you? Over."

"No. No, I'm okay. Just need to get out of here. Over."

"You sit tight, Smithy. Dave'll be there ASAP. Over."

"Okay. Over and out."

Smithy locked the Hilux, put the keys back under the front bumper, and then went and hid out of sight in the thick scrub beside the railway line.

Twenty-five minutes later, Dave cautiously pulled into the siding beside the railway line. Smithy hurried out of the scrub and jumped up into the Landcruiser as Dave reversed back and spun around.

Smithy slammed the door. "Let's get the hell outta here."

The back tyres spun in the loose metal and they shot out onto the road.

"You okay?" Dave asked sombrely.

"Yeah, I'm fine," Smithy answered. "You were right about those buggers. If it hadn't been for your two mates, I'd be dead as a bloody doornail, just like poor old Ernie."

"Is John and Tui okay?"

"Right now, I don't know," Smithy replied, shaking his head. "All we can do is hope. There's a war going on by the sound of all the firing."

"The helicopter crashed. Did you hear that?" Dave asked.

"Yeah. It made one hell of a bang."

CHAPTER 20

Mannie grinned victoriously at the sight of the helicopter on its side and the two dead soldiers lying in the river and then at the third dead soldier lying on the edge of the riverbank. Waving his arm forward, he raced off into the bush. "Come on. Those bastards can't be far. We've got them now."

Chappy immediately chased after Mannie. Nga Rangi put his hand up stopping Tuku, Himi, Pucky, and Marlene.

Puzzled, Pucky looked at Nga Rangi and asked, "What's wrong?"

Nga Rangi replied, pointing at Mannie and Chappy racing off into the bush, "Mannie's what's wrong. We came here to get away from this shit, not carry it on."

"Got no choice," Pucky said and chased after Chappy and Mannie.

Having gone a hundred metres, Mannie glanced back. Chappy was standing beside him with only Pucky following.

"Where's the others?" he asked as Pucky stopped in front of him.

Frowning, Pucky glanced back and said, "Gone dog on us."

"What...?" Mannie asked, unsure what he meant.

Pucky stepped back nervously, not knowing how Mannie would react.

Mannie's face twisted bitterly as he stormed back through the bush and went directly up to Nga Rangi. Unexpectedly, he pushed Nga Rangi in the chest, sending him crashing to the ground. Marlene let out a scream. He glared at her. "Shut up, bitch," he snapped and then turned his attention to Nga Rangi. "What the fuck's wrong with you all of a sudden?" he snapped, glaring threateningly down at Nga Rangi. "Lost your balls or somethin'?"

Leaping to his feet, Nga Rangi rushed up to Mannie and thumped him in the chest with both hands. "You trying to start another Maori war?" he shouted in Mannie's face. "We came here to get away from this shit." Again, he shoved Mannie in the chest.

Mannie went to punch Nga Rangi, but Nga Rangi blocked. Mannie shouted, "What's wrong with you all of a sudden?"

"Nothing's wrong with me," Nga Rangi said remorselessly. "It's you that's the problem."

Mannie's eyes bulged with rage, not used to having his authority questioned so forcefully.

Again, Nga Rangi shoved him in the chest. "Look what's happened here, and for what, eh? We've killed enough people and I'm sick of it." He pointed to Marlene, Himi, and Tuku. "We're all sick of it." He shook his head, disgusted. "Now the army's involved. We've wrecked one of their choppers." He shouted into Mannie's face, "Where do you think this is all gonna end?" Again, Nga Rangi shoved him in the chest. "What the hell you think's gonna happen now?"

Marlene butted in, "We all know how much Jo meant to you but do you have to carry on like a bloody maniac?"

"Shut up, bitch!" Mannie shouted. "Don't you talk about Jo like that."

"Leave her out of it," Nga Rangi cut in.

"Says who?"

"I do. This is between you and me."

Mannie tried to compose himself. "Okay, now listen up," he said, pointing at Nga Rangi. "This gutless prick's lost it. Gone dog on us. He's no fuckin' good to anyone."

Nga Rangi stood his ground. Tuku and Himi walked slowly over and stood beside him. Marlene was already standing beside Nga Rangi and lifted her chin rebelliously.

Mannie snarled, "So, there's a split in the bloody ranks, eh? Have we come this far to just give up now?"

No one answered.

"Eh...? Have we?"

Marlene interrupted, "Geez, Mannie. Can't you see how futile this is?"

He looked at her and bellowed. "Useless bloody bitch. Shut your bloody mouth." He cast a menacing eye at Nga Rangi. "As for you, you gutless wonder. What the fuck's wrong with you. We came here to do a bloody job."

Nga Rangi stared venomously into Mannie's eyes. "And what bloody job's that, eh? Kill as many people as we can? Is that what you want?"

What really unsettled Mannie most was having his authority questioned. He knew Tuku and Himi would always side with Nga Rangi. His eyes narrowed maliciously as he looked at all four. "You gutless fuckin' cowards, the lotta ya."

Nga Rangi looked around at the group and then pointed to Mannie. "You stay with this murdering bastard and you'll finish up dead for sure."

Again, Mannie snarled at him, "What a lotta shit." He threw an arm in the air. "What a lotta bullshit."

Courageously, Nga Rangi stood his ground. "We've killed a cop, one of those guys we've been chasing, not to mention four or so army fellahs. And apart from that, we've wrecked their bloody chopper." He threw his arms in the air. "You call that bullshit?"

Marlene cut in, sick of Mannie's intimidating attitude. "Don't forget the three last year."

"Yeah, that's right," Nga Rangi added regretfully. "And let's not forget the three hunters you murdered last year." Disgusted, Nga Rangi shook his head and then looked at Chappy and Pucky, hoping they might side with him. "You know, we had it made up here. We really had a chance of making something that would benefit us all." He stabbed a finger at Mannie angrily. "We were doing really well until this maniac decided to declare war on everyone who came in here."

He shook his fist in Mannie's face. "We actually could've made it, we really could've." Again, he pushed Mannie in the chest. "But you had to be the big man. Always gotta be the big man." Dropping his voice a decibel, he went on. "What chance do we have now? One-way ticket to the bloody slammer."

∗   ∗   ∗   ∗   ∗

John, Tui, and Jamie were almost back at the river. They heard loud voices and stopped to listen. "You hear that...?" he whispered. "Shouting. Someone's shouting."

"Yeah. Wonder what's goin' on?" John replied warily.

"They must be having a dispute," Tui added. "Let's get closer, eh?"

Jamie, lifting an eyebrow in disbelief, suggested, "Shouldn't we take advantage of the distraction and get the hell outta here...?"

John had a gut feeling. "Something's not right. I'd like to see what's going on."

"You sure...? They're trying to kill us."

"Yeah. I know, and I am sure."

They crept quietly through the bush to where they had a clear view of the group. Ahead, they could see Nga Rangi facing Mannie; obviously both men were very angry at each other.

Pucky and Chappy were standing beside Mannie, Marlene, Himi, and Tuku beside Nga Rangi.

Mannie's temper erupted. He swung his rifle butt at Nga Rangi's head, but Nga Rangi ducked and managed to push him away.

Mannie exploded into a rage, shouting at Nga Rangi, "Fuck you, you fuckin' coward! You and that fuckin' bitch of yours are full of shit!"

John glanced at Tui. "Having a major dispute all right."

"Wonder what's happened?"

"I'd say some of them want out," John replied.

"Could be right. There's two standing beside that tattooed bastard and three beside the other guy."

Pucky suddenly brought his rifle up, pointing it at Nga Rangi and the other three. "Drop your rifles, you gutless arseholes."

Tuku, Himi, and Marlene stood there, shocked; and for a moment, they just stared at him. Again, Pucky shouted, "I'm not kiddin'! Drop your fuckin' rifles!"

A malicious grin crossed Mannie's face. He nodded approvingly to Pucky, happy to have gained the advantage.

Pucky grinned musingly, pleased with having impressed Mannie.

Mannie pointed his rifle at Nga Rangi's head, shouting, "Do as he says or I'll blow your fuckin' head off, then I'll waste the rest of you, you gutless bloody cock-suckin' cowards!"

* * * * *

"Time we upped the odds," John said and tapped Tui's shoulder. "You get behind that bugger with the rifle. We'll get behind the tattooed bugger."

Tui nodded and quickly made his way quietly through the bush. John and Jamie crept slowly forward.

With resentment etched in his face, Mannie said, "I thought we were friends, you and me. We were such good friends once."

Rebelliously and unafraid, Nga Rangi replied, "Correction. Used to be. Used to be, arsehole, but not any more. You're obsessed with this Maori land rubbish. Can't you see it's not gonna work? None of us will walk away from this now. Not one of us."

"We still have time to get these bastards," Mannie said, trying to maintain a calm voice and appease Nga Rangi. "We've got to stop them getting out. We'll make plans after that."

"Listen to yourself, will you? Just can't help it, can you?" Nga Rangi snapped back. "Why do you want them all dead?"

"Two reasons," Mannie snapped. "They're stealing our meat and Amohia's great grandfather murdered my great grandfather. It's time I evened up that score."

"That's your score to settle, not ours. Don't we have a choice?"

Mannie said with an evil grin, "Too late for choices now, mate. Way too late for that. You've already made your choice." He smiled, shaking his head. "Not a good one."

"Amohia's one of us," Nga Rangi said defiantly. "We're not gonna kill one of our own." Frowning, he glanced around at Pucky and Chappy and then back at Mannie. "You don't care about us. You couldn't give a shit about what happens to any of us. So long as you get your bloody revenge." Nga Rangi shook his head. "You're stuffed in the bloody head. Completely insane. Did you know that?"

Mannie answered bitterly, "And you're pushin' your luck a bit too far, shit head."

"We've had enough of this bullshit. You only have Pucky

and Chappy. They're not the smartest monkeys in the tree either. You'll need more than those two to get Amohia."

Not liking the insult on his intellect, Pucky took a step toward Nga Rangi and shouted, "Who're you callin' a monkey?"

"Work that one out for yourself."

Himi got a spurt of courage. "Two short of a six-pack, I'd say."

Without warning, Pucky drove his rifle butt into the side of Himi's head. "I wouldn't say you were the smartest one around here either, drongo."

Himi went down. Marlene, shocked at Pucky's reaction, eyed him narrowly. "Can't you see this is not going to work out? You're as bad as him," she said, pointing at Mannie and then bent down and helped Himi back to his feet. Blood oozed from a gash just above Himi's ear.

Pucky lifted his rifle butt and feigned a move at her. "Shut up, bitch or you'll get the same."

Smiling, Mannie said smugly, "You lot aren't doin' that well, are you?" Forcing a laugh, he stepped up close to Nga Rangi. "In fact, from where I'm standing, I'd say you're completely stuffed."

CHAPTER 21

Jamie slid slowly forward on his stomach, getting in behind a manuka tree where he had a clear line of fire at the whole group.

John waited for his signal. Jamie gave the thumbs-up, indicating he was ready.

John passed his rifle to Jamie and then stepped out into the clearing behind Mannie. He called out, "I disagree, Te Ngongo. From where I'm standing, I wouldn't say he was completely stuffed."

Startled, Mannie jerked around at John's voice. He stood there for a moment, dumbfounded.

Pucky swung his rifle around, pointing it at John.

Tui stepped out of the bush behind him and Chappy. "Drop your rifles, all of you."

John was five metres from Mannie, and, forcing a smile, he said, "I'd do as he says if I was you guys. He's pretty nervous, especially with you buggers trying to kill us."

Pucky and Chappy glanced at Mannie, looking for direction but got none. Tui brought his M16 up to the firing position and shouted threateningly, "Drop them now or I'll put a bullet between your eyes, the pair of you."

Unsure what to do, Pucky and Chappy reluctantly

dropped their rifles. The sudden appearance of the very men they were chasing caught them off balance and completely by surprise.

"Now step back," Tui ordered.

Reluctantly, they stepped back away from their rifles.

Tui went forward and kicked their rifles behind him and then called to Mannie, "Hey, pig face. Are you deaf or something? I said drop your rifle."

Mannie cast a hostile eye at him.

John put his hand up in a gesture, meaning, forget it. Tui remembered what John had done to Mannie's rifle the previous day and stepped back behind Puck and Chappy.

John studied the group for several seconds. They were very grubby; their clothes were tattered and torn. They were all in desperate need of a shower. Nga Rangi, Marlene, Tuku, and Himi's faces said it all. They wanted out.

John nodded to Nga Rangi, indicating that he understood what had been happening. He then concentrated on Mannie.

"Looks like you're on your own," he said, forcing another smile. He studied Mannie's face for a second. "And those tats," he continued, shaking his head. "Man, you look pathetic, like a stupid clown at some run-down circus. You haven't grown up since you were a snotty-nosed kid."

"They represent my whanau," Mannie snapped.

"I've never heard such crap in my life," John replied. "Your family were a bunch of no-hopers."

"Don't go looking for trouble, John," Jamie cut in. Worried, he glanced at Tui.

Tui noticed his concern and said reassuringly, "It's okay, Jamie."

Mannie couldn't fathom out what they were on about and, without warning, swung his rifle up, pointing it at John. "Fuck you, Amohia!" he shouted and pulled the trigger. There was a loud click as the broken firing pin fell short of the detonator in the cartridge.

Jamie was aiming directly at Mannie's chest, about to pull the trigger, but again, John put his hand up.

Immediately, Mannie ejected the unspent cartridge and drove another into the breech and, aiming at John, pulled the trigger. To his horror, there was only a loud click.

Jamie's finger quivered on his trigger, ready to fire. "What the hell're you doing, John...?"

Tui glanced at him. "It's okay."

"You sure?"

"Yeah," Tui replied.

Confused, Mannie stared down at his rifle, not understanding why it wouldn't fire.

John pointed to the ejected cartridge. "Go on, pick it up. Take a good look at it."

Mannie picked up a cartridge and studied it.

John said calmly, "Remember when I dropped you in the bush?" He pointed over his shoulder with his thumb upstream. "Or can't you remember? It was yesterday."

After studying the cartridge, Mannie realized there wasn't a dent in the detonator. He thought back briefly at when he had fired at the helicopter. It had clicked then. He stood there, staring at John.

Then they heard thumping on the air. Instinctively, Mannie looked to the sky. The helicopter was way off in the distance, out of view, but heading toward them.

"Fuck you!" Mannie cursed. "Fuck you to hell, Amohia!"

Jamie stepped out from behind the manuka tree and fired a flare in the air.

Knowing only too well his time was running out, Mannie threw the cartridge at John.

John ducked to one side and then drew his stainless-steel SAS survival knife and pointed to the serrated edge. "That old blunderbuss of yours hasn't got a firing pin. I broke it off yesterday, with this." John re-sheathed his knife.

Not able to contain his fury, Mannie swung the butt of his rifle at John's head. John sidestepped and punched Mannie on the temple and then, with his foot, tripped him as he staggered back.

Mannie fell flat on his face in the dirt three metres from where Himi and Tuku were standing beside Nga Rangi and Marlene. Before anyone could react, Mannie leaped to his feet and dove, wrapping his left arm around Tuku's neck; and then drawing his hunting knife with his right, he held it to Tuku's throat.

Tui had him in his sights but couldn't risk a shot for fear of hitting Tuku.

Tuku screamed and tried to pull away, but Mannie held firm. "Geez, Man. Are you crazy?"

"Shut up, dip-stick!"

John hadn't expected this turn of events and had to think quickly. It was obvious Mannie had no consideration for anyone's life, including his two loyal friends, Pucky and Chappy.

"Some great leader you turned out to be. You used them to serve your own selfish means. You couldn't give a shit about these people, so long as you got what you want. What an arsehole." He glanced at Pucky and Chappy and sensed their indecision at Mannie's unpredictable moods.

"I bet you haven't the guts to take me on, Te Ngongo, man to man," he said, trying to entice Mannie into a duel, hoping he would release Tuku. He could see the fear in Tuku's eyes. Drawing his survival knife, he took a step closer to Mannie. "Just like your dumb old great grandfather was all those years ago. Thick as pig shit."

Jamie tried to intervene. "Don't be stupid, John."

John glanced back. "He wants a fight. I'll give him one."

Mannie snarled and then, unexpectedly, heaved Tuku

forward. Tuku tripped and sprawled on the ground in front of Nga Rangi. Nga Rangi helped him to his feet and took him back to stand beside Marlene.

Mannie knew this would be his last chance to get even with Amohia. He had to take it if nothing else. The helicopter was closing in on them and this time, the soldiers would not be so easily dispensed with.

In the warrior tradition, Mannie poked out his tongue and drew his hunting knife. "Haaaa! I'm gonna gut you like a fish, arsehole."

Slowly, he walked to the centre of the small clearing. "My great grandfather was a great warrior."

Mannie's eyes were dilated with his hatred and loathing. He spat on the ground in front of John. "I'm gonna spill your guts in the dirt then feed them down your fuckin' throat."

Again, he spat on the ground. "At least my ancestors didn't lick the arses of the pakeha. They had pride, not like your swindling fuckin' lot."

Moving cautiously around the centre of the clearing, Mannie faked a move, slashing at John's abdomen. "You're an arse licker, Amohia. Just like your fuckin' old great grandfather was. A fuckin' pakeha arse licker."

Again, Mannie darted forward, slashing at John's abdomen; but John was ready and stepped back.

"Be careful, John," Tui warned. "Watch him, mate."

Mannie circled, shifting the grip on his knife from one hand to the other. "Fuckin' arse licker."

Suddenly, Mannie lunged forward, but John anticipated the move and stepped back away from him, and then, unexpectedly, he struck like a puff-adder and punched Mannie in the face.

Stunned, Mannie reeled back, shaking his head at the unexpected powerful blow.

Mockingly, John forced a grin. "You must be sick of being punched in the head, Te Ngongo."

Mannie glanced across at Tui guarding the others. An idea came to him. Without taking his eyes off John, he began circling the clearing, little by little, a bit at a time. As he drew parallel with Tui, he faked a move at John and then, unpredictably, spun on his heel and plunged his knife into Tui's abdomen.

"Who're you calling pig face, shit for brains?" Mannie sniggered and then, head-butting Tui in the face, he ripped his knife out of Tui's stomach. Stunned, Tui dropped his rifle, his legs folded under him, and he went down on his knees.

John lunged forward; but Mannie, anticipating his move, was ready and slashed viciously at him. John withdrew managing to side step Mannie's knife.

Tui's mind slipped on the edge of conscious thought. He collapsed forward and fell to the ground. Blood oozed out between his fingers and began to pool around him.

John, devastated at seeing his friend lying on the ground with blood pooling around him, called out, "Tui...! Tui."

Jamie, rushing to Tui's aid, put his rifle down beside him, threw off his backpack, and took out a field dressing. He tore open Tui's shirt and held the field dressing tightly over the deep wound to stifle the flow of blood.

Pucky, taking advantage of the moment, tapped Chappy's hand and then pointed with his eyes at their rifles.

Chappy acknowledged with a flash of his eyebrows. Together, doing a somersault roll, they dove at their rifles, picked them up and in the same move, leaped to their feet, pointing their rifles at Nga Rangi, Marlene, Tuku, and Himi.

Jamie made a grab for his steyer, but Pucky had him covered. "Leave it!" he shouted. Jamie froze. There was nothing he could do and he felt like such an idiot. Cautiously, Pucky went over and picked up Jamie's Steyer.

Mannie grinned. "Didn't expect that did you, arse licker, and your mate's not doing too well either, is he?"

With John's concentration distracted, Mannie seized the opportunity and, faking a move, lunged at John. John stepped back but couldn't help glancing across at Tui, dropping his concentration. Mannie dashed forward unexpectedly, his knife slicing John's left forearm.

John winced at the sting of the cut. Blood quickly soaked his shirt sleeve. With ferocious intensity, an overwhelming surge for revenge charged through his body like a runaway freight train.

Mannie sniggered, "Didn't expect that either, did you arse licker?"

"You murdering piece of shit," John said, his emotions so powerful he felt he would explode.

Again, Mannie lunged forward, slashing at John's abdomen. Anticipating the move and in a well-calculated manoeuvere, John pulled back away from the arch of Mannie's blade and then darted forward, pushing Mannie's knife hand aside with his left. In the same move, he wrapped his blood-soaked left arm around Mannie's right arm above the elbow and, locking his grip, lifted up with all his strength and then head-butted Mannie in the face.

Mannie staggered, almost losing his balance, but John's arm was locked, vicelike, holding him. John then brought the butt of his survival knife down hard on Mannie's forehead, stunning him, cutting the skin to the bone.

Mannie involuntarily screamed out at the sharp stab of pain of the brutal blow. Instantly, blood pouring from the wound ran down his face like a small rivulet and dripped off his chin.

John quickly sheathed his survival knife. Reaching around his body, he took Mannie's knife from his hand, and then, tossing it on the ground, he applied a cruel wristlock, forcing Mannie over at an awkward angle.

Crouched down beside Tui, Jamie rolled him onto his

back and applied another field dressing, desperately trying to stem the bleeding. Tui had gone into shock and was trembling uncontrollably.

The sound of the army Iroquois coming in to land on the riverbank upstream caused Pucky and Chappy to anxiously look north.

Taking advantage of the distraction, Himi went at Chappy and took him in a rugby tackle around the legs. The two crashed to the ground, both struggling with the rifle. Pucky, jumping across to Chappy's defense, drove his rifle butt into the back of Himi's head, knocking him semi-unconscious.

Chappy, rolling onto his hands and knees, jumped to his feet and kicked Himi in the ribs with all his weight. Himi let out a painful groan, clutching his abdomen, his breathing erratic from the force of Pucky's kick.

Angry, Pucky pointed his rifle at Nga Rangi. "Anyone try something' like that again, I'll waste the fuckin' lot of you." He glanced across at Mannie. John had him in a wristlock, totally disabled. With indecision he began to panic and called to Chappy. "What the hell do we do?"

Chappy was in a panic also. "Dunno, but we gotta do somethin' soon or we're gonna be stuffed." He called to John, "Hey, Amohia. Let him go or I'll put a bullet in your guts."

John, with all his concentration on Mannie, didn't hear or, if he did, ignored him.

At that moment and out the corner of his eye, Nga Rangi saw two SAS soldiers slip silently out of the scrub to the right of Pucky and Chappy but behind their line of vision. They went down on one knee on the edge of the clearing, their steyer rifles at the ready.

Realizing the situation instantly, Nga Rangi created a diversion and said mockingly, "You buggers are nothing without a rifle."

Pucky glared at him, his mouth screwed up with anger. "Don't push your luck, arsehole."

Then two more SAS soldiers dashed past the first two, their rifles slung over their shoulders.

Catching the movement in the corner of his eye, Pucky swung his rifle, but he was a split second too late.

Taking Pucky's rifle barrel in one hand, the stock in the other, the SAS soldier drove the butt up into Pucky's face, breaking his nose and sending him staggering backward, off balance.

Then Chappy, realizing what was happening, swung his rifle around, but as he did so, Pucky crashed into him.

The second SAS soldier grabbed Chappy's rifle with both hands and flipped him over face down in the dirt. In the same move, the soldier drove his knee down hard between Chappy's shoulder blades, knocking the wind out of him. He shouted. "Stay down! Don't move!" The sudden attack from the SAS soldiers had taken less than six seconds.

Pucky and Chappy's wrists were tightly wrapped with duct tape. With blood streaming from his nose, Pucky shouted at the SAS soldier, "You broke my bloody nose."

"Shut it," was the only sympathy he got. The soldier spoke quietly into his intercom.

John, with Mannie in a wristlock, drew his foot back and kicked him under the chin with such force, his legs flew out from under him and he crashed down hard on his back.

John, keeping the pressure on Mannie's wrist, twisted it even further. Screaming in agony, Mannie was forced over face down in the dirt. John leaned down and whispered into his ear, "I should slit your throat, you murdering bucket of shit, and save the courts a lot of trouble." He paused momentarily, trying to control his rage. "You and your great grandfather are one and the same. Both thick as pig shit." He thumped the side of Mannie's head with his foot. "There's nothing here between your ears but hate."

"This is Maori land!" Mannie shouted into the dust.

John, looking down at the tattooed blood-covered face, said, "It hasn't been Maori land for over a 130 years. And another thing, warriors in the old days earned their tattoos like a badge of honour for battles they'd fought in and won. You're not even worth the smell of a warrior's fart, you murdering bastard. Your mother never gave birth to you. She shit you out."

A medic rushed into the clearing and went down on one knee beside Tui. He spoke briefly into his wireless radio receiver. Forty seconds later, another soldier burst into the clearing, carrying a stretcher. He lay the stretcher down beside Tui and together, the two medics eased him onto it and then, picking him carefully up, hurried off to the awaiting helicopter.

John let Mannie's wrist go and stepped back. He called to one of the soldiers, "Duct tape this bastard's wrists tight as you can. Don't want him getting loose."

Jamie took John by the arm and led him to the medic. The medic rolled John's shirtsleeve up and quickly bandaged his arm.

"Tui gonna be all right?" John asked sombrely.

The medic shook his head. "Don't know, John. He's bleeding pretty bad internally. We'll have to keep our fingers crossed."

John looked up as the helicopter lifted above the bush, heading for the Taumarunui hospital.

A soldier went over to Mannie with the roll of duct tape and was about to tie his hands behind his back, when Mannie suddenly drove his fist into the soldier's croutch. In a last-ditch effort at getting away, he took hold of the soldier's Steyer rifle, then doing a somersault roll, he came up beside Marlene. She screamed as he grabbed a handful of her hair and pointed the Steyer at her head. "Stay back or the fuckin' bitch dies!"

he shouted. "Make one false move and the bitch gets it in the head. Do you hear me?"

John and Mannie's eyes met, their hatred for each other burned so deep it showed on their faces. Mannie said in a low menacing tone, "You know I'll do it, Amohia, so tell your men to keep back."

Mannie put the Steyer over Marlene's shoulder and, releasing three fingers on the pistol grip but still pointing it at John, grabbed Marlene's hair with the three fingers and retrieved his hunting knife from the ground and sheathed it. Then with the Steyer in his right hand and with a solid grip on Marlene's hair with his left, using her as a shield, he retreated backward toward the bush. Nga Rangi took a step toward him.

John put his hand up. "Stay where you are. He'll kill her for sure."

"Too right I'll kill the useless bitch!" Mannie shouted, "Stay back!"

Nga Rangi, distraught with fear for Marlene's safety, glanced at John.

"Don't move," John advised him.

Nga Rangi could see the desperation and fear in Marlene's eyes, but he was powerless to help.

Mannie, pausing on the edge of the bush, said threateningly, "If anybody tries to stop me, the bitch gets it in the head." And then looking at John, he shouted, "Understand?"

With that, he and Marlene disappeared into the bush. Immediately, Mannie swung her around and pushed her to a run. "Get going, bitch. You slow me down and I'll blow your fuckin' head off. Got that?" Mannie pulled her head back when she didn't answer. He shouted in her ear, "You hear me, bitch?"

CHAPTER 22

Nga Rangi cast a desperate eye at John. "You gonna let him take her?"

"If we'd made a move, he'd have shot her," John replied. There was no doubt he had to go after Mannie and get the girl back. He pointed to two soldiers, Marc and Glen. "You two, come with me. We're going after them. But remember, we'll have to keep our distance or he'll kill her for sure," John added, and then glanced at Nga Rangi. "We'll bring her back, don't you worry."

"You're not going without me," Nga Rangi pleaded. "That's my wife the murdering son of a slimy pig's got. You'll have to kill me first."

John shook his head. "Look, I'm sorry, but I can't let you come. You'll have to stay here with the others."

"He's got my wife!" Nga Rangi screamed.

"I know and I'm sorry," John replied sombrely. "You were part of all this in the first place."

"Yeah," Nga Rangi agreed. "But we didn't know this was going to happen when we came here."

Tuku stepped forward in Nga Rangi's defense. "He actually tried to stop this bullshit. That's how we finished up like this."

John stabbed a finger at Nga Rangi. "Look. You stay here. We'll get her back." Then turning to Jamie, he said, "Make sure he stays here. Tie him up if you have to."

Without warning, Nga Rangi raced off into the bush. John knew there was no way he was going to catch him. He pointed at Tuku and Himi and said to Jamie, "Make sure they stay here."

John led Marc and Glen into the bush at a run.

$$* \quad * \quad * \quad * \quad *$$

Mannie, with Marlene running ahead of him, rushed through the bush as fast as they could. They came to the shortcut to the plateau. He swung Marlene around by the hair, pointing her up the track.

Unwittingly, Marlene stumbled. Mannie gave her hair a sharp tug. "You slow me down, bitch, I'll slit your fuckin' throat where you stand."

Marlene was breathing heavily, suffering from the stitch, and knew if she did anything stupid, Mannie wouldn't hesitate to kill her.

$$* \quad * \quad * \quad * \quad *$$

Nga Rangi was running as fast as he could, trying to catch up with Mannie and Marlene. Without a weapon, he was next to useless, but he had to at least try. He couldn't just let Mannie take her, knowing only too well now what he was capable of. He was vicious and unpredictable and felt very much afraid for her.

Nga Rangi slowed at the shortcut and saw the fresh footprints. To him, it was obvious where they were heading. He decided to carry on north along the river. He had more of a chance of surprising Mannie by going up the steep face by the waterfall.

John was leading Marc and Glen, following Mannie and Marlene's footprints. They were fresh and easy to follow. They came to the spot where Nga Rangi had come out onto the track ahead of them, heading north.

Cursing, he glanced back at Marc and Glen, pointing at Nga Rangi's fresh prints. "Shit...! The girl's husband is ahead of us. Damn it."

John crouched down to study the footprints when they came to the shortcut that led to the main western track. There were two sets clearly going up; another set continued toward the river.

Warily he said to Marc and Glen. "The husband's staying along the river. We'll stay with the tattooed bugger and the girl. Come on."

*   *   *   *   *

Mannie was keeping a close watch behind. He was full of bitterness and resentment at the way John had outwitted him in every way. Desperate and angry, he shoved Marlene in the back. "Keep going, bitch. Keep going."

"I could run faster if you'd let my hair go," she said, almost losing her footing from the heavy shove. "You keep pushing me off balance."

"Let you go...? Not likely, bitch." Scowling, Mannie gave her another shove in the back. "Shut up and keep going."

*   *   *   *   *

Over the last twelve months Nga Rangi had travelled this track many times. Without even losing his stride, he leaped over the fallen rotten tree trunk and came out onto the riverbank. Stitch, a constant pain in his side, was plaguing him and was slowly beginning to take its toll. With sheer determination, he forced himself to run through it, knowing it would eventually dissipate if he kept going. It was painful but he couldn't slow down. Not now.

*   *   *   *   *

Two hundred metres before the plateau, a tree root on the track tripped Marlene, and she sprawled, face down, in the centre of the track.

Caught unaware, Mannie fell over the top of her and unwittingly released her hair. In an attempt to escape, Marlene rolled onto her feet, but Mannie was on his feet equally as quick and drew his hunting knife.

He stood there for a moment, just staring at her, his eyes black with hatred. Marlene thought he was going to kill her right there and then.

Instead, Mannie backhanded her across the face with his left hand. She stumbled backward, screaming and fell into the undergrowth. "Try that again, bitch, and I'll spill your guts all over this track." He stood over her menacingly, knife in hand. "Get up or I'll gut you right here, you useless bloody bitch."

Desperate and breathing heavily with fear, Marlene was suffering from stitch and was inadvertently bent over, wincing at the pain.

Mannie sheathed his knife and picked up the Steyer. Grabbing another handful of her hair, he heaved her to her feet and shook her so violently she thought he was going to break her neck. He snarled, "Try that again you fuckin' slut and you're dead. No more second chances. Now, start running."

*   *   *   *   *

John, Marc, and Glen were only sixty metres behind them when they heard Marlene scream. John put his hand up to stop. "They're just up ahead. Keep your eyes peeled."

Cautiously, they continued, but at a slower pace, their eyes searching the surrounding bush ahead.

* * * * *

Nga Rangi was rounding the big sweeping bend, running as fast as he could, holding his hand to his side. The pain of stitch was intense, but he had to keep going; his only thoughts were of Marlene. Upon reaching the base of the steep face, he paused, bent over for several long seconds, gasping for breath.

He looked up at the top and, taking a deep breath, began the hard climb, grabbing hold of short scrub and rubbishy plants, pulling himself up, going hand over hand.

* * * * *

Mannie and Marlene raced out onto the plateau. Smoke still lingered in the air from the burned-out meetinghouse and huts. The meetinghouse was now a pile of smouldering rubble. Mannie gazed around at the destruction of what had once been their home.

With a strong grip on Marlene's hair, he dragged her to his hut to look at the devastation. The roof beams had burned through, and with the weight of the soil on top, they had caved in. He began to curse, his mouth twisting bitterly. "Fuck. Fuck...! Look at it all. Fuckin' gone, all because you and that useless shithead of a bloody husband wanted out."

Looking through the other huts, he could see most of their hard work had been reduced to ash; nothing had been spared. Where the roofs have caved in and in other places, what was left of the timber frames were still smouldering. Smoke hung over the valley like a huge blanket, trailing off into the distance toward the mountain.

Cursing, he backhanded Marlene across the face, knocking her to the ground. She let out another scream. "Fuck you, you useless fuckin' bitch." He grabbed her hair again and pulled her to her feet and then turning, pulled her backward across the plateau, using her as a shield, knowing John Amohia would not be very far behind.

* * * * *

From beside the still-smouldering meetinghouse, John, Marc and Glen looked out onto the plateau. Mannie was facing them but walking backward, pulling Marlene, by the hair with him, the Steyer pointing up at the end of the track. Mannie couldn't see them but knew they would most likely be there. He let go of Marlene's hair and wrapped his left arm tightly around her neck.

* * * * *

Nga Rangi reached the top totally exhausted. He was on the animal track just below the rim of the plateau. He saw Mannie with Marlene fifty metres away with his left arm around her neck, walking slowly backward toward him. All of Mannie's attention was on the bush up by the smouldering meetinghouse.

Nga Rangi ducked down out of sight and tried to catch his breath, his heart pounding like a jackhammer inside his chest from the exertion of the steep climb. He would be patient and wait with the hope that he would get an opportunity to take Mannie from behind.

John saw Nga Rangi along the rim of the plateau just before he ducked down out of sight. He glanced at Marc. "There's the husband along the edge. You see him?"

"Yeah," Marc replied and then glanced at Glen. "You see him?"

"I saw him. That tattooed bugger's heading straight for him."

"Hope he doesn't do anything stupid," John said anxiously. "I'll try and distract the tattooed bugger."

John called out, "Let the girl go, Te Ngongo. You can't get away with this. Surely you must know that."

"Take more than you to take me down, Amohia."

"You're out numbered. Use your head for once. Let the girl go."

"Fuck off, Amohia."

"Real Maori warriors don't hide behind women, Te Ngongo. Not in the old days, not now, not ever."

Mannie was thirty metres from the edge, still too far for Nga Rangi to mount a surprise attack.

John guessed what Nga Rangi had in mind. He turned to Glen and Marc. "Cover me. I'm gonna show myself to keep the tattooed bugger distracted." He stepped out of the bush with his rifle at his side.

"Real warriors show themselves, Te Ngongo," John mocked. "They don't hide behind women."

Mannie kept walking slowly backward, now fifteen metres from Nga Rangi.

Still too far, John surmised and called out again, "Only cowards hide behind women," he shouted, trying to hold Mannie's attention. "I can see you're nothing but a yellow-belly piece of shit."

Nga Rangi came up to a crouched position. Even with the element of surprise, Mannie was still too far away for a successful attack. Mannie Te Ngongo was no fool and not one to be underestimated.

"You're no warrior, Te Ngongo," John called again. "Neither was your dumb old great grandfather. You're living proof of that."

With his right hand holding the Steyer and his left hand around Marlene's neck, Mannie's finger quivered on the trigger, wanting so desperately to inflict serious injury on Amohia before he killed him. Marlene was choking from the tight hold Mannie had around her neck. She tried to pull his arm down away from her throat so she could get another breath, but the harder she pulled, the tighter he held her.

Not wanting to make a sound, Nga Rangi began creeping toward Mannie, picking his steps carefully.

Desperate now to breathe, Marlene struggled with Mannie's arm, twisting and struggling, on the verge of blacking out. She tried to cough to clear her throat. At that moment, out of the corner of her eye she caught a glimpse of Nga Rangi only four metres away. With eyes bulging from the huge surge of adrenaline, fear and the lack of air, her will to live kicked in; and she began struggling with fierce determination.

With her sudden burst of energy, Mannie's concentration was broken. As he glanced down at her, a movement to his left caught his eye. Nga Rangi was coming at him and he swung the Steyer around.

Marlene, afraid Nga Rangi would be shot, grabbed the barrel of the Steyer with both hands and pulled down, applying all her weight and strength. In a frantic attempt to make Mannie let go, she sunk her teeth into his forearm and bit down as hard as she could.

Mannie let out an agonizing scream as Marlene's teeth struck bone. Forced to let her go and defend himself, he brought his knee up hard into Marlene's face, momentarily stunning her. She released her grip on his arm, and he let go as she slumped to the ground.

Nga Rangi launched himself and tackled Mannie around the waist.

Locked together, they fell to the ground. Before Nga Rangi could gather himself, Mannie drove the butt of the rifle down hard between his shoulder blades, partially winding him. Nga Rangi quickly recovered and rolled onto Mannie's arm, holding the Steyer.

John was fifty metres away. Mannie scrambled to his feet and wrenched the rifle out from under Nga Rangi. Fearing for his own life, Nga Rangi reached up and grabbed the rifle in the centre of the stock. Mannie struggled with fanatic desperation, but Nga Rangi's grip was solid and he held on with all his strength.

Mannie's forefinger was caught in the trigger guard, and as the two men fought and struggled, the rifle accidentally fired twice.

Dirt flew up twelve metres to John's right. Shouldering his own rifle, he went to ground, aiming at Mannie.

Mannie managed to maintain a strong grip on the rifle. Nga Rangi was still on the ground, and as Mannie struggled against him with the rifle, he pulled himself to his feet.

Knowing it was futile to keep struggling with the rifle and wanting to get away before Amohia could get to him, he let the rifle go, sending Nga Rangi hurtling over backward onto the ground, still holding the Steyer.

John leaped to his feet and charged at Mannie. Marc and Glen burst out of the bush by the smouldering meetinghouse.

As Mannie raced for the edge of the plateau, Nga Rangi rolled onto his side and fired a quick shot at him.

Mannie felt the bullet strike his thigh. He lost his balance and fell, rolling twice, going for the edge of the plateau but came up short by two metres. His thigh wasn't painful. There was just a burning numbness.

Marc and Glen were running toward him with their

rifles in the firing position. John yelled, "Don't shoot! Don't shoot!"

Realizing how close he was to the edge, Mannie rolled and went over the short drop onto a narrow animal track. Scrambling to his feet and keeping low, he limped along the narrow track toward the river above the waterfall.

Nga Rangi was only a metre from Marlene. She was lying there, still stunned, rubbing her jaw where Mannie had kneed her in the face, unaware he was so close to her. She sat up slowly. Nga Rangi wrapped his arms around her and held her tightly. "You okay, sweetie?" he asked nervously.

"I think so," she croaked and shook her head to clear her vision.

John ran over to them. "Stay with her." Then he glanced back at the edge of the plateau. "We'll get the bugger. You take care of your lady."

Marlene looked up into Nga Rangi's dirty, blood-smeared face, still visually shaking from her harrowing ordeal. Her emotions took over as she put her arms around his neck and burst into tears. "Shit, mate, I thought you were dead there for a second."

"Thanks to your bravery, I'm okay," he said and kissed her bloodied cheek.

"I'm fine, I think," she replied, wiping the tears from her dirty blood-smeared face with the back of her hand.

Nga Rangi, happy that she was unhurt and okay for the moment, glanced along the edge, where Mannie had disappeared. He handed Marlene the rifle. "Here, you keep this just in case."

"You're not going after him," she pleaded and grabbed his arm. "Stay here with me. He's mad and dangerous, even without a rifle. He's got a knife."

"I'll be careful. Don't worry."

"Nga Rangi," she pleaded. "Don't go after him. He's completely mad."

"I'll be all right. Don't you worry," he said and touched her cheek with his palm. He turned, about to chase after Mannie.

Marlene grabbed his hand. "You're not going after him. Let the others get him. He's insane. He'll kill you, given half a chance. Stay here with me."

Nga Rangi turned and started to where Mannie had gone over the edge.

"Nga Rangi," Marlene croaked. "Stay here with me," she went on, with tears streaming down her cheeks. "He'll bloody kill you, you stubborn shit. Get your dumb arse back here."

CHAPTER 23

John and the two soldiers were searching to the right of where Mannie had gone over. John was afraid he might have already started down the steep face. Nga Rangi searched to the left. Looking down along the narrow animal track, he saw a hunting knife lying in the dirt. He recognized it as Mannie's.

Mannie had gone to ground in a small patch of scrub and ferns three metres down the steep face but still a short distance to the river. John, Marc, and Glen were searching the opposite direction.

Mannie saw Nga Rangi along the edge and went to draw his hunting knife, but his sheath was empty. He looked back along the animal track. Nga Rangi was standing there above his knife, glaring at him.

Jumping down onto the track, Nga Rangi began running toward him. John glanced back and saw Nga Rangi drop onto the animal track below the rim. He immediately knew he had seen Mannie.

As a last-ditch effort to get away, Mannie made a dash for the river above the waterfall. He scrambled up onto the narrow track and limped as fast as he could.

John suddenly saw him making for the river with Nga

Rangi in hot pursuit. He yelled to Nga Rangi at the top of his voice, "Back off! We've got him trapped!"

Nga Rangi, ignoring him, kept going. He had a personal score to settle with Mannie, and no one was going to stop him from doing what he had to do.

John sensed his determination and again, he yelled, "Back off! Back off, will you! He can't get away!"

Mannie reached the end of the track above the river and glanced back. Nga Rangi, running like a man possessed, was closing in on him fast. Time had run out. Nga Rangi would be on him in seconds. He braced himself for the imminent clash.

Nga Rangi tackled him around the thighs, and with his momentum, they went over the edge into the river.

The current caught as they fought and struggled against each other, rolling them over and over on the rocky bottom, taking them downstream. Mannie's eyes boggled when he saw the waterfall approaching only metres away.

Marlene saw them disappear from sight into the river. From where she was sitting, she couldn't quite see the river, but she knew they had to have gone in. Frantically, she tried shouting to John but could only croak. "They'll go over the waterfall."

John heard her and called back, "Don't worry! We'll get them!"

Nga Rangi struggled and fought his way around behind Mannie. Then locking his legs around Mannie's waist, his left arm around Mannie's neck, he applied a headlock.

Mannie was thrashing his arms and legs, trying desperately to break Nga Rangi's vicelike grip. He lashed out with his fist, but Nga Rangi clung to him like a leech. Suddenly, he felt the river bottom fall out from under them as they went over the waterfall.

Nga Rangi screamed in his ear as they fell, "You murdering piece of shit!"

Marlene scrambled to her feet and stumbled to the edge of the plateau and saw the two men, locked together, go over the waterfall. In disbelief, she put her hands over her mouth, trying to stifle her scream. "They've gone over the waterfall. Shit...! They'll drown...! Someone help them."

Nga Rangi took a deep breath as they plunged into the swirling, turbulent cavernous hole at the base of the waterfall and were driven deep into the whirling-washing machine action of the water. The current caught and carried them out away from the never-ending wall of water that plunged down on them.

They surfaced twenty metres downstream and as they broke the surface, Nga Rangi drew a deep breath and shouted in Mannie's ear, "You bastard! You murdering bloody bastard!"

John, Marc, and Glen were along the narrow animal track, trying to get a better view of the river below. John saw the two men surface. Mannie was thrashing around, trying to keep his head above water, but Nga Rangi brought his weight to bear over them, forcing them both under. Twenty seconds later they surfaced, and again, Nga Rangi brought his weight to bear over them, forcing them under.

John dropped onto his backside and began sliding down the steep face. It was quicker and easier. Marc and Glen followed suit.

"He's trying to drown the tattooed bugger," John said. "He's got balls. I'll give him that."

"He's tough all right," Glen added.

At the base, the three soldiers rushed out onto the riverbank as Nga Rangi forced them under again.

John could see they were still in three metres of water. "Too deep here," he said and pointed downstream. "It's shallower down further."

"The husband's going to drown that bugger if we don't get to them soon," Marc replied as the two men surfaced with Mannie's arms whirling in a splashing, thrashing frenzy. Again, Nga Rangi brought his weight over the top of them and forced them under.

Hurrying into shallower water, John, Marc, and Glen waded out ahead of the two struggling men.

Mannie felt the bottom with his feet and, with the last of his fading strength, pushed up. As they surfaced, instinctively he splashed and thrashed in an attempt to reach the riverbank, but Nga Rangi kept the pressure on with his headlock and, again, forced them under.

Mannie's lungs were burning from the lack of air. He rolled them over and, reaching behind, punched Nga Rangi's ribs in a desperate attempt to rid him from his back, but Nga Rangi held firm.

Sensing Mannie's intentions, Nga Rangi rolled them back, putting himself on top again, Mannie underneath.

Mannie's face was red as a beetroot from the pressure of Nga Rangi's headlock. He seized Nga Rangi's left arm with both his hands and pulled down with all his strength, but he couldn't break the vicelike hold.

John and Marc, in the river up to their chests, took hold of the two struggling men and began dragging them into the shallow water.

Mannie, having swallowed copious amounts of water, was choking and coughing, struggling to breathe.

Getting angry and frustrated with Nga Rangi for not letting go, John shouted at him, "We've got him now! We've got the bugger! Let him go! Let him go, for chrissake!"

Nga Rangi, face red with rage, refused to release his headlock. For him, Mannie had ruined not just his and Marlene's life but the lives of everyone in their group. He was a ruthless psychopath, a maniacal killer, and thought only of his own selfish twisted needs and didn't deserve to live.

It took the combined strength of Marc and John to break his grip on Mannie's neck. John then tried to drag him away from Mannie, but Nga Rangi still had his legs locked around Mannie's waist.

"For chrissake, release him!" John shouted angrily. "Let the bugger go, will you!"

Nga Rangi finally let go but not before he gave Mannie a powerful kick to the head.

John managed to drag him up onto the riverbank while Marc and Glen dragged Mannie to the river's edge, his chest heaving and gasping for breath, coughing and choking, completely exhausted. They picked him up bodily and dragged him onto the riverbank and laid him face down. Then stripping the bootlaces from his boots, they tied his hands behind his back.

Marlene, terrified and with her heart in her mouth, had been watching the struggle in the river from up on the edge of the plateau. Her major concern was that if Mannie broke free from Nga Rangi's headlock, he would kill him without hesitation. Now that the three soldiers had taken control and with Mannie and Nga Rangi now on the riverbank, she jumped down onto the narrow animal track and began her descent.

John pointed at Nga Rangi. "You stay where you are this time and don't move. We don't want another fiasco like this last one."

Upon hearing the helicopter hovering above them, John looked up and saw a soldier in the open cockpit door, pointing downstream.

"They want us to go down further," John said. "They'll pick us up down there."

Mannie was lying just two metres from Nga Rangi. Nga Rangi lashed out with his boot and caught Mannie a glancing blow on the side of the head. "You murdering bastard. We had it made up here before you decided to stuff everything up. What are we all going to do now, eh?"

"Shut your fuckin' mouth, you gutless coward!" Mannie shouted. "This is Maori land!"

"Maori land my arse," Nga Rangi scoffed. "You're stuffed in the bloody head. You're completely insane."

"It's my ancestral land," Mannie snapped.

"Okay, you two," John interrupted. "Enough of this nonsense. The helicopter's waiting for us."

Marlene burst onto the scene, and before anyone could stop her, she kicked Mannie's wounded thigh. "You bastard!" she screamed.

"Yaaahh!" Mannie cried out in agony

She aimed her foot at Mannie's head and connected his jaw. "You were going to slit my throat, you psychopath." Dropping onto her knees and with both fists, she punched his dirty blood-smothered face. "Gut me like a fish, slit my bloody throat, you said." She spat in his face. "You're insane. Absolutely insane, you horrible piece of shit."

Mannie yelled at John, "Get this mad bitch off me! Get the slut away from me!"

John wrapped both arms around her in a bear hug and lifted her away. "Calm down. Calm yourself, will you. We've got him. He can't get away now."

Marlene had let all her fears come out at once. Breathing heavily, her face puffed up red with her rage, she shrugged John away. She glared venomously down at Mannie. "You filthy piece of shit."

John cut in, "Time to get going."

Marc and Glen lifted Mannie to his feet and started

walking downstream to where the helicopter had landed. Mannie's limp was quite pronounced, and with his trousers being wet, the blood had dispersed through the material, making it look worse than it was. His arm, where Marlene had bit him, was swelling and bleeding quite badly.

Marc pointed to Mannie. "Leg's bleeding quite bad."

Nga Rangi cut in before Glen could answer, "Should've been his stupid bloody head."

"His arm's not much better," Glen added.

"The medic'll sort him out once we get to the chopper," John replied and then put a hand on Glen's shoulder. "Been one hell of a day, mate, I can tell you that."

"Yeah. You're certainly not wrong there."

Sadly, John shook his head and said, "Just hope Tui's gonna be okay." Scowling, he shoved Mannie's shoulder as he limped along the riverbank. "Keep going, shithead. Pity it's only a scratch. As the other fellah said, it should've been your stupid bloody head."

Looking back, Mannie's said angrily, "I'm gonna get you one day, Amohia!"

John cuffed the side of his head. "You won't get me. You've got nothin' up here."

Marc, seeing John's anger mounting, stepped in. "Okay, okay. Back off, eh? Where he's going he won't see daylight for at least twenty years."

Mannie glanced back again. "Fuck you, Amohia! Fuck you and your whole fuckin' family to hell!"

Glen shoved him in the shoulder. "Shut up. Just shut up and keep moving."

They reached the helicopter, and as another soldier came to assist them, John pointed to Mannie. "You'll need to tie him properly."

The soldier put a pair of handcuffs on Mannie and then did the same to Ritchie. Zac was strapped to a stretcher, ready to go in the helicopter.

Marlene, having calmed down, said sadly to John, "What's gonna happen to us now?"

"I'm not sure. You'll have to wait and see what happens when we get to the cop shop," John told her. He studied the couple for a second or two. "How'd you two come to be mixed up in this anyway?"

Nga Rangi explained how he and Mannie had lost their jobs and that they had been on the dole for some time. He also told him how the black supremacy gang in South Auckland had killed two of their friends and completely destroyed their house with a Molotov cocktail, forcing them to move in with Mannie temporarily. Mannie came up with the idea of moving to Pokaka before the Molotov cocktail incident, and that unwittingly brought their moving date forward.

At first, Nga Rangi explained, he wasn't that happy with the idea, but after the petrol bombing of their home, it seemed to have a lot of merit, and the more they discussed it, the idea grew on them. Not wanting to leave anything out, he told him about Jo, how she had attacked three hunters who were spying on them and how she had accidentally broken her neck. Mannie was totally distraught and went after them and shot them out of grief. After that, he became obsessed with claiming back this land, especially now with Jo buried up there by the vegetable garden.

"I saw the vegetable garden. But that grave we found yesterday only had two bodies," John said. Both Marlene and Nga Rangi bowed their heads. "Where's the other one?"

Nga Rangi pointed across the river. "Down there a bit further. Not far from where your friend was shot."

With a heavy heart, John looked across the river thinking about Brian and how he had died.

Jamie interrupted, "Come on. Gotta get going."

John led Nga Rangi and Marlene to the helicopter and climbed aboard.

The pilot picked up the microphone. "National Park Police. Eagle Two. Do you copy? Over."

"Copy that, Eagle Two. Go ahead."

"We have the perpetrators onboard. I repeat. We have the perpetrators onboard. We've got three wounded, one reasonably serious, so we'll need an ambulance. Can you organize that? We'll come back for the deceased once we've dropped these ones off. ETO approximately thirty minutes. Over."

"Copy that, Eagle Two. Can do. Over."

*   *   *   *   *

Thirty-five minutes later, the helicopter landed in the empty school grounds across the road from the police station in Buddo Street, National Park.

Dave, waiting in the doorway, saw them fly in and land. He rushed across the road as John disembarked.

"You okay?" he asked nervously.

"I'm okay," John told him soberly. "Don't know about Tui though," he said and then pointed to Mannie. "This maniac bastard stabbed him in the stomach."

"Yeah. I heard the report from the pilot on the radio when they took him to the hospital," Dave replied sadly.

Nga Rangi, Marlene, Tuku, and Himi were led across the road to the police station by two soldiers with John and Dave following behind.

As they went in through the front door, John put his hand on Nga Rangi's shoulder. "I'll see you get a good lawyer. Don't you worry. I'm sure something can be worked out."

"Thanks, we'd appreciate that. We can do with all the help we can get," Nga Rangi said gratefully.

John looked at Mannie as Smithy escorted him into the

police station. "Put that bastard in a cell on his own, Smithy. You never know what that piece of crap's liable to do."

Jim cut in, "Jeepers creepers. These people smell. Their body odour is foul."

"I'm not much better, mate," John replied. "It's been a couple of hard days in the bush."

Zac was carried in on a stretcher with his leg bandaged. Ritchie had his forearm bandaged. Both glared at John as they were put in a cell to wait for the ambulance.

Nga Rangi, Marlene, Tuku, and Himi were being processed; and as Mannie was being escorted to a cell, Nga Rangi snapped, "I should never have listened to you, you dumb bastard!"

"You're the dumb bastard," Mannie responded heatedly. "You think they'll give a toss about you?"

As Jim, the on-duty policemen, opened the cell door, Mannie turned to John. In a low menacing tone, he said, "I'm gonna get you one day, Amohia."

Jim took off Mannie's handcuffs.

"Piss off, dick brain," John scoffed and shoved him into the cell. "You're too bloody stupid. Just like your great grandfather."

Marlene went over to Mannie's cell. He looked her in the eye and with an evil grin, he said, "You stupid bloody slut. You think they'll be sympathetic with you if you tell them everything? I don't think so."

He made a grab at her through the cell bars. Marlene stepped back and spat into his face. "You horrible bastard. I don't know what Jo ever saw in you. If she was here today, she'd be absolutely disgusted. You're nothing without her. You're as rotten as they come."

"Leave my Jo out of this, you fuckin' slut!" Mannie screamed.

Marlene turned to John and said, "Jo was such a nice person, my very best friend. Far too good for this animal."

"Anything would be better than him. Animals only kill to survive. This," John said, emphasizing the this, "is nothing but a piece of rotting dog shit."

"You wait, arsehole," Mannie assured him. "One day I'll settle that score for my great grandfather."

"Like I said, you're too bloody thick and stupid."

Nga Rangi was standing beside Marlene. He looked at Mannie. "We could have had a real good life up there on the mountain if you hadn't gone completely insane. And for what? You tell me, shit for brains."

"You really think they're gonna be lenient on you?" Mannie shouted, spittle flying from his mouth. "You're dumber than the dumbest shithead I've ever seen."

John, disgusted at Mannie's attitude, cut in, "Unlike you, he wanted what was good for the group. You and your so-called Maori land, your ancestral land, as you call it, was gifted to all the people of New Zealand by your ancestral chief, Amohia, my great grandfather. Your great grandfather didn't like it and wanted to make a stand and fight for it." Sadly, John shook his head. "Too many people would have died pointlessly. Can't you see that? It was a consensus of the tribe. The whole tribe," he repeated. "Why would the whole tribe listen to one dumb, thick-as-pig-shit bastard when they all knew it was for their own good?"

Mannie's eyes narrowed. "It was part of my whakapapa. I would have preferred to have died than let them take it."

"If that had happened, you and I wouldn't be standing here having this conversation. Can't you see? Most of our ancestors would've been wiped out. Where's the sense in that?" He took a breath. "None of it was ever part of your whakapapa." John broke off and was about to walk away. He hesitated for a second and then turned back to Mannie. "It was gifted to all the people of New Zealand, to the whole country, way before you and I were ever thought of. It was never yours to claim back in the first place."

"It should never have been gifted!" Mannie shouted.

"Amohia saw sense," John replied angrily. "And we are fighting them right now to get the mountains and the land back by due process. In the courts."

"What a waste of bloody time that is. It's more than a 130 years since then and what's happened, eh? What's fuckin' happened? I'll tell you. Nothin'. Not a single bloody thing."

John walked slowly back and stood in front of Mannie's cell, shaking his head. "That's not true," John corrected him. "They are going through due process as we speak. We will get it back, but on our terms, not theirs."

Mannie sniggered and made a grab at John, but John was just out of his reach. Mannie was holding onto the bars and, out of sheer anger and frustration, shook them as hard as he could and shouted, "That's bullshit! Plain fuckin' bullshit and you know it! They should have listened to my great grandfather and fought the buggers for it!"

"Tell me. Why would the tribe listen to one dumb bastard with no status whatsoever, with no speaking rights at a hui, when they all agreed with Amohia in the first place, especially under the threat of annihilation? It was done for the survival of the tribe in the long run."

Mannie made a grab at him through the cell bars, shouting, "Fuck you! Fuck you, you fuckin' bloody bastard!"

"Amohia, my great grandfather, the paramount chief, listened to his people. He listened and appreciated their points of view and analyzed their thoughts. That's what made him a great and wise chief. He wasn't greedy. He asked everyone what they thought before he made a decision. It was a decision that was not taken lightly and one that was made for the benefit of the whole tribe. Now just to make this quite clear so you know where your family stood then. They had no speaking rights at any hui and no status at all within the tribe. They were considered then and still are thought of today. Nothing has changed in all this time. They're still and will always be as thick as bloody pig shit."

John was now standing in front of the cell right in front of Mannie. Mannie, breathing heavily, his nostrils flaring, his eyes dilated black with rage and hatred, was holding onto the cell bars.

Like a stroke of lightning, John's hand flashed through the bars and whacked him across the head. "You're a chip off the old bloke, you know. Just like them in every way. Thick as bloody pig shit."

In the traditional warrior stance, and with knees slightly bent, his right hand quivering above his shoulder, tongue protruding out and down, eyes fierce, John glared directly into Mannie's eyes.

"Haaaaaa. Tangata te whenua." (Power of the Land)